# ENGLISH SPY MYSTERIES

## SERIES 1 OMNIBUS

### RACHEL AMPHLETT

## ALSO BY RACHEL AMPHLETT

*Detective Kay Hunter series:*

Scared to Death

Will to Live

One to Watch

Hell to Pay

Call to Arms

*Dan Taylor spy novels:*

White Gold

Under Fire

Three Lives Down

Behind the Wire

*Standalone novels:*

Look Closer

Mistake Creek

Before Nightfall

CONTENTS

PART ONE
**Assassins Hunted** 1

PART TWO
**Assassins Vengeance** 155

PART THREE
**Assassins Retribution** 291

**From the Author** 449

# PART ONE
# ASSASSINS HUNTED

# ONE

*Cyprus, present day*

'There's a man holding a gun to Stefano's head.'

For a fleeting second, Eva's first thought was that Alex was talking about a character on the show playing on the television in the front room.

Then, she wondered what the hell he was doing changing the channels and watching something wholly inappropriate.

Finally, before the digital clock had blinked to the next second on the hour, she registered the frightened tone in his voice, and her head jerked up from the magazine she'd been reading.

Above her head a ceiling fan spun, pushing a cooling breeze between the open window of the dining area through the room and out towards the hallway. Moths dive-bombed against the window's fly-screen that separated her from the outside world. The pages of the magazine article fluttered under her fingers, then her hair lifted off her shoulders as she spun on her heel.

She dropped her coffee mug as she moved, the sound of it smashing against the tiles following in her wake as she reached out to grab the kitchen bench to turn the corner without slowing down.

Eva cursed under her breath as her bare feet crossed the minefield of plastic building bricks Alex had left strewn across the floor in his haste to answer the intercom, before she raced to where he stood staring up at the wall next to the front door, fixated at the image streaming via video link from the condo's gatehouse.

Almost within touching distance, she realised he was still dressed in his school uniform, instead of the pyjamas she'd asked him to change into twenty minutes ago. Her throat constricted at the sight of him, his vulnerability all too evident as he shifted from one foot to the other.

His hair sticking up on one side from where he'd been lying on the sofa, his blue eyes widened at the flickering image on the screen, before he turned to her, his mouth open in a little "o" of shock.

Eva held her finger to her lips, shook her head, then beckoned to him, fighting to keep her face calm and not let him see the fear that was crawling through her veins.

He blinked, then moved away from the camera's range,

edging along the wall to where she stood, her heart pounding.

He tried to slip his hand into hers, but she gently brushed it away and ruffled his hair.

'Stay here,' she whispered.

She lifted her chin, not waiting for his response, and instead took a deep breath and stepped in front of the monitor.

She swallowed.

Stefano, the security guard that manned the small security office from noon through to eight o'clock in the evening five days a week, was staring at her, sheer terror in his eyes.

She'd spoken to him on a regular basis, often stopping to chat after collecting Alex from the private ex-pat school he attended. He was in his late teens, and had taken the job to pay for his evening classes. He dreamt of becoming a chef, he'd said. Finish the course, then apply to some of the best cookery schools in France.

She'd asked him, once, how he'd got the job, as she'd wondered how effective the young man would be if threatened.

He'd rattled off his martial arts qualifications, the training the security company had given him, and she'd relaxed a little.

Perhaps a little too much.

Now, the barrel of a gun pressed into his brow so hard, she could see the skin puckering under its weight.

The owner of the gun was off camera, out of sight.

Alex was still small enough that he could only reach the lower button on the console to activate the video connection, and she silently counted her blessings that he couldn't stretch up to touch the other controls.

Keeping her eyes on the image in front of her, she clicked her fingers once to make sure she had Alex's attention, then made a movement with her hand; a movement she'd spent three years praying she'd never need to use.

She wondered, for a moment, if he'd remember the training because it had been a few weeks since they'd practised, and then she heard his tiny feet pattering away down the hallway towards the door next to the kitchen, the one that led to the special room that she'd insisted the condominium be built around. His footsteps stopped, and the sound of four staccato *beeps* reached her.

She waited until she heard the door slam shut, then counted to three.

On the screen, Stefano's shoulders moved up and down, and even before pressing the intercom to connect their voices, she knew she'd hear his breathing, hard and panicked.

She punched the button, and didn't waste time on niceties.

'Who are you?'

No response.

Stefano's eyes widened as the gun was pressed harder

into the side of his skull, and Eva saw a tear roll down his cheek as his hand moved forward.

*No, no – don't open the gate!*

'Who are you?' she repeated. 'What do you want?'

She fought the tremor in her voice, her brain already planning, evaluating, discarding the different ways the scenario could play out.

Before she could move her lips to form another question, the front of Stefano's skull exploded, blood and gore striking the screen as his body slumped forward.

She cried out, covering her mouth with her hands.

On the screen, a hand pushed Stefano's body out of the way, and a figure wearing a black mask bent down until his dark eyes blazed from slits in the material, straight at the camera.

'You,' he said. 'We want you. *And* the boy.'

The screen went blank, and Eva stepped away from the wall, terrified.

*How had they found her?*

She'd been so careful, severing all ties to the old days. She bit her lip, cursing herself. She'd missed something, evidently. Somehow, they'd tracked her down.

*How long had they been watching, waiting?*

She turned and ran to the front door, bent down to the mat and tugged her old running shoes onto her feet. She straightened, and sprinted to the kitchen, where she started pulling open the cupboard doors, lifting a bottle of cleaning fluid out and placed it on the counter-top.

She glanced at the closed steel door, the red light on the entry keypad blinking a steady beat, and bit her lip.

The Caretaker had told her the room would hold, that no matter what happened to the house around it, the space would be impenetrable.

Alex had enough supplies inside to last four weeks; easy-to-open packets of snacks, and plenty of water. If she missed her daily call to the Caretaker, he'd come. Wherever he was in the world, whatever hellhole he was currently inhabiting, he'd come.

She reached out to the cooker hob and turned the four gas outlets on full, then opened the oven door.

Within seconds, the putrid stench had begun to fill the space, and she ran across the room to close the window.

Dashing back past the kitchen bench, she grabbed the bottle of bleach, and moved back along the hallway, flicking off light switches as she went.

She ran into the living room, switched off the television and the table lamps, and the house finally plunged into complete darkness. Leaving the room, she pulled the door shut, then lunged for the front door and wrenched it open. She checked the security screen was locked, then uncapped the bottle of bleach, pushed the door so it was only ajar, then reached up and balanced the bottle on top of it.

Her chin jerked down at a slight movement at the end of the short path that led to the expensively paved road that curved round the exclusive housing estate, and she stepped back into the shadows of the house.

In her mind, she ran through last-minute checks.

The back door was already locked; unless she or Alex went out into the garden, which was rare, it was never opened. The kitchen window had been the only room open in the house as she'd planned to put the air conditioning on upstairs half an hour before she went to bed. Alex felt the cold, and so it would be another month before he'd acquiesce to the unit in his bedroom being used.

*That was it.*

She darted back towards the kitchen, covering her nose and mouth with her sleeve, and tried not to gag at the stench.

She spun in the centre of the room, her eyes fully adjusted to the gloom as she spotted possibilities, but nothing that would be guaranteed to work, before she lunged across the tiles to the floor and grabbed the remote for the air conditioning unit that had been set into the wall above the dining table.

A moment after she'd touched it, a crashing sound reached her ears as the intruders began to tear at the security screen at the front door.

She dropped to the floor and crawled across it on her hands and knees, reached up, and pushed the kitchen door closed.

Next, she placed the remote control on the floor so that it faced the closed door, lining it up with the spring that prevented the door from hitting the plaster wall when it was opened.

She leaned down, her cheek touching the tile, gauging the

position, and shifted the remote a little to the left, then straightened and dashed towards the secure door.

As she punched in the last number of the four-digit pin code, she heard a loud *thump* against the back door, and then the security screen door at the front of the house gave way.

She felt a momentary note of triumph as one of the intruders cried out, no doubt blinded by the bleach that had spilled out over his head, then she pushed open the door and stepped over the threshold.

Alex was standing in the middle of the room, a torch in one hand, his thumb in his mouth. He removed it as she entered, and looked up at her, his face contorted with fright.

'Mummy?'

Eva slammed the door shut behind her, felt the structure shudder as it settled back into place, then launched herself across the floor towards him, scooped him up in her arms, and pulled him into the far corner of the room.

She sat on the floor, hugging him to her chest, and stared at the steel door.

'Cover your ears, Alex,' she said. 'It's going to get loud.'

# TWO

*British Embassy, Berlin*

Miles Newcombe slid the manila folder under his arm, the Queen's seal on the outer cover as faded as the stamped "Top Secret" lettering printed underneath it, and snatched two plastic coffee cups from the dispenser next to the machine.

He slipped the first cup into place, pressed a button, then wrinkled his nose as the hot liquid spat into the cup, and took a step back.

The beans were burnt, again, and the aim of the jet was temperamental at the best of times.

He peered down at his wrinkled shirt, and wondered when he'd get time for a shower and change of clothes.

The signal had been received at nine minutes past seven the previous evening, mere moments before he was due to leave the office. Twenty-one minutes later, and it would have been someone else's problem.

Instead, he'd phoned his wife, and apologised profusely. His gaze had drifted to the photograph on his desk as he'd hung up the phone, and he'd wondered how much of his kids' childhood he'd have missed out on due to his career, if he and his wife had been able to conceive.

The coffee machine spluttered to a standstill, and he swapped the cups over, leaving the first to stand on top of the vending machine. He peered over his shoulder at the beige-painted corridor that led towards the secure reception area. The soundproof lining of the walls lent a muffled, cocooned effect to the offices, the muted interior a poor reflection of the beautiful city outside.

The machine coughed, and checking the second cup was full, he adjusted the folder under his arm, then picked up both plastic cups at the rim, trying to ignore the burning sensation that scorched his fingertips.

He turned and hurried along the corridor towards Room D-41, questions churning his thoughts.

The contents of the folder had been disturbing.

If Philip Petersen hadn't retired last July, it wouldn't have come to this. Management would have phoned Petersen at home, demanding he return to the office immediately.

Instead, Miles had been handed the folder – after it had been retrieved from the secure archive three floors under where he now walked, a complex library of secrets hidden beneath the German streets.

He passed one of the rare windows in this area of the building, its bulletproof tinted glass lending a smoky aspect to the early morning city skyline, before turning right to face a closed door.

He glanced down at the full cups, contemplated the folder under his arm, then raised his chin and glared up at the security camera before jerking his head towards the door.

The camera stared back at him, its opaque lens taunting him below a single red flashing light.

Nothing happened.

'For fuck's sake. Pay attention,' he murmured.

He kicked the door twice, then glared at the camera once more, and raised the coffee cups a little.

An electronic *beep* sounded from the other side of the door, then it swung outward.

He stepped back, sloshing hot liquid over his hands, and the folder slipped from his precarious grip, dropping to the floor.

Miles swore as two pages escaped from it, fluttering to one side and landing on the carpet tiles.

'Whoa, sorry, Miles.'

He glared at the bespectacled man who peered around the door, thrust the coffee cups at him, then crouched to retrieve the folder and its contents.

'You're supposed to monitor the camera feed, Nathan,' he grumbled.

'Sorry, I was—'

'Yes, I know. Watching the interview room.' He stood,

flicked the folder under his arm, then reached out for one of the cups. 'Lead the way.'

He kicked the door shut and followed Nathan Crowe into a small darkened room; the only available light was provided by a row of six computer screens that illuminated Nathan's face as he pulled out one of the two swivel chairs for Miles, who put his coffee cup on the desk below the screens and sank into the cracked leather upholstery.

Crowe ran a hand through dark unruly hair, his brown eyes troubled as he returned to his seat in front of the computer.

Somehow, the Section's systems had failed Eva Delacourt, and they needed to find out how.

Miles placed the folder on the desk, a little to the left of the coffee cup but still within easy reach, and raised his gaze to the large panel of glass above the screens.

His research proved one thing – the man assigned to watching her was unaware of what the woman was truly capable of, and that troubled him.

'How's she doing?'

Nathan leaned forward and pointed at the screen nearest to Miles. 'Her heart rate is up, but that's only to be expected. Humidity in the room hasn't changed dramatically since she arrived.'

'So, she's not panicking?'

'Not yet. Should she be?'

'We'll see.'

'What's her background?' asked Nathan, leaning across the desk and placing his hand on the folder.

Miles tugged it out of his reach and yawned. 'Special operative. Hasn't seen active service in three years. Until last night, that is.'

He sipped the coffee and contemplated the woman sitting at the small table in the interview room.

She looked bored, her head propped in one hand, her elbow on the table, while she traced patterns on the table surface with a finger, her eyes firmly fixed on what she was doing.

'Has she looked in the mirror?'

'No.'

'Huh.'

'She obviously knows it's a fake.'

'Of course,' said Miles. 'She's been on this side of the room often enough in the past.'

'Oh.' Nathan sat back in his chair and stared through the window. 'I didn't know that.' He frowned, then turned to Miles. 'So, what *has* she been doing?'

'Keeping her head down,' said Miles. He flipped open the folder and glanced at the executive summary, a one-pager that he'd typed up at one o'clock that morning, and one that he'd already committed to memory.

'Okay, so we know she's been living in Cyprus for just under a year,' he explained. 'In plain sight, under an alias that changes every twelve months when she moves country.

Before you joined the Section, she was in Prague, then moved to Bermuda, then Cyprus. She bases herself somewhere with a British ex-pat presence, usually in a gated community.'

'Why that particular order of location?'

Miles shrugged. 'No reason that I can see. It just is what it is. She was due to move again in two weeks' time.'

'Where to?'

'Copenhagen.'

'What about the job she had in Cyprus – at the British Embassy? Was that a ruse to keep her close?'

'Or a ruse for her to keep an eye on us.' Miles rubbed his chin and flipped the folder shut. 'Where's the boy?'

'Next door, in D-43, watching cartoons.' Nathan pointed to one of the other monitors.

'Any indication from the psych report how he's holding up?'

'He seems fine, all things considering. Asks for his mother every now and again, but seems to be okay when they've told him she's just next door and helping us with some stuff.'

Miles sighed. 'Poor mite.' His thoughts turned to his own nephew, only three years younger than the boy, and wondered how he would cope in the same circumstances. He shook his head to clear the thought. He didn't want to contemplate such a scenario.

'All right,' he said, and stood, stretching his arms over his head. He stifled a yawn and snatched up the folder before turning to the inner door. 'Let's see what she's got to say for herself.'

'How did they find her?' asked Nathan. 'She must've made a mistake.'

Miles shook his head and thought of the documents he'd been reading all night. 'Eva Delacourt doesn't make mistakes,' he said. He pointed towards the two-way mirror between the office and the interview room.

The woman sat forward and put her head in her hands, momentarily letting her true emotions show, and obviously not caring who saw the gesture.

'Someone knew where she was. Someone sent the strike team there.'

'Well, that was a monumental fuck-up.'

'Indeed.'

## THREE

Eva raised her head from her hands as a man entered the room, and immediately noticed how dishevelled he looked.

Maybe she wasn't the only one having a rough time of it, then.

He looked to be in his late thirties or early forties, his light brown hair just starting to recede from his forehead. His green eyes were bloodshot, but she couldn't tell whether that was from lack of sleep, too much coffee, or both.

'Hello,' he said, and held out his hand as he approached. 'I'm Miles Newcombe.'

'Hello, Miles,' she said, returning the handshake. 'What's your role in all this?' She cast her eyes around the room and then pointed at the mirror. 'Are you in charge, or are there several layers above?'

His mouth twitched. 'There are a few layers, yes.'

She leaned back in her chair and watched as he dropped a

notepad and a manila folder on the desk between them and settled himself into the chair opposite. She noticed the wedding ring on his left hand, and pitied the woman who had married him. He was obviously a career-spook, no doubt of that.

She sighed, and pointed at the folder. 'That's what my life comes down to, is it? A flimsy file?'

Miles loosened his tie, rolled it up, and placed it on the desk. 'I'm wondering how much of your life is in here, actually.' He glanced at it, but didn't open the file. 'It *does* seem a bit thin, given some of the stories I've been hearing tonight.'

'Where's Alex?'

'Next door, watching cartoons.' He smiled. 'He's a nice kid.'

'You've got children of your own?'

'No.'

His demeanour changed slightly, and Eva picked up a sense of loss in his tone. She decided not to press him, however, and instead edged forward on her chair and folded her arms on the desk. 'Have you done a psych evaluation already?'

'He's fine. I'm sure with your care he'll be able to put it behind him over the coming months.' He finally flipped the folder open, and clasped his hands together so they covered the front page.

She managed to read some of it though, then relaxed as she realised the typed words were simply a timeline of her documented past. No surprises. Good to know he'd done his homework.

She allowed herself to relax a little, and settled in to answer his questions.

'Your flight from RAF Akrotiri was okay?'

'Yes. Thanks.'

'How long was it before you were able to leave the property?'

'What's left of it, you mean?' Eva leaned back in her seat. 'Two hours, by the time the fire service had put the flames out and then the local police called the embassy.'

'Any issues?'

'None. I showed the policeman in charge my diplomatic credentials, and he provided a car and driver to get us to the RAF base straight away.' She broke off, a small smile crossing her lips. 'I think he was glad to be rid of us. The neighbours were certainly giving him a hard time.'

'That's something, I suppose.' Miles rubbed his chin and turned a page. 'Were you able to salvage anything at all?'

'No. I'm even wearing borrowed shoes.'

He glanced down and she shuffled in her seat so she could move her foot out from under the table.

'They're rather, er, fetching.'

She shrugged, and straightened. 'They'll have to do.'

'I'll have someone take a note of your measurements; we'll send someone out to get a change of clothes for you and Alex.'

'Thanks.'

'Can you tell me exactly what happened?'

'I'm presuming you'd like to hear it all "from the top",' she said, accentuating the words with her fingers.

He nodded. 'If you wouldn't mind. You know how it is,' he added with an apologetic shrug. 'Better to hear what happened with my own ears.'

Eva began to walk him through the events of the past twenty-four hours, starting with a précis of how her day had been prior to Alex calling to her, and the gatehouse guard's murder.

As she began to talk, Miles took a pen from his shirt pocket and began to take notes. She was slightly surprised that he favoured a fountain pen, thinking it a little old-fashioned, but she kept churning out the words, watching as his large looped handwriting began to fill page after page of the large notepad he'd brought in with him.

She stopped after fifteen minutes and reached out for one of two glasses that had been left on the table, and nodded her thanks as Miles filled it and the other for himself from a plastic jug.

She took a few sips, then pointed to the notepad. 'Isn't this being recorded?'

A faint smile crossed his lips. 'I prefer to take notes,' he said. 'It helps me absorb what I'm hearing.' He raised his eyes to the ceiling. 'Of course, if I miss anything, then we've got a back-up.'

His gaze fell to her, his eyes sparkling.

*He's loving this,* she realised. *Probably the most excitement he's had here in years.*

'Right, where were we?' He flicked over the page, checked his last note, then looked up at her. 'The remote for the air conditioning unit. Why?'

She shrugged. 'They were professionals. Unless they had a complete rookie with them, none of them were going to hit a light switch after smelling all that gas. I had to force their hand.'

Miles frowned. 'The explosion that levelled the house?'

Eva nodded. 'Whoever was leading the intruders from the front door had to open the door into the kitchen if they were going to try to breach the panic room. I popped the back off the remote to expose the batteries to be sure, then lined it up so the door would hit it when they pushed it open, causing an explosion.'

She watched, fascinated, as he wrote the word "boom" and then drew a little cloud around it. She tore her eyes away as he raised his head.

'What about accents?' he said. 'Recognise anyone's voice?'

She took a moment, closed her eyes, and tried to remember. 'There was one man. When the first intruder came through the front door and the bleach landed on him, he yelled, and I heard another man speak.' She opened her eyes. 'Eastern European, I think.'

'You're sure?'

'Yes. Definitely not Russian, but perhaps one of the old Eastern Bloc countries.'

'Do you know how many there were?' he asked.

'No,' she said, and frowned. 'Although I'm assuming a minimum of six. Three through the front, three at the rear.'

He nodded. 'Spot on.'

'How many were left?'

'None.'

'Ah.'

'Yes,' said Miles. 'Therein lies the problem. No-one to question to find out who they worked for.'

'Damn,' replied Eva. 'I'll try to remember that next time.'

He rolled his eyes. 'It was merely an observation.'

'So,' she said, as she crossed her arms over her chest, and leaned back in her chair. 'How the hell did they find me?'

'You've got no ideas? Anything at all?'

She shook her head, exhaustion threatening now that the adrenalin had well and truly worn off. 'No,' she murmured. 'And that's what worries me.' She uncrossed her arms and eased forward. 'I haven't seen *anything* these past few weeks. I would've told the Section otherwise.'

He sighed, and threw his pen down. 'That's what we thought.'

# FOUR

Miles pushed the door closed, stalked over to the spare chair in front of the computer screens, and slung the folder next to his empty coffee cup.

He sank into the chair and ran a hand over his eyes.

Nathan broke the short silence that followed. 'Do you think she's telling the truth?'

'Yes,' Miles mumbled from behind his hand.

'Shit.'

After a pause, Miles heard the other man's chair squeak and waited for the next question.

It didn't take long.

'Miles – all I know is what my job description entails. Why was she in hiding?'

Miles sighed, pushed the chair away from the desk so he could stretch out his legs, and folded his arms across his chest, wondering how the hell he was going to come up with a strategy to fix the problem that would meet with the Section chief's approval.

'It's because of her fiancé. His name was Douglas Bolton,' he began, keeping his eyes on Eva through the glass. 'Doug worked at the British Embassy in Prague as a cultural attaché.'

'He was a spy?' Nathan leaned forward, resting his arm on the desk as if to stop himself from falling out of his chair.

Miles glanced at him, then back to Eva. 'Yeah. He was a spy.' He paused. 'More like a messenger, really, without wanting to make it sound insignificant. He passed on messages between us, the CIA, and various informers. He used the diplomatic communications channels to get information in and out of the country.'

'What sort of information?'

Miles eyed the folder, then looked away. 'Sensitive information.'

'What happened?'

'The Section received intel to suggest his life was in danger, so we had them both moved to a safe house in the city,' said Miles. 'The admin staff at the embassy were told Doug and Eva were going on a holiday for a few weeks. Except after two weeks, it became apparent that if they stayed there, Doug's contacts would deteriorate – the sort of informers he had links to, they'd never talk to anyone else.'

'So, the Section chief sent them back?'

Miles nodded. 'Doug agreed, though. He'd just made contact with a new informant who wanted to defect when the Section pulled them out, and there was still time to make contact without it seeming suspicious. He was as keen as us to see it through.'

'What about Eva? What was she doing all that time?'

Miles ran his hand over his jaw. 'She was assigned as Doug's close protection officer as a way of taking a break from her work for the Section after a particularly difficult job.'

'Was she in danger too?'

'No more than usual.'

'So, how was he killed?'

'He was walking down the front steps of their house in Malá Strana towards his car. The driver was standing with the passenger door opened.'

'Armed?'

'Of course.' Miles leaned forward and balanced his elbows on his knees. 'As Doug reached the pavement, a motorbike appeared from a side street, sped past, and the pillion passenger took out Doug and his driver. Single shots to the head.'

'Shit.' Nathan leaned back in his chair, and Miles caught the note of admiration in his voice despite the seriousness of the events. 'That's one *hell* of a shot to take once, let alone twice.'

'There are only a handful of likely candidates we know of that could possibly have done it,' said Miles.

'So that's why she's been in hiding,' said Nathan. 'The shooter and the accomplice were never caught.'

'Right.' Miles jerked his thumb at the wall. 'Plus, she had the boy to worry about. He was only three at the time.' He pushed a newspaper clipping across the desk to Nathan, its headline screaming out the terror of the assassination of a high-profile British Embassy official in the historical enclave of Malá Strana.

He swallowed, the thought of his nephew having to be told that his father had been assassinated in cold blood sending a shiver up his spine and across his shoulders.

Nathan snatched the clipping from the desk, pushed his glasses up onto his forehead and squinted at the grainy photograph that depicted the front of a three-storey house, its front door obscured by plastic sheeting that led down to the pavement to maintain the crime scene. 'And so she's been hiding ever since.'

Miles nodded.

Nathan's gaze drifted to the woman on the other side of the glass, and he flicked his glasses back onto his nose. 'That can't have been easy with a kid in tow.'

'No, it can't have been.'

'Anything to suggest *why* her fiancé was shot?' asked Nathan.

'Only rumours,' said Miles. 'But we can't prove it, because no-one got the chance to ask him before he died.'

'What sort of rumours?'

'We thought he might have been passed some information, something explosive,' said Miles. 'I was only a junior analyst at the time, but whatever it was died with him.

Housekeeping got to the house at the same time as the emergency services and turned the place upside down. Eva was brought in for questioning, too – standard procedure in the circumstances, but she knew nothing of his activities. He never discussed it with her. Both of them were true professionals.'

'Shooting from a motorbike though,' mused Nathan. 'That's the Israelis' preferred method of dispatch, isn't it?'

'It was also Eva's method. She was one of our best assassins until she took a break from that and joined the contingent at the British Embassy.' Miles scratched his earlobe as he stared through the glass at Eva. 'It's the reason why we think he was deliberately targeted. Retaliation for one of her hits.'

# FIVE

Miles turned at the sound of the keypad on the door being activated, then stood as the Section chief entered the room.

'Sir. I didn't know you were in the building so early.'

'I think it's going to turn into a long day for all of us.' The elder man pointed through the glass. 'Anything of use?'

'Honestly, no,' said Miles. 'We've been through it a few times, from different angles. I'd say her memory is perfect. No deviation from the story at all.'

He watched, warily, as the Section chief stared through the glass at Eva.

Gerald Knox had been his boss for only a year since Petersen had retired, and he'd yet to get used to the man's grating manner.

It wasn't Gerald's fault, of course. Recruited into MI6 straight from university, he held an enviable track record of running successful overseas operations, and had a reputation as being an impeccable strategist. Rumour had it that the man was still gunning for the top job, despite the fact his own retirement was only two years away. However, his style of management left a lot to be desired; one moment he could be fractious, demanding to know every detail of an active operation; the next, driving his team by playing to their egos.

Knox pointed at the manila folder. 'What do you make of it all?'

'Either the people who arranged the attack on her got lucky, or we've got a serious leak.'

Knox's eyes opened wide. 'A leak?'

Miles shrugged. 'I can't think of any other explanation,' he said. 'She's one of the best we have. The whole operation has been running without a hitch for three years – so well, in fact, that we've only had a watching brief assigned to it for the past nine months,' he added, indicating Nathan.

'That's worrying,' said Knox, his gaze returning to the woman sitting in the interview room.

'Sir? I wonder if it'd be possible to have Eva relocated to a hotel for the next few days?' said Miles. 'Under guard, of course,' he added as Knox's eyebrows shot up. 'Maybe if we get her and Alex into some nicer surroundings than this, she'll be able to relax a bit. Perhaps that will trigger a memory from one of them; something we can use.'

'I don't know, Newcombe. Seems awfully risky.'

'I understand, but at least that way, Nathan here will have time to finish going through the camera feed from the complex. If he finds anything, we can run it by her – see if she recognises anyone.' He glanced over his shoulder through the mirror. 'Let's face it. She's got nowhere else to go.'

Knox rubbed at his chin. 'I suppose that would work. It's not ideal, of course.'

Miles held his breath. He desperately wanted a chance to continue working on the case, now that he knew the woman's background. And then there was Alex, an innocent caught up in a horrendous attack. His fingernails dug into the palms of his hands. He'd vowed to himself that he'd find those responsible, and he didn't want to let the boy down.

'All right,' said Knox. 'Let me talk to her. Set some ground rules. We'll go from there. Come on – both of you.'

Miles caught the surprised expression on Nathan's face, then hurried after Knox, who had already opened the door to the interview room.

'Eva,' said the Section chief, offering her his hand. 'I'm Gerald Knox. I believe you knew my predecessor, Philip Petersen.'

Eva stood, and Knox seemed surprised at her height. She shook his hand, then raised an eyebrow as Nathan followed Miles through the door.

'Ah, so the man behind the mirror makes an appearance?'

Miles ignored the faint blush that crossed Nathan's face. 'Gerald is our Section chief,' he explained. 'He'd like to ask you a few more questions. Nathan here is the analyst assigned to your operation. I hope you don't mind?'

'Not at all.'

Her mouth quirked as she gestured to the seat in front of her.

Miles leaned against the wall behind his boss, and folded his arms over his chest as Gerald eased himself into the plastic chair and crossed one socked ankle over the other.

Nathan appeared flustered, then copied Miles's stance and tried to look relaxed.

'It seems you've attracted the attention of some rather nasty people,' Knox began. 'I'm glad to see you and Alex are none the worse for wear.'

'Thank you,' said Eva. 'What are you doing about finding out who tried to kill us?'

Knox held up his hand. 'Bear with me,' he said. 'First of all, are you absolutely sure you had no idea the attack was imminent?'

From where he stood, Miles noticed the dangerous flash in Eva's eyes, and silently willed her to keep her cool.

'No, nothing,' she said eventually. She checked her watch, then glared at Knox. 'We've been through it at every angle for the past eight hours.'

'Newcombe here has suggested that we move you to a hotel for a few days, under guard of course, so that you can recover,' said Knox. 'Given your track record, however, I'm presuming that you would rather take on a more active role in the investigation, would that be correct?'

Eva leaned forward and folded her arms on the desk. 'Yes. Yes, I would.'

'I thought so.' Knox leaned back, and Miles could imagine the smug look that had crossed his face. 'Then I suggest the following course of action. Newcombe here will be assigned as your case officer. You will report to him while the investigation is ongoing. The boy can stay with you, of course.'

Knox turned in his seat to face Miles. 'The pair of you will work together to find out how the hell the house in Cyprus was compromised, and who attacked you. Newcombe, you'll report direct to me. The usual lock-down protocols apply – understood?'

Miles nodded. 'Understood.'

'Good.' Knox pointed at Nathan. 'The pair of you can work through the camera feed from the hotel, correct?'

Miles heard Nathan swallow before he answered.

'Er, yes – that's correct. Sir.'

'Good. Go and grab whatever you need. You're going with her.'

Nathan's eyes widened. 'I am?'

'You are,' confirmed Knox. 'So, if you're ready, we'll adjourn to my office and work out the detail, shall we?'

He rose and offered his hand to Eva. 'No doubt we'll talk soon. In the meantime, try to get some rest, and then work with Nathan to see what you can find out. I need to know how badly the rest of your mission has been compromised, understand?'

'He can't be serious,' said Eva as Nathan followed Knox from the room. She left her seat and approached Miles. 'I've got enough on my hands looking after Alex. You can't expect me to babysit your computer guru as well.'

'You won't be babysitting. He's been out in the field before.'

'Not like this, I'll bet.'

'You don't have a choice. He's going with you.'

'He's an *analyst*, for goodness' sake!'

Miles spun on his heel and glared at her. 'You don't get it, do you? When Douglas was shot, the programme got removed from the active operations system. Mothballed. No-one else knows about it.'

'So, why does Nathan know about it?'

'He was tasked with making sure it didn't fail. That no-one ever found you. Call it a watching brief, if you like.'

'Can we trust him, given what's happened in the last twenty-four hours?'

Miles sighed, threw the manila folder onto the table, and sank into one of the chairs. 'Eva, he's the one that tried to tell us a week ago that someone had found you.'

'What?'

'I'm sorry,' said Miles, holding up his hands. 'We didn't believe him.'

'You bastards.'

# SIX

Eva followed Nathan into the hotel lobby, her fingers wrapping around Alex's small hand as her gaze roamed their surroundings.

For government-sponsored accommodation, it was opulent, and she wondered what UK taxpayers would think; then she realised that Knox had placed them here because the very nature of the establishment ensured a better degree of privacy.

The staff would be used to VIPs, and wouldn't bat an eyelid at some of the Section's demands that would have had to have been made to assure her and Alex's safety.

She shifted the canvas holdall in her right hand containing the selection of clothing and toiletries one of the Section's enterprising admin staff had put together, and checked her watch.

She needed sleep, to recharge.

She couldn't concentrate without rest, and she desperately wanted to soak in a bath and ease the past twenty-four hours out of her pores.

Movement at the top of a marble staircase to her right caught her attention.

A black-suited man stood at the top of the stairs on the landing, trying to blend in as a member of staff. The tell-tale bulge under his jacket spoilt the effect, but a normal person wouldn't notice.

Eva exhaled, trying to loosen the tension in her body, and realised Nathan had spoken.

'I'm sorry, what?'

'I said I'll get our room keys, shall I?'

'Okay. Thanks.'

Alex tugged at her sleeve and pointed at him as he walked away. 'Who's he?'

Eva turned, then sighed as Nathan jogged over the marble tiled hotel lobby towards the reception desk. 'A computer nerd.'

Alex giggled. 'Nerd,' he repeated.

'Shh,' said Eva, fighting the urge to smile, despite her frustration. Instead, she concentrated on finding her bearings, noting the staff exit behind the reception area and the double doors leading to a bar, and counting the fire exits.

Her eyes drifted over the people that milled about the lobby, consigning each into a mental filing system; potential Section personnel, hotel staff, hotel guests, and—

She swallowed, and kept her gaze sweeping the lobby,

while her mind worked overtime.

A man was sitting at the bar, his body angled so that he could lean against the ornate brass rail that surrounded the serving area, whilst watching the lobby.

She calculated the distance, and then lowered her gaze to Alex. The boy was staring open-mouthed at the large chandelier hanging above their heads, his eyes sparkling in wonder.

Out the corner of her eye, Nathan was in the final throes of obtaining their room keys, and she hurried towards him, studiously ignoring the double doors through to the bar area, keeping her body between Alex and the man that sat there.

'Nathan, move!' Eva ignored the startled exclamation from the reception desk, grabbed the room keys, then took Alex by the sleeve and hurried towards the elevators.

'Wait!'

She hitched her bag up her arm. 'Press the button, Alex. Hurry.'

Alex did as he was told, then looked over his shoulder. 'What's wrong?'

'Never mind. Turn around.'

The elevator emitted a low *ping* as Nathan hurried towards them.

'Can you believe this place?' exclaimed Nathan. He raised his gaze to the ornate chandelier hanging from the ceiling that had held Alex spellbound. 'I could get used to this.'

'Here's a hint,' she said. 'Don't.'

'What's the rush?'

'I'll tell you in a minute.'

They rode the elevator car in silence, until it stopped on the sixth floor and the doors opened.

'Hold on,' said Eva.

She handed her bag to Nathan, then pushed Alex towards him and eased herself from the elevator.

As she stepped into the hallway, she looked left, then right. Her breath caught in her throat as she made out two dark-clothed figures halfway along.

They faced the elevators, one with a finger to his ear, the other with his hand behind his back, as if to pull a weapon from his belt.

The first dropped his hand, and moved towards her, gesturing to the two doors to her left. 'We managed to find adjoining rooms,' he said. 'There's a kitchenette and diner, and the refrigerator has been fully stocked. You should make yourselves comfortable.'

'Thanks,' said Eva, then turned back to the elevator and beckoned Nathan and Alex forward. 'Come on,' she said, and led them along the hallway to the first door.

They waited while the second security guard opened it for them and conducted a brief search, before he stepped aside.

'We'll wait in here while you check the other room,' said Eva, and brushed past, knocking his arm. 'Sorry.'

The agent shrugged. 'Both rooms were checked only twenty minutes ago.'

Eva peered over her shoulder and raised an eyebrow. 'All the more reason to check it again.'

She waited until Nathan and Alex had stepped over the threshold, then slammed the door shut and locked it.

'Right,' she said, keeping her voice low. 'I don't care what those two say. Be alert, and keep your voice down. I'd imagine the Section has installed listening devices.'

'Why would they do that?' Nathan said, spinning on his heel to face her and dropping the bags to the floor.

Eva held up her hand to silence him, then put a finger to her lips. 'Be careful what you say,' she murmured. She turned her attention to Alex. 'Go and put the television on,' she said. 'Find a cartoon channel. Turn up the volume.'

Alex nodded and hurried across the room, pulled out the television remote control, and began flicking through channels. Soon, the sound of a familiar cartoon theme song filled the room, the volume increasing within seconds.

'What are you doing?' hissed Nathan.

Eva pointed at the door to the suite. 'How long have you worked with the two men that are standing out in that corridor?'

'What?'

'How long?'

'I've never seen them before in my life,' he said, confusion in his eyes.

'So, how do you know you can trust them?'

'They're from the Section,' he said.

'But how do you know you can *trust* them?' persisted Eva.

'Have you seen their credentials? Did Miles tell you their names, or who had organised them to be here with us?'

Nathan lowered his gaze, and ran his hand along the kitchen worktop that separated the space from the living area. 'No.'

'How long have you worked with Miles?'

'A few months.'

In the background, the noise from the cartoon grew louder until Alex dropped the remote onto one of the plush lounge chairs and made his way back towards the kitchenette.

'That's what I thought,' said Eva.

'What are you thinking?' he asked.

Eva peered across to the closed door to the hallway, then leaned forward so she could murmur into his ear without being easily overheard. 'We're leaving. Now.'

# SEVEN

Samuel Parkes drained the glass of sparkling mineral water, swung away from his bar stool, and strode towards the lobby.

He'd already noticed the four agents milling about the staircase and reception area, so kept his gait relaxed as he exited the bar. Instead, he adjusted his cufflinks and straightened his tie, then checked his watch.

Plenty of time.

He was sure Eva had seen him, which was a shame. He preferred the element of surprise, but the hunt always excited him, no matter the circumstances.

He'd been surprised to hear that she'd escaped unscathed with the boy after the assault on her home in Cyprus, but revelled in the challenge that lay ahead.

He ignored the agent he passed as he made his way towards the elevator. The man was young, probably inexperienced, and like his colleagues had most likely underestimated the woman they'd been sent to guard.

And her enemies.

When he'd first received the phone call, he'd sat down at the kitchen counter of his two-bedroom apartment. He'd never admit it to his contact, but his legs had started shaking. He still wasn't sure if had been from shock, or excitement. The one hit he'd hoped for, dreamt of, prayed for, was his.

And he owed her.

He adjusted the sleeves of his black suit jacket, smoothed a hand over close-cropped sandy coloured hair, and then reached to the open collar of his crisp white shirt and ran his finger and thumb over the thin gold chain around his neck.

It had belonged to his grandmother, a devout Christian, and when the chain slipped between his finger and thumb and found the engraved crucifix, he closed his eyes for a brief moment and murmured a silent prayer.

Vengeance would be his.

He pressed the button between the two elevator doors nearest to him, and waited, whistling under his breath as the numbers counted down from the upper levels. He'd already worked out which floor she'd be staying on – it was a simple case of waiting and watching the agents as they prepared for her arrival. From his perch at the bar, he could observe the bank of elevators with ease. Without fail, each agent had punched the button for the sixth floor at some point or other over the past hour.

A soft *ping* preceded the left-hand elevator's arrival, and

Parkes stood to one side as an elderly couple stepped into the lobby. The old man nodded his thanks, and Parkes smiled politely before stepping into the elevator.

His senses picked up movement behind him before he heard the footfall, and his eyes found the mirrored wall at the back of the elevator.

One of the agents had reached out to stop the doors closing.

Parkes held his breath, keeping his face calm and his shoulders relaxed. By his count, there were already two agents outside Eva's hotel room, so this guy was either following him, or checking on his colleagues. He favoured the latter.

He turned and reached out for the panel, pressing the button for the floor below Eva's room, figuring the obviously inexperienced agent would relax once he could write off Parkes as a non-threat.

Sure enough, the agent leaned across with an apologetic smile, and pressed the button for the sixth floor.

Parkes moved to one side, linked his hands in front of his crotch, and waited.

The elevator slowed as it approached the fifth floor, before the familiar *ping* announcing its arrival filled the car. The doors opened, revealing an empty hallway. No guests waited to enter the elevator.

Parkes spun around, the heel of his open hand slamming underneath the agent's nose, driving the cartilage upwards.

The man slumped to the ground, his body convulsing as bone fragments entered his brain.

Parkes punched the button to keep the doors open a little longer, checked the hallway was still deserted, then crouched and dragged the now lifeless agent from the elevator.

Dumping the body on the ornate carpet, he then brushed off his suit, straightened his tie, and stepped back into the elevator.

Now he only had to deal with the two agents outside Eva's door, and the hunt could begin in earnest.

# EIGHT

'Why? How?'

Eva jutted her chin towards the window. 'We've been compromised. When the car pulled up, I noticed this side of the building has a fire escape. That window will open out onto it.'

'You want us to climb out there?'

'Grab what you need from your bag,' she said. 'You'll need your passport, cash, and anything that identifies you. Leave everything else behind.'

She watched as he moved across the room to where they'd dumped their bags and began to rifle through the outer pocket until he withdrew his passport.

'Is that everything?' she asked, craning her neck to see around his body.

'Yes,' he scowled over his shoulder, and then stood. He

patted the pockets of his jeans as he walked towards her. 'Everything else is here.'

'Good.' She moved away from counter, lifted one of the ornate chairs that had been placed against the wall next to the television, and carried it to the door that led to the hallway.

She moved slowly, grateful for the plush carpet that silenced her footsteps. Once next to the door, she lowered the chair, and rested her ear against the door's surface, blocking out the sound from the television with her hand over her other ear.

She held her breath, straining to hear through the health-and-safety specified fireproofed woodwork. A faint murmur of voices carried briefly from the other side, but appeared to be several paces away down the hallway, not right outside.

Satisfied, she dragged the chair towards her until it touched her toes, then moved and wedged it firmly under the door handle before returning to the main living area.

'Why are you doing this?' Nathan leaned forward on the kitchen bench, his eyes troubled.

'I don't trust the Section,' she whispered.

Nathan's eyebrows shot upwards. 'Why ever not?' he hissed.

'Gut feeling,' she said, then sighed. 'Helped along by the fact that you told them over a week ago that mine and Alex's life could be in danger, and they did absolutely nothing about it.'

'That seems a bit extreme,' argued Nathan. 'After all, the

communiqué I sent was probably one of hundreds they have to read every day.'

She shook her head. 'Don't make excuses for them. What if your report was deliberately ignored?'

'Why would they do that?'

'I don't know,' said Eva. 'I've never worked with any of you before. So, I don't know if I can trust them.'

'If you don't trust them, then why do you trust me?' asked Nathan, his voice uncertain. 'Why are we even having this conversation?'

'I *have* to trust you,' she said. 'You're the only one left in the Section that knows the systems and can get me the information I need. And you tried to warn them my life was in danger. So, I figured you're one of the good guys. Quite possibly the only one left.' She turned and blew a low whistle at Alex.

When he drew closer, she leaned down and took his arm. 'Go and check the window,' she said. 'Unlock it, but don't open it out all the way. Just a little, understand?'

Alex nodded, then hurried to do as he'd been instructed.

She held out her hand to Nathan. 'Give me your mobile phone.'

'Why?'

'You can stay here, if you want.'

Nathan sighed, reached into the pocket of his jeans, then handed over his phone. He watched Alex cross the room, then turned back to Eva and pointed at his phone in her hand. 'What are you going to do with that?'

Eva grabbed a towel from a neat pile next to the sink, unravelled one of the larger ones, and removed the memory cards and batteries from both his phone and her own. Next, she placed the parts on the square of material before covering them with the other half of the towel. She pulled open the cupboards until she found a complimentary steam iron, then glanced up to see Nathan staring at her, his mouth open, and winked.

She then smashed the contents of the towel with two precise blows.

Nathan held up his arm to shield his eyes from the pieces of plastic that escaped the material and shot through the air, then glared at her. 'Wasn't that a bit extreme?' he hissed.

'Not really,' said Eva, holding up the iron and examining the now-pockmarked surface. 'I never liked ironing.'

Eva ignored the glare Nathan gave her, and used the towel to collect the remnants of plastic that had managed to escape across the countertop.

She bundled the towel, then knotted the top of it and threw it across the room to Alex, who caught it with a grin on his face.

'What's the point of keeping that?'

'I don't want anyone putting them back together,' she said. 'I'll scatter the parts.'

Nathan folded his arms across his chest. 'Don't you think you're being a bit too paranoid?'

'No,' said Eva. 'I don't. There's a man downstairs. I noticed him when you were getting the room keys.'

'What man? Where?'

'In the bar, off to the left of the reception desk.'

'Where do you know him from?'

'I've seen him somewhere before, a long time ago.'

'You weren't just a diplomat's fiancée, were you?'

'No.'

'And you haven't been in witness protection either, right?'

'No.'

'Why is he so important? Why run?'

'He used to be a trained killer,' said Eva, her tone patient. 'Wet work. Unsanctioned hits, that sort of thing.'

'You say "used to",' Nathan persisted. 'What if he's just working in a different role now?'

'I doubt it very much.'

'What makes you say that?'

'Because he isn't meant to be here,' said Eva, peering through the net curtains. 'He's meant to be dead.'

# NINE

Eva edged along the wall alongside the window, the net curtain billowing in the gentle breeze.

The scent of exhaust fumes mixed with the cold air that blew through the open window, freezing now that she had moved away from the sanctuary of the hotel room's reverse-cycle air conditioning.

Lifting her gaze to the opposite building, she watched and waited until she was sure no other surveillance was apparent; the windows of the building opposite were sparse and appeared to mark the rear of offices converted from an eighteenth-century residence, while the street below was deserted.

She checked her watch.

*Two o'clock.*

The locals would have finished their lunches, and with any luck their guard would be down, muted by good food.

And, with luck, not the sort of time for her enemies to draw attention to themselves.

It was as good a time as any.

She glanced over her shoulder at Nathan, and beckoned to him.

'You go first,' she said. 'Straight down the fire exit and crouch behind the bins at the bottom, near the wall, okay?'

'What are you going to do?'

'I'll wait until you're halfway down, then I'll send Alex. Keep him with you,' she said. 'When you're both down, I'll follow.'

She saw the flash of concern in his eyes, reached out and put her hand on his arm. 'Please. Trust me.'

He leaned out the window and peered down the length of the building to the cobblestones below. His Adam's apple bobbed in his throat, and then his brow creased. 'Where are we going once we leave here?'

'Train station,' said Eva. 'We need to put as much distance as possible between ourselves and Berlin.'

'They'll be looking for us, won't they?'

Eva nodded. 'Of course. But hopefully by the time they realise we've gone, we'll have a good enough head start. Even if they check the CCTV cameras at the station, we'll be long gone.'

'They'll know which train we're on,' he protested. 'They'll be checking the CCTV cameras at all the stations leading out of the city.'

'They'll know which train we *left* on,' she corrected him.

'We're going to have to be smart about this, Nathan, and that means we change trains a few times to make sure we shake them off.'

His gaze rested on the locked door to the hallway. 'Are you sure about this?' He turned back to her. 'Absolutely sure?'

'Yes.' She shrugged. 'If I'm wrong, we get told off for slipping past our security detail. If I'm right…' Her eyes fell on Alex. 'We stay alive for a bit longer. Hopefully long enough for me to work out what the hell is going on.'

Nathan sighed. 'Okay.'

She stepped aside as he brushed past her and watched him clamber over the low windowsill and onto the steel fire exit.

He edged across the narrow platform, then began to lower himself down the steps. He stopped as he was about to slip from view. 'You never asked how I found out about the threat on your life,' he said.

She held his gaze. 'But I believed you anyway,' she said.

She saw his jaw clench, and then he began climbing once more, the sound of his feet on the steel treads floating up to where she stood long after he'd disappeared from sight.

Alex joined her, his fingers wrapping around hers as he leaned forward, copying her stance.

She swallowed, wondering how much he remembered; whether he recalled the terrifying ordeal that had been their escape three years ago, or whether the whole experience had been consigned to some deep part of his memories.

She gave his hand a quick squeeze. 'Come on, Alex – it's your turn.'

She helped him over the windowsill, casting her eyes around the surrounding buildings and street below.

*Please let this work.*

'Go,' she whispered.

Once Alex was safely on the platform, he dropped into a crouch and crawled towards the ladder. He turned, stretched one foot tentatively towards the first rung, and glanced up at her.

'Go,' she urged.

He nodded, then settled his weight on the ladder and began to slip from view, his hands gripping the sides of the metal structure as he descended.

She waited until the top of his head was out of sight, then followed, holding onto the windowsill until she'd found her balance on the steel structure.

She hurried across the platform, peered down the first ladder to make sure Alex was clear, then turned, placed her hands on the handrails either side of the treads, and began to lower herself.

She was halfway down the ladder when she heard the unmistakable bark of gunfire.

Her head jerked up at the sound, a fraction of a second before she picked up speed, sliding down the last four rungs of the ladder rather than waste time climbing.

She reached the second platform as a second shot resonated through the open window from the floor above.

She took a moment to lean over the fire exit to check Alex's descent.

He was almost at the last platform, Nathan's face peering up at him, beckoning him. His eyes met hers, and she quickly put her finger to her lips before gesturing to him to get Alex to hurry.

That done, she turned and moved towards the next ladder, her fingers wrapping around the handrails before she dropped in a fast, controlled slide using the instep of her new ankle boots to slow her descent.

She fled across the third platform moments before a splintering crash reached her ears.

# TEN

Parkes tested the weight of his gun in his hand, then pressed against the right-hand wall of the elevator as it completed its short journey to the sixth floor.

As the doors slid open, he reached down and selected the button to keep the doors open, gambling on the agents' inquisitive nature and heightened senses. They'd be expecting their colleague, so he reckoned their first instinct would be concern when he didn't appear from the elevator.

Sure enough, he heard a muffled curse, then the footfalls of the agent that had lost the argument coming closer.

The man's pace was steady, assured, and not the sound of someone expecting to be attacked.

Parkes brought the gun up to chest height, and waited.

The agent stopped before reaching the elevator.

'Dave? Everything okay?'

Parkes let out a groan.

The agent fell for the ruse, and stepped into view.

Parkes didn't hesitate; he shot the agent in the chest, then dropped to a crouch and sprang from the confines of the elevator, firing as he did so.

The second agent fired once, a shot that went wide and ploughed into a ceiling panel before he cried out, sinking to the floor, his hand against his stomach.

Parkes ran forward, and as the agent raised his head, shot him between the eyes.

He spun on his heel, returned to the elevator, and used the gun to jam the door open. He'd still have to contend with the other three, but putting one out of action was better than nothing.

He reached down to the first agent he'd killed and picked up his gun, noting with a satisfied grunt that it still held a full magazine, and removed a key card from the agent's pocket. He jogged to the door of the room the second agent had been standing outside, and swiped the card across the locking mechanism.

He entered the room, and quickly deduced that it hadn't been used.

He moved swiftly through the suite, checked the bathroom and bedrooms, and then returned to the living area, his senses alert.

A sound from the adjoining room caught his attention, and he ran out the door into the hallway, and tried the next room.

*Locked.*

Parkes stood back and aimed the gun at the lock, then turned his head and fired.

Splinters of wood showered his hair, covering his jacket.

He brushed away the detritus, then raised his weapon once more when the door refused to open against his weight.

Two shots obliterated the top of the chair that had been placed under the handle, and he aimed a low kick at the door.

His eyes immediately picked up the net curtains flowing in the breeze.

He raced to the open window, craning his neck to peer down the fire escape that hugged the wall, and then cursed.

## ELEVEN

'Move!'

Eva grabbed Alex's hand and pulled him along the alleyway towards the back of the hotel.

Beyond the exit from the alley, cars flashed by on a busy street, and pedestrians hurried back and forth, oblivious to Eva, Alex and Nathan as they emerged as one onto the pavement.

'Here,' said Eva, and led the way to a subway entrance.

'Won't there be cameras?' said Nathan.

'I hope so,' said Eva. 'We'll use those to our advantage – send them on a wild goose chase with any luck.'

She reached the bottom of the stairs, then followed the subway signs to the nearest platform.

Her eyes flickered over the signs, her brain translating the German easily.

'This way – hurry!'

Eva picked up Alex, and held him tight to her chest as she ran towards the platform that headed north.

As they reached it, a roaring sound began to emanate from the tunnel, and a hot wind preceded the headlights of a train. It slid to a halt, and Eva and Nathan stood to one side as passengers disembarked, before climbing on board.

Eva selected a seat that gave her a view of all the exits and sank into it, turning Alex in her arms.

As the train pulled away from the platform, Eva glanced across the aisle to Nathan.

He was panting, his hair slicked to his forehead.

She pulled Alex closer on her lap and peered over his fair hair at the passengers at the other end of the carriage.

A couple of tourists pored over a map at the far end, pointing and laughing as they compared the pages in their hands with the route displayed above their heads, while an old woman glared at them from four seats away, then rose to her feet and shuffled towards the doors as the train began to slow once more.

Eva caught Nathan's attention. 'Two stops,' she said. 'Then we have to hurry, understand?'

'Got it.' He ran his fingers through his hair. 'I didn't realise I was so unfit.'

'You have to keep up.' Eva shifted Alex from her knee, but kept a hand on his arm. 'We're not out of trouble yet.'

'Okay.'

The train gathered speed once more.

Eva had no idea how much back-up the Section would send their man, but she wasn't going to underestimate them.

Nathan leaned forward. 'Those were gunshots, weren't they?'

'Yes.'

'And you think it was the man you saw in the lobby?'

'Yes, I do.' Eva gave up struggling with Alex and let the boy climb across to the seat next to hers. 'And those two agents that were posted outside our door won't have stood a chance.'

'But, why?'

Eva swallowed. Nathan's face was distraught. How could she even begin to tell him what she'd done, what she'd kept hidden? And now someone had discovered her, and she was on the run again. Her gaze fell to the small figure beside her, and she fought down the ache in her throat that threatened tears.

She was so damn tired of running.

The train burst out of the tunnel, bright sunlight piercing the windows, making her squint.

'Get ready,' she said, then cleared her throat and steadied her voice once more. 'We're getting off here.'

The train slowed and through the window, she noticed the urban sprawl had thinned a little, pockets of houses and apartment blocks replacing the busy metropolis.

As they disembarked, Nathan reached out and took Alex's hand before Eva could. He glanced up apologetically, but she shook her head. The gesture had been so natural, she didn't have the heart to reprimand him.

She wondered what his history was. With the rush of them being sent to the hotel, and then the sheer panic of their escape, she realised she'd never had the chance to ask him about his background.

She still trusted him though. There was something about him that meant she simply couldn't believe he'd cause her or Alex any harm.

At least, she hoped so. It was what her instincts told her, and they hadn't been wrong so far.

Especially about the Section.

How else had their attacker found them?

'What do we do now?'

Nathan's question interrupted her thoughts, and she realised both he and Alex were staring at her, expectant looks on their faces.

'We cross the platform,' she said, and led the way towards a footbridge that crossed the tracks. 'Then we get on a train that's heading south and get as close to the Czech border as we can.'

Nathan picked up Alex and hurried up the steel steps after her. 'Why didn't we do that in the first place?'

'There were CCTV cameras at the subway we entered,' she explained. 'There are only a few here, and they probably won't get to check these for a couple of hours or more. They'll be expecting us to head north, to go back to the UK.'

'And we're not?'

'No. We're not.'

Alex wriggled in Nathan's arms, and he set him down at the top of the steps. The boy reached out for Eva's hand, evidently determined to walk down the stairs on his own rather than be carried.

She smiled a little. He was at the age where one moment he'd be all grown up, determined to forge ahead on his own, before changing his mind and reverting to the little boy that she loved so much.

'Look,' she continued, 'they'll be watching all major stations and airports for us. If I was them, I'd be banking on my heading north so I'd put most of my manpower there. Of course, they'll be checking south of the city as well, but I don't think it'll be as heavily patrolled.'

Nathan frowned. 'You're absolutely convinced it's the Section that did this?'

'Whose idea was it for us to be placed in a hotel in the first place?'

'Miles.' Nathan exhaled. 'Shit.'

Alex giggled.

'Sorry.'

'It's okay. He's heard worse.' Eva smiled. 'Sorry you got dragged into this. You're a bit out of your depth, aren't you?'

'I guess.' Nathan glanced over his shoulder at the approaching train. 'I did all my fieldwork training, but then I got assigned to this project. Spent most of the last six months at a desk.'

'Don't apologise,' said Eva. 'If you hadn't reported a

breach in the system, no-one would have believed me about the attack in Cyprus, and—'

'What?'

The noise of the train drawing to a halt next to the platform put paid to any conversation. Instead, Eva peered through the window of the carriage and, noticing it was deserted, pulled Alex in after her and sat down.

Nathan joined her as the doors slid shut and the train pulled away.

'What did you say?'

Eva checked Alex was settled into his seat and happy to watch the scenery pass by the window, then turned her attention back to Nathan.

'It's why they assigned you to go with me to the hotel.'

'What do you mean?'

'Think about it,' said Eva. 'We're the only two people that know about my existence, and the Section puts us in a hotel together.'

'And then send an assassin to kill us,' finished Nathan.

'If you hadn't flagged the breach—'

'They wouldn't be trying to kill me as well,' said Nathan. His gaze fell to the window as the train re-entered the tunnel and began powering through the city on its journey south. 'Shit. I hate being right.'

## TWELVE

'What the hell happened, Greg?'

Miles slammed the door to the room that had been allocated to him, and glared at the two analysts that looked up from their computers, shock on their faces.

'We don't know,' the elder of the two men admitted. 'We think something spooked her.'

'You think?'

'She was already on the move before the gunman reached her room.'

Miles ground his teeth, forcing the anger down, and held up his hand. 'Okay, status report. What do we know?'

'They checked in at eleven seventeen, collecting separate key cards for their rooms,' said Greg. He pointed at two computer screens displaying a frozen image from the hotel's security cameras. 'We've got two angles on these. One from the reception desk, the other from the front door.'

Miles leaned closer to the two screens. 'What's the layout, Jason?'

'The elevators are to the right of the reception desk as you enter the hotel lobby,' said the younger analyst. 'On the left is the bar, separated from the lobby by double doors.'

'Okay, got it. Play the recording.'

Miles stood with his arms folded across his chest as the screens flickered, and the camera feed returned to its starting position.

Greg had cued it from the moment Eva, Nathan, and Alex entered the hotel, the small boy turning his head from side to side, a look of wonder on his face as he gaped at the extravagant surroundings.

Nathan hurried towards the reception desk, efficiency in his movements as he left Eva to check in. Within moments he could be seen talking to the two receptionists, one of them laughing at something he'd said, before her colleague had turned to her computer and started the check-in process.

Miles realised he was holding his breath as he watched Eva.

Although to a casual observer she appeared to be bending to Alex's will, letting him point and tug at her sleeve to get her attention, Miles could see the way her eyes swept the lobby, looking for any signs of threat.

He watched the way her head jerked up, and noted that it had only taken her moments to spot the men he'd put in place to protect her. She was professional though, and did nothing to alert anyone around her that heavily armed men were walking around one of the most prestigious hotels in Berlin.

Her gaze shifted to her right, assessing the elevators, and no doubt the fire exits and staff areas that would have already been checked for potential threats by Miles's team.

Then she looked to her left, towards the bar, and Miles thought his heart would punch through his ribcage.

'Stop the tape!'

Jason leaned forwards and hit a button, then waited, his hand hovering over the controls.

'Move it back to when she looks at the entrance to the bar,' said Miles. He glanced at Greg. 'Do we know if the doors were open at that time?'

Greg leafed through his notes, his eyes flickering over hastily scribbled details he'd managed to glean from the security detail so far. 'Yes. The bar opened at eleven, so the doors from the lobby would've been open.'

Miles pointed at the screen. 'Play it again. Pause it when I say so.'

The three men watched in silence as the recording began, the two cameras clearly showing Eva leading Alex through the lobby.

At first, she appeared wary, her chin jerking slightly as she noticed the Section's security men for the first time.

Then, she turned her head to her left, and her whole demeanour changed. She'd looked away quickly, but her shoulders stiffened, and she quickened her pace towards the reception desk.

It was subtle, but enough to convince Miles. He straightened, his mind racing. 'Do we have any footage of the bar area?'

'Negative,' said Greg. 'Nothing at all.'

'Okay,' said Miles. 'Replay the footage from the whole morning from both camera feeds. From first light to an hour after Eva left the building. I want every single person who went anywhere near that side of the lobby to be accounted for. Identification, home addresses, and whether they're staff or otherwise, understand?'

'Got it,' said Greg, his fingers already flying over his keyboard.

Miles turned as the door opened, and raised an eyebrow as Knox entered.

'I heard about the attack,' he said, loosening his tie as he approached. 'What happened? Is she alive?'

Miles pointed at the screens. 'Something spooked her. She got out just in time.'

'What spooked her? Not our men?'

'No – she'd seen them and didn't bat an eyelid. Almost as if she expected us to have people there.'

'So, what scared her off?'

'Greg – play that sequence again,' said Miles.

He watched and waited while Knox was shown the footage, and then leaned forward to stop the recording. 'She saw someone,' he said. 'I'm certain of it. Someone was in that bar, and whoever it was frightened her.'

Knox's brow furrowed. 'Are you sure?'

'No,' said Miles. 'But at the moment, that's the only reason we've got to explain her actions.' He frowned. 'My guess is that she recognised the shooter before he had a chance to get to her room, and escaped down the fire exit, taking Alex and Nathan with her. We're pulling CCTV footage from the nearby subway stations now.'

Knox ran a hand over his jaw. 'I have to say, Newcombe, this is extremely troubling. Eva is one of our best assets. She's had her cover blown, and her life and that of the boy are still under threat. And now she's on the run. Presumably because she thinks we've got something to do with the attack.'

'I'm going to need more manpower, sir.'

The Section chief sighed, and motioned Miles over to the far corner of the room. 'The problem is,' he said in a low voice, 'the more people I bring on board, the more her life could be at risk.'

'You think someone here could be involved?'

'I don't know what to think. When was the last time you knew of a deep cover operation like this being exposed so badly?'

Miles exhaled. 'True.'

'Let me see what I can do about some extra manpower. We're going to have to be careful, though,' said Knox. 'Right,' he said, and pointed at the two analysts that stared up at him from their desks. 'No-one leaves this building until we find her, understood?'

'Yes, sir,' said Miles, ignoring the glares from his team. 'We'll let you know as soon as we have something to report.'

'Make sure you do,' said Knox. 'And find out who that shooter was, where he's gone, and how we're going to stop him. This is an absolute disaster, Newcombe.'

'Sir.'

# THIRTEEN

Eva wiped the condensation from the window of the train carriage with her sleeve and peered out into the night, cupping her hands around her face to block out ambient light.

As the train slowed, a station drew into her line of vision, and a nameplate loomed out of the darkness, illuminated by the light from the train carriages.

She dropped her hands and turned to Nathan.

'It's this one. Let's go.'

They hurried along the length of the carriage and as the train crawled to a halt, Eva swung the door open, climbed down onto the platform and then turned to take Alex from Nathan before he joined her and slammed the carriage door shut.

No-one else alighted from the train.

The conductor's whistle blew from the end of the train,

echoing the piercing shriek emitted from the stationmaster's whistle at the far end of the platform, and the carriages began to ease forward.

'Move,' said Eva, and led the way into the shadows of a low structure she guessed to be a waiting room.

The interior was dark, and there were no other passengers to be seen.

They averted their eyes as the last of the train carriages passed, the slam of the door to the guard's cabin reaching her ears before a final rush of air tugged at her clothes, and then the train's rear lights disappeared into the night.

'Wait,' she whispered. 'Don't move.'

She craned her neck to peer around Nathan, hugging the sleeping form of Alex to her chest while she tried to gauge the stationmaster's movements.

She froze, as at the far end of the platform he stopped moving, and seemed to be waiting.

Eventually, perhaps deciding that whoever had disembarked had already left the vicinity, he shook his head and shuffled across the poorly lit platform to his office.

A door closed, the lights beyond their hiding place dimmed, and silence descended upon the train station.

'What is this place?' hissed Nathan.

'We're near the border with Germany and the Czech Republic.' She jerked a thumb over her shoulder. 'Half a mile that way is the official border.' She pointed to her left. 'But we're going that way. It'll probably take us a couple of hours to cut through the fields.'

'What about border control?' asked Nathan.

'Negative,' said Eva. 'The Czech Republic signed up to the Schengen Agreement with its neighbours, so that makes border crossings easier. Despite more stringent controls on main roads because of the migrant crisis, we should be okay. My guess is that if we cross through one of the small towns, we won't be stopped. They probably won't even have anyone manning the crossing at this time of night.'

'Are you sure?'

'No. Keep an eye out for any customs officials once we're in sight of the signs for the border, just in case.'

An hour and half later, Eva's new ankle boots were covered in mud and her jeans were clinging to her calves.

The route across the fields and through hedgerows had been hard going, hampered by having to carry a fitful and exhausted Alex.

Eva had been grateful when Nathan offered to carry him, and between them they managed to keep going, one bearing the extra load when the other began to stumble.

'Why Prague?'

'It's where all this began,' said Eva. 'I thought maybe we'd find some answers there.'

'Wouldn't it have been better to head for the UK, regroup there and work out what's going on? '

'Better, maybe. But not safer.' A breeze lifted her hair off her forehead, and she shivered. 'The way things are going, I don't know if we'd ever make it back there alive.'

The moon scuttled back behind a cloud, but not before she'd seen the look of shock that crossed his face.

'Better that you know the truth, Nathan.'

'Easy for you to say.'

She stopped and held up her hand as a rushing sound reached her ears.

'What's that?'

'The main road. We need to put some distance between us and the border before we venture out onto it though. We'll raise too much suspicion otherwise.'

'What's your plan?'

'We'll hitch a ride to the outskirts of Prague. It's only sixty miles away.'

'Isn't that risky?'

'No. We'll say we were dumped by an unscrupulous taxi driver who decided to ditch us just over the border. Follow my lead. We'll be fine.'

Twenty minutes later, they found a small stream beside a hedgerow and despite the cold, waded in and washed the worst of the mud from their shoes and jeans.

'We'll dry out fast enough,' said Eva, ignoring the biting chill that now nipped at her skin. 'We'd stand out a mile with all that mud over us.'

They pushed through a break in the hedgerow and stepped onto a grass verge that bordered the main road leading towards Prague.

Nathan checked his watch. 'It's one o'clock in the morning. We'll never get a lift at this time of night.'

Eva cast her eyes along the deserted highway, and then pointed to her right. 'Okay, well Prague is that way, so let's keep going.'

Despite Nathan's foreboding, vehicles did pass them as they walked. After what seemed an age, and an inordinate amount of unsuitable vehicles, including two motorbikes and a large truck, Eva spun round at the sound of an approaching car.

'This one,' she said, and pushed Nathan to the edge of the pavement. 'Make sure he stops.'

She pulled Alex until he was standing in front of her, and placed her hand on his shoulder. 'Nearly there,' she murmured. 'Then you can sleep.'

Alex grumbled under his breath, but remained where he was.

Eva lifted her eyes from the downy fluff of his blond hair to the glare of the approaching headlights, and let her desperation show.

Nathan lifted his hand as the vehicle drew closer, stepping off the kerb as it slowed.

The driver lowered his window as the car stopped, his features etched by the pyramid of light that shone from the halogen lamps above.

'Co je špatně?'

'Thank you so much for stopping,' began Nathan in broken German, and glanced over his shoulder at Eva.

She took the hint; he'd struggle to maintain the lie and needed her to take over.

She took Alex's hand and led him towards the vehicle, smiled at Nathan as if he was her knight in shining armour, then turned her attention to their very real saviour.

'*Sprechen Sie Deutsch?*'

'Ah – *ja*! I speak a little German,' he beamed. 'That will have to do.'

'We're so sorry to trouble you,' she continued in fluent German. 'We only arrived this morning. Our taxi driver dumped us two miles away from here.' She swore under her breath, her disgust apparent. 'We didn't know he wasn't a legitimate driver. He's stolen all our luggage.'

The driver of the vehicle cursed, and nodded. 'It is a problem,' he said. 'So many unscrupulous people, taking advantage of tourists.' He smiled at Alex. 'Where are you from?' he asked.

'Australia,' said Eva, and hoped to hell her German disguised the fact that her accent was pure English. 'We were wondering – if you wouldn't mind—'

The driver held up his hand to stop her. 'Where do you need to go?' he asked.

Eva exhaled with real relief. 'Into the city,' she said. 'If you can get us to—' She frowned, and paused as if to try and recall, '—Smíchov, we'd be very grateful. We can pay you – we have cash.'

'No, no – I won't take your money,' said the driver, and climbed from the vehicle. He held out his hand. 'I'm Markus.'

Eva smiled. 'Natasha,' she said, 'and this is my husband, Simon. This little imp is Alex.'

She deliberately stuck to Alex's real name – it was safer, and less likely to confuse him in his exhausted state.

Markus opened the back door and ushered Alex and Eva to the back seats, then gestured to Nathan to take the passenger seat. 'It's only a little out of my way. We'll be there in no time.'

Eva leaned over and fastened Alex's seatbelt for him while the driver jogged back to the open driver's door, swung it shut and eased the car back onto the highway.

As the the vehicle picked up speed, she exhaled some of the tension she'd been holding back.

They weren't out of danger yet, not by a long shot, but they were moving again – and in the right direction.

'Do you have somewhere to stay in Smíchov?'

'Yes,' said Eva. 'My sister keeps an apartment there. Luckily she's expecting us.'

'A nice area,' agreed Markus. 'Very close to everything.'

He indicated, and overtook a large double-trailer truck with Polish plates, the powerful car surging forward before sweeping back into the right-hand lane once more.

'Would you like me to take you to the police station in the morning?' he asked, his eyes finding hers in the rear-view mirror. 'You and your husband should report this as soon as possible.'

She shook her head. 'That's very kind of you,' she said. 'But we'll go and see them once we've phoned our travel insurers and the embassy.' She leaned over and ruffled Alex's hair. 'At the moment, we're just trying to get to our destination and keep our fingers crossed this one thinks it's a big adventure.'

Markus smiled and nodded. 'I have two nephews,' he said. 'I understand.'

Eva let the conversation end, and the occupants of the car spent the rest of the journey into the city centre in companionable silence. She was grateful Nathan spoke no German – it stopped Markus asking too many questions.

Instead, she watched Nathan's reflection in the window next to his head. He seemed lost in thought as he looked out at the streets as they passed by in a blur.

She resisted the temptation to look over her shoulder at the sparse traffic on the road behind them. She would be followed, she knew, but for now she had to trust that her quick thinking had put some distance between her and her pursuers – whichever side they were on.

# FOURTEEN

*Berlin*

Miles fought down the sense of frustration that was threatening to overwhelm him and instead paced the room, his eyes roaming over the different feeds from the various CCTV cameras around the hotel.

Knox had found three more analysts to work with him, but had been reluctant to part with more from the Middle East section.

'The fewer people that know about this, the better,' he'd said. 'Let's keep this close.'

Miles appreciated what the Section chief was saying, but it didn't help the fact that he was understaffed and desperate to find Eva, Alex and Nathan. Worryingly, there was no sign of the assassin who had killed five of the Section's agents, either.

The only lead they had so far for him was a grainy feed from the hotel bar's CCTV camera. The images were saved onto a different server than the rest of the hotel, and were recorded at one minute intervals rather than continuously. Greg was running the images through a software application to try and clean them up.

'Who's checking car rental companies?'

One of the new analyst's hands shot up in the air, although his eyes didn't leave the screen in front of him. 'Nothing to report. I'll keep monitoring it, but at this stage it looks like they've use another mode of escape.'

'Nothing on the taxi radios, either,' said Jason.

'Well, they won't have got far on foot, and Eva wouldn't risk it with Alex in tow,' said Miles. 'That leaves the train station, subways, and bus stations. Get on with it.'

He ran a hand through his hair, knowing he was taking out his frustration on the team, but unable to stop himself. His mind raced while he tried to fathom who had found out that Eva was in the hotel before she'd even arrived, let alone how they had found out she was in Berlin. The flight plan hadn't been logged until the RAF plane was an hour north of Alicante the previous night.

Desperate, he returned to his desk and began to scroll through the reports that were coming in.

He cursed himself for being so complacent. He should have

known that whoever organised the attack on the condo in Cyprus wouldn't stop there. Somebody wanted Eva and Alex dead, and was prepared to do anything to ensure that outcome.

Guilt washed over him. He had no doubt Eva could look after herself, but he had put Nathan in that situation and the man had undergone no current field training. Not for situations like this. In his haste to find answers, he had put three lives at risk.

'Miles? I think I've got something.'

His head jerked up from his screen at the sound of Greg's voice, and he made his way over to the other man's desk.

Greg pointed at the frozen image on the screen. 'I found him.'

Miles leaned forward. On the screen, Greg clicked through a series of images. A man dressed in a black suit entered the bar at two minutes past eleven, sat on a bar stool and twisted around so that he could see the lobby. He waved over a waiter and ordered a drink, which he then ignored.

'This is the only person in the bar,' said Greg. 'I've already put a call through to the hotel and sent them this image. They confirm the man isn't a guest.' He flicked to a different image, this time from the CCTV camera in the hotel lobby. He pointed at the screen. 'He walked in off the street at ten to eleven.'

Miles stabbed his finger at the monitor. 'Find out who that is. Where he's from, why he's here. Everything.'

'Why do you think he's involved?'

'Watch Eva in that footage from the hotel lobby. She's

relaxed, almost, when the embassy car drops them off. Her shoulders are slumped; she's tired. Yet within two minutes, her whole demeanour changes. Why?' He tapped the screen again. 'Because she saw him.'

Miles picked up his mobile phone and called Knox. 'You'll want to see this. We've got a match on the gunman. Greg's emailed you the image. What—' He waited while Knox barked out an instruction. 'Okay. I'll see you in a minute.'

He ended the call and turned to Greg. 'Knox is on his way down.'

He didn't have to wait long. Within five minutes, the familiar beep of the security pad on the door being activated reached his ears, and Knox strode in.

'Show me.'

Miles pointed at the screen next to Greg's desk and joined the Section chief. 'Run Gerald through it,' he said, lowering himself into one of the spare chairs and folding his arms over his chest.

Out the corner of his eye, he saw Knox's jaw clench as the suspect's image filled the screen, the analyst taking them through the whole sequence of images, from when the man entered the bar until the moment he left – only minutes before the killing began.

Knox remained silent as the photographs flashed before his eyes, and Miles was about to ask him what he thought, when the Section chief spoke.

'Miles? Step outside a moment, would you?'

Knox jerked his head towards the door, then walked away and opened it, not waiting to see if Miles followed.

Miles cursed under his breath, then pushed his chair back and hurried to catch up with him. He closed the door and found Knox standing a little further up the corridor, leaning against the wall, his arms crossed over his chest. He looked troubled.

'What is it?'

Knox glanced up as he approached, then checked to make sure the corridor was empty.

'The man in the CCTV image,' said Knox. 'His name is Samuel Parkes.'

Miles frowned. 'You know him?'

Knox's mouth formed a thin line. 'I should do. I recruited him.'

# FIFTEEN

*Prague*

'Where are we going?'

Nathan matched her pace, and Eva could hear the impatience in his voice. She felt responsible for him, aware that he'd been thrust into a situation that was beyond his comprehension. She owed him an explanation, and soon.

'Somewhere safe, I hope,' she said. 'We're nearly there.'

In fact, they'd already passed the apartment a block back, and she was now circling round to lead them down the street that passed along the rear of the building. So far, she'd seen nothing suspicious, but she wasn't prepared to let down her guard yet.

'Why did you insist on speaking German to the Czech guy who gave us a lift?'

'It'll buy us some time if the Section can't determine where we are, or which direction we went. They'll put out an alert for a missing English couple with a little boy in tow. If Markus sees it, hopefully it'll take him a while to put two and two together or, better, not at all.'

She bent down and gathered Alex into her arms. He'd stumbled, exhausted, and she needed to get him to safety so that he could rest. A fractious child would only draw attention to them, something they could ill afford at such a late time of night on a quiet street.

After persuading Markus to drop them off close to the city centre, she'd set a quick pace towards the old safe house. She knew it was a risk, but no-one in the Section knew about it.

The property had been part of an inheritance, and one that had been kept a secret through necessity, the papers hidden in a safe deposit box in a London bank vault.

Three years ago, it had been cared for by a part-time manager; those days had long passed, and her contact assured her that no interest had been taken in the building for the past few months.

It would have to do.

Alex's weight slowed her progress, and she fought off the weariness that threatened to engulf her.

'I can take him, if you want?'

'That's okay, I've got him.'

'You're exhausted.'

'We're nearly there.'

Headlights flashed further along the street in front of them, and Eva jerked to a stop.

'Get down,' she hissed, dropping to a crouch beside a parked vehicle. She prayed none of the residents in the narrow buildings lining the street looked out from their windows.

Nathan copied her stance, and they peered through the car's windows as the vehicle drew closer, and then passed them.

Its brake lights flashed when it had gone a few more metres, and then the driver stopped and reversed into a parking space on the opposite side of the road.

Doors opened, before being slammed shut, and the voices of a young couple wafted across the street towards them.

Eva and Nathan stood, and she flashed him a guilty smile. 'Sorry.'

He shook his head. 'You've got some explaining to do when we get to wherever we're going.'

'I know. I will,' she said. 'I promise.'

She led the way along the street towards an alleyway. She checked over her shoulder once, then led the way past discarded takeaway cartons, the back door to a Chinese fast food outlet casting bright light over the asphalt.

She hurried past, avoiding the temptation to look through the door into the busy kitchen, in case someone saw her face, and then stopped at a door set into the side of the opposite building.

She slid Alex to the floor, made sure he stayed close, then reached into her pocket for a set of keys.

After her interview at the Berlin office, Miles had automatically assumed they had belonged to the house in Cyprus, and had handed them back to her, a rueful expression on his face.

Now, she inserted the larger of the two keys into the door, and breathed a sigh of relief when the lock turned smoothly.

'Come on,' she said, and ushered Nathan and Alex over the threshold.

A small window set above the door allowed light from the Chinese takeaway to filter through the dirty glass, illuminating a narrow corridor that led away from the door and towards a flight of stairs.

Eva brushed past Nathan, picked up Alex, and led the way down the passageway, ignoring an archway in the wall to her left.

As she reached the stairs, she realised Nathan wasn't following, and stopped, glancing over her shoulder.

He was standing stock-still, staring through the opening in the wall, a look of wonder on his face.

'A bookshop?'

She wandered back to join him, running her eyes over the bookcases that ran in several rows through the space to where she knew a counter to be at the front of the shop.

She pursed her lips. 'It's guaranteed to go up in flames very quickly if we need to cover our tracks.'

'Oh.' Nathan ran his hand along the nearest dusty and cracked spines before he shook his head and caught up with her. 'That would be a shame,' he murmured.

Eva said nothing, turned on her heel and trudged up the stairs ahead of him, ignoring the mustiness from months of neglect that permeated the stale air around her.

At the top step, she lowered Alex, noticing the way his legs wobbled as he reached the floor, and put her hand on his shoulder to steady him.

She turned her attention to the door that blocked their path, then punched a series of six numbers into the key pad set into its surface, and stepped back as the locking mechanism released with a loud *clunk*.

Again, she stepped aside to let Nathan and Alex pass, before closing the door behind them and flicking a switch set in the wall.

Four lamps set on small tables dotted around the room flickered to life, casting a muted glow around the large space. Faded sheets covered various items of furniture, their forms reduced to shapeless lumps in the poor light.

Eva crossed the room and began pulling one of the sheets away, revealing two sofas and a coffee table.

Nathan followed her lead, and began to help, uncovering a dining table and four chairs.

'Looks like this place was abandoned in a hurry.'

'It was.'

'So, what happens now?'

'I need to make a call. There's someone who can help us.'

Nathan frowned. 'You destroyed our mobile phones.'

Eva reached into her coat pocket and pulled out a phone. 'I took this from one of the other agents.'

'Wait. What? You stole that?'

Eva glared at him. 'You have a better suggestion?'

'What if the call is being traced?'

Eva glanced over her shoulder at Alex, who had curled up on one of the sofas and was drifting to sleep.

'Given that we heard shots fired, I'm pretty certain the previous owner is no longer with us,' she hissed. 'Aren't you?'

Nathan folded his arms across his chest. 'Who are you going to call?'

'It's not as simple as that.'

Eva selected the internet connection on the phone, opened a familiar email website page, and logged in.

'You're going to use the "drafts" folder, aren't you?'

She nodded. 'It's not the best way, but it's the easiest in our circumstances. My contact will be checking this regularly now, waiting for me to get in touch.'

She hit "save", then pulled the battery and SIM card from the phone and crushed them under her heel.

'What do we do now?' asked Nathan.

'We sleep,' said Eva, and rubbed her eyes. 'I'm shattered.'

## SIXTEEN

*Berlin*

'What do you mean, you recruited him? When?'

Miles glared at his boss.

'About ten years ago,' said Knox. He handed over the folder he'd been clutching to his chest. 'He was one of our best assets.'

'Was?' Miles snatched the file from the Section chief and opened it, running his gaze down the neatly typed overview that had been clipped to the inside front cover.

'He went rogue a little over three years ago. Despite our best efforts to trace him, he was too well trained. He disappeared.'

'Until now.' Miles closed the folder, took a few steps away and ran his hand over the stubble covering his jaw. 'What the hell happened three years ago, Gerald? What isn't in the dossier about Eva?'

'Everything we know about Eva is on file, Miles,' said Knox. 'Listen, I know you need more manpower to bring this to a successful conclusion but like I said, we need to keep this locked down.'

'I understand. We're doing our best.'

'Keep up the good work,' said Knox as he turned away. 'I'll be in touch.'

'Sure.'

Miles waited until the Section chief disappeared from sight, then exhaled and leaned against the wall, staring at the ceiling.

'Something doesn't add up,' he murmured.

He strode back into the room, snatched up the manila folder containing all the paperwork about Eva, then told Greg to phone him on his mobile if there were any developments and made his way to the cafeteria.

The place was deserted, but he chose a table at the back of the room in a corner away from any windows, and began to leaf through the documents once more.

When interviewing Eva earlier that day, he'd concentrated on the events of three years ago, sifting through the file to try and extract memories from her, to find out how her Cypriot location had been compromised.

Now, he pushed that aside and instead began to go through the papers that documented her recruitment process.

As his eyes skimmed the typed words, a lump formed in his throat. While he'd been working his way through the bureaucratic ranks of the British secret service, Eva had undertaken a brutal training regime, and had been spat out the other end minus twelve other recruits that had attempted the course with her.

After that, there had been no more recruitment programmes like it. Too many injuries, the report said, both physically and psychologically.

He blinked, then picked up her active service sheet.

She'd been busy.

He traced his finger down the list of confirmed kills, his jaw slack. Some of them he'd seen in newspapers, reported as accidents or deaths by natural causes.

He'd imagined, on nights where he lay awake in bed unable to get back to sleep, that the Section probably maintained a black ops capability, but until now, he'd kept that to himself. He'd simply never been part of such an operation, so it was easy to reconcile his work with the security of the nation.

Yet here it was. Proof that they were involved.

He pushed Eva's file to one side, then flipped open the folder Knox had given him. His eyes widened as he read, working his way through each document in turn, until he stopped, and realised his hands were shaking.

'Holy crap,' he murmured.

He let the page fall to the table, and rubbed his hand over his mouth.

As the document settled, his eyes opened wide, and his hand shot out to stop the page sliding over the edge of the table.

'That's not possible.'

He pulled the document closer, his eyes flickering over the staccato nature of the communiqué, his mind racing, before pushing the chair back and rising to his feet, trying to ignore the slight tremble in his fingers. Instead, he gathered up the remaining documents, shoved them into the folders and hurried back to the team of analysts.

If he was right, Eva was in a lot more trouble than any of them had first imagined.

# SEVENTEEN

*South-east Poland*

The interior of the large steel and concrete building fell silent as Maxim Kowalski stalked through the open double doors, his guards closing the metal panels once he was clear.

A group of men stood in the middle of the space.

No-one spoke; most were terrified.

Maxim's reputation was something the younger members of the group had feared as children in the neighbouring villages; they'd witnessed first-hand the way in which Maxim controlled his territory and dealt with dissenters.

The boldest of them had later joined his underground army, weary of being destitute. The promise of money, drugs, and as many young girls as they could want, in return for unwavering allegiance.

Power was a strong aphrodisiac, and something that Maxim used both to control his own men and retain his grip over the local population.

Except Maxim wanted more.

He dug his fingers into his palms as the soles of his boots echoed off the concrete walls. He could smell the fear emanating from the group of men as he approached, and it did nothing to allay the fury that was coursing through his body.

Hunting down the boy had taken years of work; the past three years of his sordid life had revolved around tracking his movements, planning to kidnap him, then watching helplessly as each opportunity slipped by because the Section moved the boy, and the hunt began once more.

Until last month, when Maxim finally traced him to the gated community in Cyprus favoured by embassy workers and ex-pats alike.

Weeks of planning, getting his team in place one by one posing as tourists, so as not to alert the authorities. They'd travelled into Cyprus via Greece, buying European Union passports from a backstreet vendor in Athens, finding it easy to obtain fake identities within a country struggling with debt and an influx of refugees from the Middle East.

Days spent following the boy and the woman from a distance, noting the weak spots in their routine. There hadn't been many, and the team were growing frustrated by the time they realised the chink in the woman's armour was the half-hearted security at the compound that she'd grown to rely on.

Yet, despite all that, the woman had outsmarted his best men, who now lay in various states of decomposition in an Akrotiri morgue, their identities unknown thanks to his foresight to strip them of any identification that could lead back to their home country.

And she and the boy had disappeared once more.

Maxim felt warmth in his palm and, lifting his hand, realised he'd drawn blood. He stopped, licked his skin clean, then glared at the assembled men.

'Where is she?'

'Last seen in Berlin, Maxim,' said an older man, his black hair shot through with grey. He met Maxim's glare with an unwavering stare of his own. 'Our contact sent his man after her, yet he was also outwitted.'

Maxim snorted. 'She's just a woman, Vadir.' He gestured towards the doors. 'No more than one of those bitches out there that snivel around your heels and take your drugs.' He ground his teeth. 'This is our last chance. She knows now that nothing has changed in three years.'

'She doesn't know who we are,' insisted Vadir. 'Nothing was ever traced to you back then, and nothing will be traced back to you now.'

Maxim stuffed his hands into the pockets of the heavy coat he wore. The edges of the forest were cold, even at this time of year, and it would only grow colder over the coming weeks. No sunlight penetrated the building despite the small windows inserted into the high walls, and he longed to return outside.

Instead, he began to pace, in an effort to control the panic that was beginning to rise within him in the confines of the building, as well as work off some of the anger that threatened to overwhelm him.

He needed to stay calm, to think, to plan.

'All right,' he said. 'Use your contacts. Find out where she could have gone.' He spun on his heel to face his men. 'Hunt her down.'

# EIGHTEEN

*Prague*

Eva twitched the curtain and surveyed the street below.

She'd woken at the sound of a car pulling up outside, wiping sleep from her bleary eyes as she'd stumbled out of the bedroom and across to the front window in the living area.

'Who is it?'

Nathan moved by her side, his voice no more than a murmur.

'Only the owner of the place next door,' she said, checking her watch. 'Opening time.' She let the curtain fall back into place. 'Did you sleep okay?'

'Yes. Thanks.' He stepped aside to let her pass. 'What's the plan for today?'

'I've got some stuff to sort out.' Eva sank onto one of the sofas and curled her legs up under her. 'There are some things here I need to go through,' she said. 'It might take me a while.'

Nathan perched on the arm of the sofa opposite. 'What sort of things?'

She met his gaze. 'Some files, to start with.'

'I'm guessing you mean you've got copies of Section documents.'

'Some of them, yes. It's okay, they're in a safe. Only Douglas and myself knew the combination,' she added when his jaw dropped.

'You realise that's a breach of the Official Secrets Act?'

'Nathan, my whole life has been a breach of one law or another. I'm past caring.' Eva stood and stretched her back muscles. 'I want to find out who the hell betrayed me and put Alex's life in danger.'

'Do you really have no idea why someone wants you dead?'

'What exactly do you know about me?'

'What's that got to do with it?'

'Humour me.'

'You're Eva Delacourt. You've been in a government-run witness protection scheme with your son, Alex, ever since an unknown assassin killed your fiancé, Douglas Bolton. You're still considered a high-risk target because of your own past as an assassin, which is why your location is changed every eighteen months to two years. There have been no threats on your life for three years, which is why you were only assigned a watching brief. Me.'

'No-one else in the Section knows about it?'

'Well, they probably do now after yesterday's events. But, no – it was just me, Miles, and Knox. And, I suppose, Petersen – your old boss. After all, he was the one that put you both into the witness protection programme in the first place.'

Eva sighed. 'That's what I thought. Did you have sight of what my next location was going to be?'

He shook his head. 'That wasn't known. Not at the time. Miles told me it was Copenhagen when he was interviewing you. The way they run it, they'll have three or four options being set up at the same time. They choose the final one at the very last minute, to try to prevent anyone finding out.'

Eva stood up, then moved across to the window and checked the street below once more.

'Have you heard from your contact?'

She shook her head. 'He won't email back. He'll be here if and when he can.'

'What if he doesn't show up?'

'He will.'

'Yes, but how long will we have to wait for him?' Nathan said, pacing the room. 'I mean, there's a very good chance the Section will have traced our movements by now – I've seen the technology they've got.' He checked his watch. 'I reckon we've got twenty-four hours at most before we'll have to move.'

'Nathan, I know.' Eva held up her hand. 'I know. Look, I really need to check through my stuff. Can you keep Alex occupied when he wakes up?'

'Sure, why not?' said Nathan, his tone exasperated. 'I'll just stay here and babysit, shall I?'

'There's no need to be like that,' said Eva. 'I'm sorry you've got involved, really I am, but let's just deal with it, shall we?'

'Fine.'

Eva brushed past him before he could utter another word, and made her way back along the passageway to the bedroom. She glanced over her shoulder before closing the door, and pulled a chair across the rug until she could prop it under the door handle.

'That'll have to do.'

She moved to the large bay window, checked the net curtain was securely in place, then crouched down next to the window seat. She swore as a nail broke under her efforts to move the wooden seat cover, then felt the surface give way, and pulled it free.

Setting down the lid, she knelt next to the exposed metal door of the fireproof safe, and wiped the grease from her fingers.

The tell that she'd left in place under the seat hadn't moved, so evidently the Section had never discovered her hiding place after Douglas's death.

Nor had her enemies.

She chewed her lip. Maybe she, Alex, and Nathan stood a fighting chance after all.

In her heart, she knew she wasn't going to keep running this time; at some point, she'd draw on all her resources and take the fight to those who wanted her dead.

First, though, she had to ensure Alex remained safe – he was her only focus for now.

Eva checked over her shoulder.

The door remained shut, the faint sound of voices reaching her ears, and she realised Alex had woken up.

She reached out and turned the locking mechanism on the safe, then lifted the lid. She pushed aside a clip of photographs she knew she had to resist the temptation to look through, or else she'd lose her composure.

Instead, she pulled out a stapled set of handwritten notes and ran her fingers over them. Lifting them to her face, she inhaled the last remnants of Douglas's scent that still clung to the pages.

She blinked away the tears that threatened to form, and cleared her throat.

'Concentrate,' she murmured.

After they'd left his official residence and hid above the bookshop for those last precious days, Douglas had insisted on writing everything down about the case he'd been working on. At the time, Eva had shrugged, her attention on ensuring the small apartment remained under the radar, and not on his need to justify his movements over the past few weeks.

She folded the pages and put them to one side on the floor next to her, then emptied the safe of its most useful contents.

Passports, first – alternative ones for her and Alex that she'd procured as a back-up; ones that she'd never really expected to need. A third passport joined them; she'd already committed to ensuring Nathan's safety, and so with a bit of handiwork she could create a new identity for him using Douglas's spare.

She'd never told Douglas about the passports. Their relationship hadn't left room for her to explain the intricacies of her life, and for a brief moment she wondered what could have been, if she'd foreseen what was going to happen and had insisted on them disappearing instead.

She spent another half an hour poring over the information she'd obtained from the Section's secret files, but none of it gave her any indication as to how or by whom her location had been compromised.

Finally, she pulled out a cloth bag from the safe, reached inside, and extracted two bundles of cash – one in Euros, the other in American dollars.

Closing the safe and putting the window seat back in place, she gathered the items together, and fetched a small backpack from the top shelf of the wardrobe.

She froze at the sound of the door entry system buzzing in the hallway, then crossed the room in an instant and tore the door open.

'Wait.'

Nathan was already standing next to it, pointing at the screen.

'This man says he knows you,' he said, and inclined his head towards the image on the screen.

The figure of a man glared back at them, his pale eyes half-hidden under a black woollen hat that had been pulled so hard onto his head, it covered his eyebrows. His jaw appeared slightly stubbled, and his nose bore the signs of a retired boxer. A black coat covered the top half of his body, the collar pulled up under his chin.

He jerked his head at the door, then held up his hand, and a tray of three takeaway coffee cups and a milkshake filled the screen.

Eva exhaled, some of the tension from the past twenty-four hours slipping from her body. 'Decker. Thank God you're here.'

She hit the door release, then walked through to the living area to wait.

'Hang on,' said Nathan as the sound of the stairs creaking reached them. 'Who is this man?'

'He used to have the dubious reputation of being one of the best assassins in Europe,' said Eva. 'And he can be temperamental, so my advice to you is, play nice.'

# NINETEEN

*Prague*

Not only had Decker brought coffee, he'd also had the foresight to bring food provisions, and now the smell of cooking filled the small kitchen.

Eva had introduced Decker to Nathan, and had explained how their presence at the apartment had come to be.

'You were lucky you saw Parkes in the hotel lobby,' he said, taking a plate loaded with bacon, eggs, and toast from her and joining Nathan at the table. 'I don't know that you'd have had a chance to escape otherwise.'

Eva spun round from cooking her own food at a loud clatter.

Nathan shrugged apologetically, and picked up his knife

and fork once more. 'Sorry,' he mumbled. 'I'm still finding it hard to believe people are trying to kill us.'

Decker shook a liberal helping of salt and pepper over his breakfast, passed the condiments to him, and began to eat. 'You'll get used to it.'

Eva plated up her own food, and sat next to Alex. She ruffled his hair as he glanced up at her. 'Eat it all,' she said. 'Then you'll grow up to be big and strong.'

'Like Decker?'

A smile split the hard features of the brute of a man sitting opposite. 'Like me.'

Alex grinned, and attacked his food once more with gusto.

'What are your immediate plans?' asked Decker.

'I've gone through the files I'd hidden here,' said Eva. 'The man in the lobby, Samuel Parkes, was hired by Gerald Knox but turned rogue. The accepted rumour was that he left the secret service after being offered a lot of money to do so.'

'Is that when Knox sent you after him?'

'Hang on. What?' Nathan spun in his chair to face Eva. 'What did he just say?'

Eva shook her head, and waited until she'd finished her mouthful before speaking. 'Petersen sent me. At the time, he wanted to keep Knox's involvement to a minimum – said it'd be a conflict of interest if he sent an assassin to catch his own assassin.'

'I can't imagine Knox took it that well.'

'If he did, he didn't show it,' said Eva. 'I think he was as relieved as Petersen that the problem was addressed quickly without casting aspersions on the Section.'

'How did you...' Decker raised an eyebrow, and inclined his head towards Alex.

'Alex, could you fetch the rest of that bacon on that plate next to the stove for Decker, please?' said Eva, and waited until Alex was out of earshot. 'Poison.'

'And you were sure it worked?'

She nodded. 'All the signs were there. And it was reported the next day that a man had been found dead in that apartment matching Parkes's description. Petersen showed me the clipping. I've got a copy of it on my file.'

'So, he's got some influential friends,' said Nathan. 'If he can get a newspaper to help fabricate his death.'

'True.'

Decker leaned back as Alex approached with the extra food and put it on the table next to his elbow. 'Thanks, kiddo. Do you want some of this?' he asked Nathan, then heaped the bacon onto his plate after the man had shaken his head. 'I wonder why he waited three years to come after you?'

'I don't think his contacts knew where to find me,' said Eva. 'Let's face it,' she added, pointing at Nathan, 'only he and Miles knew my exact locations – even Knox didn't know where I was until my cover got blown.'

'But there was a gap of six months between you, er, dealing with him, and what happened to Douglas,' said Nathan, keeping a wary eye on Alex in case the boy suddenly realised what they were talking about. 'So why not come after you during that time?'

'Maybe he was too sick,' suggested Decker. 'If he was poisoned—,' he held up his hand to silence Eva's protests, 'then it may have taken some time to recover. Whatever was meant to kill him, didn't, but every poison will take its toll on the body somehow. Perhaps by the time he was well enough to contemplate revenge, it was too late – Eva was in hiding.'

'Can I get down, please?' said Alex.

'Of course,' said Eva, and watched as the boy trotted off to the living room, before the sounds of him playing with his toy car reached her.

She pushed her plate away and sighed. 'How the hell does someone survive poisoning? It's usually so effective.'

Nathan spluttered on his last mouthful and reached out for a glass of water. He eyed it suspiciously.

Eva rolled her eyes. 'You're one of the good guys,' she said. 'Drink.'

'Where did you get the poison from?' asked Decker.

'One of the Section's contacts acquired it for me. I made the pick-up an hour before the hit, then got the hell out of there.'

'So, no time to check it was the right stuff?'

Eva leaned her elbow on the table and tapped her chin. 'No.'

'You're saying it was deliberately just enough to make him sick, but not enough to kill him?' said Nathan.

Decker nodded. 'Exactly. Eva would have waited to see

the poison take effect, and then cleared off before anyone spotted her, am I right?'

She nodded. 'Right.' She leaned back in her chair, stunned. 'Why on earth would I be sent to kill someone, if the Section wanted him to survive?'

'I don't know,' said Decker. He pointed at her with his fork. 'But every minute you stay here, it gets more dangerous for you and Alex.'

'No-one in the Section knows about this apartment.'

'Can you be certain of that?'

Eva swallowed. 'The place hasn't been touched since Douglas and I left here three years ago, Decker.'

Decker narrowed his eyes. 'They're good, Eva. Remember that.'

'I'm certain of it.'

'All right. I trust you. What are you going to do?'

She looked down at her hands. 'I thought I might see if I can talk with Scott Lancaster. He might have heard things in my absence. Maybe he's heard something I can use to get a toe-hold in this mess and find out what's really going on.'

'That's too dangerous, Eva. You have no idea if you can trust him.'

'I have to try, Decker. I have to find out what's going on.'

'Then work fast,' he said, standing and collecting the empty plates. 'Before we run out of time.'

## TWENTY

'Who is Scott Lancaster?' asked Nathan. 'I've never heard of him.'

'He was the cultural attaché for the American embassy when Douglas was alive,' said Eva, taking a dish he handed to her and wiping it. 'A CIA operative, of course. He used his position to help the secret services of both the US, and the UK when they deemed it appropriate.'

'Which unfortunately wasn't the same as telling us when they knew Douglas was in danger,' growled Decker. 'Otherwise he'd still be alive today.'

'Is that true?' Nathan's hands hovered over the soapy water.

'Yeah,' said Eva.

She handed the dishcloth to Decker, picked up her mug of coffee and leaned against the kitchen table as the two men finished the washing up.

'That's terrible,' murmured Nathan.

'Bastards,' spat Decker. He glared over his shoulder at Eva. 'Which is why I stand by my original comment. You can't trust him.'

'I'll be careful.'

'What's your plan?' asked Nathan, drying his hands and joining her.

'I did a bit of research earlier while you were keeping Alex occupied. There's a new gallery opening tonight on Nekázanka. He'll be there, I know it.'

'How can you be so sure?'

'People come out of the woodwork at these things. You never know who's going to be there, what contacts you might make,' she said. 'It's not a case of simply attending a gallery opening; it's a networking opportunity, and everybody that has something to buy or sell – including secrets – will be there.'

'Not to mention the fact it'll be held in such a public place, so you stand a fair chance of keeping out of trouble,' said Decker. He leaned against the workbench and crossed his arms over his chest. 'I'll need to get a tuxedo. What time does it start?'

'You're not going,' said Eva. 'You might be recognised. On my own, I stand a chance. The two of us there, together, after everything that's happened?' She shook her head. 'Too risky.'

His arms dropped and he took a step forward. 'You're not going on your own.'

'I know. Nathan can come with me.'

'I can?'

'You can stay here and guard Alex,' said Eva to Decker, ignoring the wide-eyed look Nathan wore. 'He's more important. I won't be able to concentrate if I think someone will come for him while I'm out.'

Decker ran a hand across his closely-cropped hair and swore, and Eva knew she'd won the argument.

'You can watch cartoons, if you like.' She laughed when Decker's stony gaze met hers, and pointed at Nathan. 'We'll be fine. We'll have a glass of champagne, eat some canapés, congratulate the gallery owner on a successful opening, and then ask Scott some questions. We'll be in and out in under an hour, promise.'

'I hate this plan already,' said Decker.

Nathan snorted. 'So do I.'

---

Eva slid back the plastic shower curtain, climbed over the edge of the bath and pulled the threadbare towel from the metal hook on the back of the bathroom door.

Steam filled the small space, creating whorls of cloud that enveloped her body as she towelled herself dry. She reached out and flicked the switch for the extractor fan, her lip curling as it rattled once, and stopped.

She tucked the towel under her arms, pushed the twisted end between her breasts, and rubbed a hand across the mirror over the sink.

She blinked at her reflection.

The hunted eyes that had stared back at her in the interview room at the embassy in Berlin were gone. The old ruthless calculating look had returned; the one she hadn't seen for years.

After she and Alex had gone on the run, it had taken her nearly a year before she'd even contemplated sleeping in a different room to his. Instead, she would read to him until he fell into a deep slumber, and then curl up next to him.

When he'd begun to complain that she took up too much room, she'd simply put a pillow and a blanket on the floor next to his bed and slept there.

Until they'd moved to Cyprus.

Somehow, with a large British military presence on the island, she'd thought she could relax, that no-one would find her, or dare to attack.

A ragged sigh escaped her lips, and she sniffed, once.

'Pull yourself together,' she said, then picked up her hairbrush and began tugging at the wet tangles that framed her face. 'Concentrate.'

She applied a bit of make-up, put on clean underwear, then opened the door to the bedroom, stepping over the threshold through the cloud of steam that followed.

She snapped off the power, silencing the pathetic attempts of the extractor fan to restart, and padded across the floor to the bed where she'd laid out a dress for the evening.

Eva pulled the satin material over her head, zipped up the

back, and then cursed as her fingers struggled with the clasp of her necklace.

She turned at a knock at the door.

'It's open.'

The handle turned and Nathan peered around the door.

'Nearly ready?'

'Yes,' she said. 'Just a minute.'

'Here,' Nathan said, and stepped closer. 'Let me.'

'Thanks,' said Eva, and turned, holding the ends of the necklace until she felt his fingers over hers. 'Whoever designs jewellery clasps definitely doesn't wear them.'

He chuckled, his warm breath brushing her neck. 'But it's a perfect piece of engineering.'

She felt her lips twitch. 'Is that so?'

'It's modelled on a lobster claw – very effective.'

His fingers moved away, and she let her hair fall.

'How do you know all this stuff?' she asked. She leaned across the dresser and picked up the matching bracelet.

'I like learning,' replied Nathan, and held out his hand for the bangle.

She handed it over, then turned her wrist upwards, and concentrated on his hand as he looped the bracelet over hers.

A wave of emotions and memories washed over her.

Douglas dashing around the bedroom of his official residence in Malá Strana, cursing as he tried to find a matching silk handkerchief to his tie, their car waiting downstairs as they tried unsuccessfully to get to the opera on time.

Dancing with him on a polished floor, the lucid notes of a string quartet on the radio filling their senses.

Afterwards, laughing their way through the apartment, past the kitchen, to here—

'Eva? Are you okay?'

She shook her head, and pressed her fingertips to the skin under her eyes. 'I'm fine.'

Nathan had her hand between his fingers, a look of concern etched across his features. 'You're not,' he murmured. 'But you do a good job of pretending you are.'

She went to snatch her hand away, but his grip was firmer than she'd imagined. She tipped her chin upwards until their eyes met.

'Don't,' she whispered.

'Why not?'

His black eyes shimmered as he held her gaze.

'I'm not going to discuss it.'

'So, you push everyone away, is that it?'

'You're going to be late.'

Eva jerked away from Nathan's grip at the sound of Decker's voice.

He stood in the doorway, one hand on the frame. 'Everything okay in here?'

'Yes.'

'Taxi's outside the Chinese takeaway.'

Eva snatched up a small handbag from the bed, checked its contents one last time, and led the way from the room, brushing against Decker's arm as she passed. She stopped, squeezed his hand, then made her way to the living area.

She pursed her lips and blew some of the tension away, squaring her shoulders.

*I can do this.*

'Alex, Nathan and I are going out for a few hours. Decker's going to stay with you,' she said, crouching down to where the boy had sat on the carpet leafing through a book. 'Behave yourself, okay?'

"kay,' he said, then reached out for a hug. 'See you later.'

'You'd better be in bed by the time we get back,' she teased, then straightened and nodded to Nathan. 'Okay, let's go.'

Decker followed them to the front door, opened it and stood on the threshold for a moment. 'All clear,' he said, then stepped aside to let them pass. 'Call me with updates.'

'Will do.' Eva followed Nathan down the steps and towards the waiting taxi.

He stood holding the back door open for her, and held up his hand as she approached.

'Are you sure you want to do this? Be out in the open like this?'

She nodded. 'There's no other way. Let's go.'

## TWENTY-ONE

*South-east Poland*

Maxim paced the bare wooden floorboards, and chewed at his already destroyed nails. It was a tick that he had developed while in prison, and while he detested the constant reminder of his time being incarcerated, he couldn't stop.

His rage was all-encompassing. If his men hadn't been killed in Cyprus by the bitch, he would have killed them himself. Even Parkes, supposedly once the Section's best assassin, had failed.

He had one advantage over the Section, however. He traded using money and fear. It was only a matter of time before his network of contacts found her.

He had to be patient.

He spat out the ragged end of another nail, and spun around at the sound of footsteps in the hallway outside.

'What is it?'

Vadir hovered in the doorway, as if afraid or unsure whether to enter. 'We just received word that the Section's analyst, Nathan Crowe, was seen boarding a train to Prague late yesterday afternoon. He never arrived, nor did the woman and child.'

Maxim shivered as goose bumps spiked his skin. It was an interesting development, and one that he hadn't anticipated.

The thought worried him further. Was he losing his edge? Surely after three years out of active duty, she shouldn't be outwitting him like this?

'Was he alone?'

'At first, we thought so. We went back through some CCTV images though, and it looks like they split up. She went with the boy, and got in a different train carriage.'

'Have they been any sightings of them in Prague?'

'No. Because of the migration crisis, the border checkpoints have stricter controls. They must have disembarked the train before reaching it, and made their way to Prague from there.'

'Have there been any reports of stolen vehicles?'

'We've been through all the police reports. There's nothing. She can't have walked all the way to Prague from there, not with the boy. She must have hitchhiked.'

'You have lookouts at the house in Malá Strana?'

'Yes. There's been no sign of her, but we'll keep them posted there until you order it otherwise.'

'Let me know as soon as you hear anything. In the meantime, arrange for a strike team to be on standby in Prague. They need to be ready at a moment's notice.'

# TWENTY-TWO

*Prague*

'Remind me again why you think this is a good idea,' said Nathan as he opened the back door of the taxi for Eva, and held out his hand to her.

She took it, climbed from her seat and waited on the kerb while he paid the driver.

As the car sped away, she led Nathan towards the gallery, the façade lit up with strategically-placed lanterns to welcome the guests. 'Scott worked closely with Douglas,' she said. 'They socialised together as well, away from their embassy duties. I'm hoping he might tell me a bit about those private conversations that will shed some light on what's going on.'

'How well do you know him?'

Eva shifted her purse from one hand to the other. 'I don't,' she admitted. 'But he and Douglas got on really well, so I'm banking on that.'

'Seems like one hell of a gamble.'

'It's the only idea I've got at the moment.'

'I don't speak Czech,' hissed Nathan as they drew closer to the reception line.

'Neither does anyone else here,' Eva assured him. 'Speak English, tell them you're a freelance computer analyst, and you'll be fine.'

'Great.'

'And smile,' said Eva. 'Put your party face on.'

'Come on then,' said Nathan, as Eva looped her arm through his to climb the short flight of steps up to the entrance. 'Before I change my mind.'

A suited doorman smiled as they approached, and opened the large wooden and glass-panelled door.

As she stepped over the threshold, Eva's senses were overcome by the scent of too many different perfumes in one space, conversation that assaulted her hearing, and a pervading tone of one-upmanship from the conversations she overheard as they passed.

'Smell that?' asked Nathan.

'This year's signature fragrance?'

'No. Bullshit.'

Eva bit her tongue to stop herself from laughing in the crowded space, and glared at Nathan.

Despite the dangers of the past forty-eight hours, his eyes were sparkling.

'Admit it,' she said. 'You're enjoying this, aren't you?'

He shrugged. 'Eva, I'm used to being cooped up in an office all day with a computer. Hanging around with you, I could be dead tomorrow, so I might as well enjoy myself. Here,' he said, taking two champagne flutes from a passing waiter. 'Let's drink to a successful mission.'

Eva clinked her glass against his and savoured the cool liquid as it cleansed her parched throat. She'd tip the rest into an ornamental plant at the first opportunity, but she allowed herself the pleasure of one taste without guilt.

She touched her glass lightly against Nathan's once more. 'Make it last,' she warned. 'No more than one of these, okay? Just in case,' she added, when he choked on his drink.

'You do realise you've spoilt the taste of vintage Krug for me forever?'

'I'll make it up to you,' said Eva, before movement at the back of the room caught her eye. 'Come on. There's our man.'

Eva led him around the perimeter of the room, slowly closing in on her quarry. Each time he was waylaid by another guest, she pretended to be deep in conversation with Nathan about one of the works of art on the wall.

Her senses alert, she was jerked back to attention at a tap on her arm.

'You do realise this is a Lavert, don't you?' Nathan said,

wonderment filling his voice as he stared at one of the paintings.

'Never heard of him,' said Eva, keen to move closer to the tall American that held court in the corner of the room.

'The latest enfant terrible out of Paris,' explained Nathan. 'I'd hate to think how much this collection is worth,' he added, as his gaze breezed past Eva and onto the surrounding walls. 'Hey – your man is free. Quick.'

Eva snapped to attention, and strode towards the American cultural attaché.

He became aware of the crowd parting before her, such was her determination to reach him before anyone else, and his eyes opened wide as she approached.

'Eva?'

'Hello, Scott.'

She accepted the kiss on her cheek with decorum, then introduced Nathan. 'This is my friend, Nathan,' she said. 'Have you got a minute?'

'What are you doing here?' asked the American. 'How are you? It's been what, three years?'

Eva took a deep breath. 'Whoever killed Douglas found me,' she said.

'Christ, Eva. You could've tried small talk first.' Scott's jaw clenched, and his gaze swept the room. He drained his drink before placing his glass on a small table next to him. 'Come with me,' he said, taking her by the arm and steering her towards a door at the back of the room from which the staff reappeared with trays full of drinks and canapés. 'It's not safe to talk out here.'

Eva made sure Nathan was following, and waited until Scott had taken them through the doors, along a short corridor, and into a room that turned out to be the office for the gallery.

'You shouldn't have come here,' he hissed, slamming the door shut. 'It's not like the old days. It's not safe.'

Nathan raised an eyebrow. 'That would be the old days, when Douglas got shot?'

Scott ignored him. 'Where are you staying?'

Eva shook her head. 'You know I'm not going to tell you that,' she said, keeping her voice even. 'Don't take this the wrong way, but someone's tried to kill me twice in the past three days.'

'What's going on, Eva? Is this about Douglas's murder? They never found the killer, did they?'

'No. Care to elaborate?'

'I know nothing about that. I found out about Douglas's death after it happened, and you were already gone by the time I got to the house. I couldn't get to you because your own government officials wouldn't let me through the door.'

'I didn't accuse you, Scott. I simply want to know what else Douglas was working on. It might help me find out who wants me dead, after all this time.'

'I have no idea.'

'It's okay, you can tell me,' said. Eva 'I realise there were some things he couldn't tell me at the time, but I'd really like to know.'

'Where have you been, Eva?' Scott's brow creased. 'What did they do to you?'

Eva rubbed at the goose bumps prickling her skin. 'I can't tell you,' she said. 'I'm sorry.'

Scott sighed and checked his watch. 'I've got a room full of guests out there, Eva, so why are you here? What do you want?'

'I'm not sure what's going on,' she admitted. 'That's why I'm here. I was hoping you could help me.'

His eyes narrowed. 'How?'

'What's the chatter on the network? Anything unusual?'

'Like what?'

Eva bit her lip. If she pushed too hard, Scott would guess where she'd been, and she wasn't sure if she was ready to divulge that information to him. Yet.

'A shooting in Berlin. At a hotel.'

Scott folded his arms across his chest. 'What's in it for me?'

'I'll never tell them I spoke with you,' promised Eva, and jerked her chin at the door. 'Those people out there will never know what you really do for a living.'

Scott swore and stepped away from her.

Nathan moved towards the door to make room for the man as he paced the small room, his fists clenched.

'Do you have any idea how long it's taken me to build this cover after what happened three years ago?' he growled. 'I nearly lost my job when my government found out I'd been socialising with Douglas Bolton.'

'Tell me what's being said on the wire.' Eva began to walk towards the door. Her hand had grasped the handle before she heard a sigh.

'Okay, stop.'

'What have you heard?'

'An incident, at a hotel in Berlin,' said Scott. 'That's all. They're reporting it as a drugs bust gone wrong. Shots fired, five men dead, and the perpetrator has escaped.'

Eva raised an eyebrow.

'That's it, I swear,' said Scott, his hands raised.

Eva turned and opened the door. 'I don't believe you,' she said, and stepped out into the passageway.

'Eva! Wait!'

She heard Nathan's indignant exclamation a moment before a strong hand wrapped around her arm and pulled.

Eva spun on her heel, broke Scott's grip and used his own momentum to slam him against the wall, ignoring his cry of pain.

'I'm done with being played,' she hissed in his ear.

'You didn't have to do that.' Scott straightened, his fingers finding the blood that trickled from his nose.

'Here,' said Nathan, and passed him a silk handkerchief.

'Thanks.' Scott glared at him.

'Any time.'

Scott held up the handkerchief, his eyes resting on

Douglas's initials embroidered into one corner, his eyes flickering to Eva.

She ignored his raised eyebrow and kept her stance as wide as she could, blocking any escape he might be thinking of making.

'I want the truth, Scott. Now.'

He sighed. 'Okay.' He dabbed at his nose a moment longer, then shoved the handkerchief in his pocket. 'The Section put out an alert on you and him.' He jabbed his finger at Nathan. 'About six hours ago, the CIA received a Code One alert on both of you.'

Eva felt the colour drain from her face.

Nathan's eyes widened. 'What does that mean?' he asked, looking at each of them in turn.

'It means they've changed the game,' Eva whispered.

Scott nodded. 'They sure have.'

'Wait. What? What's a Code One?' said Nathan.

Scott tried to smother the triumphant look in his eyes, and failed. 'It's a shoot to kill order,' he said. 'According to the Section, you're both a national threat to UK security. So,' he added, standing to one side and pointing to the back of the building. 'You might want to take the fire escape again.'

Eva met his gaze. 'You bastard,' she said. 'You know everything that's happened in the past forty-eight hours. Why won't you help me?'

'Because, sweetheart,' said Scott, lowering his face until his broken nose almost touched her own, 'you always were bad news.'

Eva ground her teeth, pushed away and began walking back in the direction of the gallery. 'Come on, Nathan. We're leaving.'

'What about the back door?' he asked, hurrying after her.

'I won't be scared into running away,' she fumed, and shoved the door open, narrowly missing a waiter carrying a tray of empty glasses, and ignoring the startled looks from the nearest guests. 'We leave the way we came in.'

## TWENTY-THREE

Eva reached into her clutch bag as they descended the carpeted staircase and pulled out her mobile phone.

She pressed the speed dial for Decker, then cursed under her breath as the voicemail service kicked in after three rings.

She tucked the phone back into her bag while Nathan nodded at the doorman who raised a finger to the brim of his hat as they passed by and out into the cool night air.

She tried to cool her frustration. She'd known Scott would be difficult to deal with, and would probably expect a favour in return, but she didn't expect his downright dismissal of her.

And the fact that someone in the Section had put out a Code One on both her and Nathan was disturbing – they were evidently being set up for something, but what?

What had she missed three years ago?

She squared her shoulders, and took a deep breath. If they wanted a fight, they'd get one. She just had to work out what she was fighting for first.

As they left the façade of the art gallery and began walking, her old instincts kicked in.

Something was wrong.

Very wrong.

Her head jerked to the left as she sensed movement on the opposite side of the road.

Two men had emerged from the shadows. One of the figures had his wrist close to his head. The other checked the traffic, his hands in his pockets.

Eva pulled out her phone again, and redialled Decker's number.

*Still nothing.*

She peered to her left as she dropped the phone back into her bag, adrenalin fuelling her frayed nerves.

The first man dropped his hand, then leaned forward and tapped his colleague on the shoulder. The man's head turned, and Eva felt her heart lurch.

She ran through the scenarios in her head.

One, Decker was simply busy with Alex and couldn't answer his phone.

Two, for some reason Decker had left the apartment with the boy, and couldn't answer his phone.

Three, the apartment had been compromised and—

Eva tightened her shawl around her shoulders, and slipped her arm through Nathan's, then increased her pace to match his long strides, cursing her decision to wear heels.

He jerked slightly in surprise, then relaxed under her touch. 'Well, this is nice.'

'Don't get the wrong idea,' she murmured. 'We're being watched.' She tightened her fingers on his forearm. 'Don't turn around. Keep walking. Act normal. Tell me about where you grew up.'

'Where I grew up?' he spluttered. He followed her lead though, and they began walking at a brisk pace along the street. 'Why?'

'It'll help keep your mind off being followed, and it'll help *me* give them the impression they haven't been spotted.'

'*They*? How many of them are there?'

'Where did you go to school?'

He sighed. 'Oh, have it your way. Abingdon Boys Grammar. In Oxfordshire. It's a mid-sized town, I suppose. Army barracks nearby. Went from there to Cambridge – bit of a spook tradition, I suppose…'

Eva let his low voice wash over her, straining her ears to listen to their pursuers' footsteps.

Behind them, a car horn blasted, closely followed by a squeal of tyres and a loud string of Czech cursing. After a few seconds, the vehicle sped past them, and turned left at the next intersection, its brake lights flashing briefly before it disappeared from sight.

'You didn't hear a word I said, did you?'

She glanced sideways. 'Your favourite colour is green.'

'What?'

'You told Alex. When we were at the hotel lobby, before we came to Prague. Your favourite colour is green.'

He stopped and glared at her. 'What the hell has that got to do with anything?'

Her mouth quirked. 'I listen to everything you say.' She heard movement in the street behind them, and looked over her shoulder, then swore.

'Run!'

She grabbed his hand and pulled him into an alleyway off to their right, away from the main street, and prayed it wasn't a dead end.

The brickwork next to her head exploded as a muffled *crack* reached her ears.

'Shit, they're *shooting* at us!'

'I know,' said Eva through gritted teeth. 'So, keep up.'

The alleyway narrowed before gently curving to the left, and Eva's heart leapt at the sight of another street beyond. 'Thank goodness.'

Her feet blistered in the high heels as she led Nathan across cobblestones, careful not to roll her ankles. If she sprained them, they'd never escape.

They were only a few metres away from the exit when a car screeched to a stop on the pavement, blocking their path.

Eva and Nathan slid to a halt, their breathing heavy.

'Oh, no.' Nathan groaned.

The driver's door opened and Decker leaned out.

'Get in!' he bellowed.

'Go!'

Eva led the sprint towards the car, slid across the bonnet and took the gun Decker thrust through the passenger window at her, then sighted it on the alleyway.

Nathan ripped open the back door.

'Hi, Nathan.'

Eva nearly dropped the weapon. She wrenched open the door and peered between the front seats to see Alex slip from the back seat.

He bolted from the car and wrapped his arms around Nathan's legs.

She glared at Decker. 'You brought Alex? Are you crazy?'

'You think leaving him at the apartment was a better idea?' he snarled. 'They're onto you, Eva.'

'We'll talk about this later.'

A gunshot sounded from the direction of the alleyway, and a split second later, the car took a direct hit.

Eva straightened. 'Get in!' she yelled, and fired twice.

Nathan spun round, sheltering Alex, and shoved the boy back into the car.

Eva heard a muffled grunt, then Nathan fell into the car, pulling the door shut. She fired twice more, and saw one of the figures closing in on them tumble to the ground before she launched herself into the vehicle.

'Go!'

Decker floored the accelerator so hard, Eva's head snapped back.

She slipped the safety on the gun, then strapped her

seatbelt across her chest, and allowed herself a few seconds to catch her breath.

'Christ, that was lucky.' She glanced in the wing mirror. No vehicles were following – yet. The uninjured pursuer was standing at the entrance to the alleyway, his hand to his ear once more.

'How did you know?'

'Bad feeling,' said Decker. He swung the car away from the street, narrowly missed an oncoming delivery truck, then settled the car into the outer lane and increased his speed.

'Where are we going?'

'Somewhere safe. You haven't been there before, so they shouldn't be able to trace you.'

'Where?'

'You'll see.' She saw his eyes flicker to the rear view mirror. 'Too much excitement for someone,' he said, and jerked his head towards the back seat. 'Look.'

Eva spun in her seat.

Alex was crouched over Nathan who had lolled back in his seat, his eyes closed.

His face was pale, contorted.

She frowned, her heart rate increasing.

Something wasn't right.

Alex shifted and turned round to her, holding up his hands. They were covered in blood.

'Help,' he said.

## TWENTY-FOUR

*Berlin*

Miles shoved open the double doors, and ignored the crash as the handles hit the thin plaster walls.

The woman behind the mahogany desk rose as he approached, as if she anticipated his next move.

'He's not to be interrupted.'

'Out of my way.'

'He's on the phone to Number Ten.'

'I don't care if he's talking to the Queen. Open the door.'

She glared at him, but refused to move. He was about to weigh up his career prospects, wondering whether it was worth manhandling her out of the way, when the door was wrenched open and Knox peered out.

'I heard a commotion. I might have known it was you, Miles.'

'We need to talk. Now.'

The secretary's eyes shot upwards at the tone directed at her boss, and glanced over her shoulder at him.

'It's all right, Joyce. Miles and I need to talk. Please make sure we are not disturbed.'

Miles mumbled a "thanks" in her direction as he passed, and followed Knox back into the office. The man stepped to one side, waited while Miles walked in and then shut the door.

'What the hell is going on, Gerald? I've just been informed that a Code One has been ordered. On Eva.'

'It's not what you think.'

'It's a kill order.'

'It didn't come from me.'

'Then from whom?'

'From the top.'

'You mean Number Ten?'

'The Prime Minister is aware of it, yes.'

'Jesus, Knox. We have to get them out of there. We can't let this happen.'

'It's out of our hands.'

'What do you mean?'

'From now on, until the Code One is lifted or executed, we're to provide a watching brief. That's all.'

'This isn't right, Knox. You know isn't right. Eva didn't kill those five agents. We have images of your rogue assassin.'

'The people at the top have taken the view that she was colluding with him.'

'But what about Nathan and the boy?'

Knox shook his head. 'The teams have been told to preserve life if they can.'

'"If they can"? Are they even going to try?'

The Section chief remained silent.

Miles growled in frustration and launched himself from his seat. He couldn't sit still. He had to do something.

'There is another option open to us, Miles.'

He spun on his heel. 'What?'

'You find Eva before they do.'

## TWENTY-FIVE

*Prague*

'He's been shot.'

'Alex?'

The car swerved a little.

'No, Nathan.'

'How bad is it?'

Eva forced her heart rate down and tried to concentrate.

'Nathan? Can you hear me?' she said, her hand on his knee. 'Where did the bullet hit you?'

'Shoulder,' he gasped. 'Hurts like hell.'

'Okay. Let me take a look.'

She reached up and turned on the interior light.

'Eva? Not a good idea,' warned Decker.

'I just need a second.'

In the yellow light of the ceiling bulb, Nathan's left shoulder was a mass of blood and torn clothing.

She snapped the light off, her mind racing. She needed to stop the bleeding.

She twisted and leaned back between the seats.

'Take off your coat,' she said to Alex. 'Give me your sweater.'

Alex squirmed in his seat until he could shrug the heavy wool coat off his shoulders, then pulled his sweater over his head and handed it to her.

She snatched it from him, bundled it up into a tight ball and held it against Nathan's shoulder.

He'd closed his eyes again, his lips parted slightly as his breath caressed the back of her hand. His face was pale, a thin line of sweat forming on his forehead.

Eva shuffled closer, and tried not to swear as the handbrake caught on her hip, then reached out and pressed two fingers against Nathan's neck.

'His pulse is faint,' she said over her shoulder.

'I know someone who can help,' said Decker.

'How far?'

'Not far. Keep the pressure on.'

Eva turned her attention back to Alex. 'Here, move across so you can hold this for me. I can't keep the pressure on at this angle, and we don't have time to stop and change seats.'

The car bucked and swayed as Decker navigated the narrow city streets. Eva lost track of time and direction, and didn't look up until the car slowed and he applied the handbrake.

He had parked outside a tall narrow terraced house, dimly lit, in what appeared to be a side street.

'Keep a lookout while I grab him.'

She slipped from the passenger seat, kept her gun lowered, and let her eyes sweep the street.

'What is this place?'

'It's okay,' said Decker. 'You can trust him. He's helped me out a couple of times in the past.'

---

Eva nibbled at a fingernail, the top of Alex's head against her shoulder.

Her gaze roamed aimlessly over the whorls in the slate floor tiles of the kitchen, the acrid stench of antiseptic permeating the air despite the closed door to the treatment room.

Exhaustion threatened, but she wouldn't sleep, not until she knew Nathan was out of danger. Not until they were far away from the Czech Republic.

'Hey.'

She glanced up.

Decker held out a steaming mug of coffee. 'Take this. You're going to need it.'

'Thanks.'

He pulled out a chair and sat next to her, wrapping his

large hands around an identical mug. 'Why on earth did you come back to Prague?'

'I thought I might be able to retrace my steps,' she said quietly. 'I thought I might have missed something last time.'

'And?'

She twisted in her seat. 'I don't think this is just about the Section wanting to get rid of me to avoid the embarrassment of my existence,' she said. 'There's something else going on.'

Decker's gaze dropped to the sleeping boy in her arms. 'You think this has something to do with what Douglas was working on?'

'Yes.'

He blew across the top of his coffee before taking a tentative sip, and then settled back, balancing the mug on his knee. 'You owe him the truth, after this.'

'I know.' Her eyes found the closed door that led through to the doctor's treatment room. 'Do you think he'll be okay?'

'I think he's tougher than either of us have given him credit for.'

'He was shielding Alex.'

'It was an incredibly brave thing to do.'

'He didn't hesitate,' said Eva. 'I saw him. He took one look at those men rounding the corner and turned his back to make sure they couldn't hit Alex.'

'I know.'

Eva fell silent. She knew the signs of shock well enough. She took a sip of the coffee, and nearly gagged at the amount of sugar Decker had heaped into it.

'Drink it,' he said. 'The sugar will help.'

She nodded, and took another sip. 'Thanks.' She sighed. 'I should've foreseen this. I've become complacent.'

'Don't be so hard on yourself,' said Decker. 'You were busy looking after this one.' His gaze softened as he glanced at Alex. 'You've kept him alive for three years, Eva. They never found you in all that time.'

'Shame I couldn't shoot both of them. I'm out of practice.'

His mouth quirked. 'Those were good, clean shots you made.' He jerked his head towards the door. 'And your quick thinking has probably saved his life. Don't beat yourself up.'

'Three years ago, I would have gone to Scott armed to the teeth.'

'Three years ago, you thought you could trust him.'

'You think he was responsible for what happened tonight?'

Decker shrugged. 'I'm not sure. Bloody coincidence though, wasn't it?'

'Do you think he was telling the truth, about the Code One?'

'What do you mean?'

Eva handed him her empty mug and waited until he'd put it on the kitchen counter with his, and shifted Alex's weight in her lap.

'What if there's someone else after us?' she said when he returned. 'What if this isn't about the Section at all?'

Decker rubbed his fingers over the stubble on his chin. 'Go on.'

'The deal Douglas was working on, when he died. I remember that last week he was alive, when we were hiding at my apartment, before the Section told us it was safe to go back to his house. He was on edge about something his contact had told him.'

'Did he ever tell you what it was?'

She shook her head. 'That's what I was looking for when you arrived this morning.' Her eyes opened wide. 'The files at the apartment—'

'Don't worry. They're in the car.'

'There's something in there, Decker. I just haven't found it yet.'

'Well, when our analyst is well enough, maybe we can get him to help us, yes?'

They both turned their heads at the sound of the door opening.

The doctor appeared, drying his hands on a small towel. He looked tired, his brows knitted together as he approached.

Eva and Decker stood as one, and she handed over the weight of the sleeping boy to Decker gratefully, noting how carefully he gathered Alex into his big arms and rested his head against his shoulder.

Alex snuffled once, then fell asleep again.

Eva turned her attention to the doctor. 'Well?'

'He's going to live,' said the doctor.

Eva exhaled, and tried to ignore the shaking that had begun in her legs. 'How bad was it?'

'He lost quite a bit of blood,' said the doctor. 'But the bullet only grazed his shoulder – it didn't penetrate any major arteries.' His eyes found Decker's. 'With plenty of rest over the next week, he should recover just fine.'

'He'll be somewhere safe,' Decker assured him. 'I'll make sure of that.'

'Thank you so much,' said Eva. 'I can't tell you how grateful I am.'

'How much do we owe you?' asked Decker.

The doctor shrugged. 'Nothing,' he said. 'You know how it is.'

Decker reached out and grasped the man's hand. 'And you know where to find me, if you need me, yes?'

'Yes.'

'Can we move him now?' asked Eva. 'We should go.'

'She's right,' said Decker. 'It'll be light in five hours. I'd like to be a long way away from here by then.'

'Bring the car round the back,' said the doctor. 'I've given him a shot of morphine. I'll give you another dose you can give him in a couple of hours if he needs it.'

'I'll meet you round there,' said Decker, and edged out the room to the front door, Alex in his arms.

The doctor led Eva into the treatment room.

The iron tang of fresh blood still hung in the air despite the freshly washed-out sink and trays. Her eyes found the prone figure on the bed in the corner, his chest bare, his shoulder bandaged.

The doctor nudged her arm. In his hands, he held a folded blanket.

'Take this to keep him warm,' he said. 'I had to cut away his shirt and jacket.'

'Thank you,' she murmured.

They both jumped at a loud knock on the back door, before the doctor hurried across and peered through the spy hole set into its surface.

'It's okay, it's him,' he said.

Between Decker and the doctor, Nathan was soon buckled into the back seat of the car, the blanket tucked up to his chin.

Alex slept next to him, his thumb in his mouth.

Eva glanced at the blood stain that covered the seat between them, and shuddered.

'I'll ditch the car, don't worry,' said Decker. 'Come on. We need to move.'

Eva leaned down, brushed Nathan's hair out of the way, and kissed his forehead.

'You saved Alex,' she whispered. 'I owe you.'

## TWENTY-SIX

*Tuscany, Italy*

Eva squinted in the sunlight after leaving the cool shade of the house, and dropped her sunglasses onto her nose.

The afternoon was drawing to a close, the coppery ochre sky broken up here and there by clouds dusting the horizon beyond the slim cypress trees bordering the property.

The terrace ran the length of the converted farmhouse, a building constructed from the strong limestone and sandstone that peppered the region.

Olive trees spread out below her position, a tangled grove of gnarled and twisted branches that bore fruit rich for picking.

'Come and eat.'

She turned at the sound of Decker's voice.

He was standing next to a wrought-iron table laden with plates and bowls, wine glasses, and a bottle of the local red wine.

Eva's stomach rumbled. 'I'm eating way too much,' she said, her eyes roaming over the crusty bread, olive oil, cheeses, and vine-ripened tomatoes.

He grinned. 'You're in Italy. No such thing.'

Eva pulled out a chair, and beckoned to Alex to join them. The boy had already gained more colour in his face, the events of the past week put behind them. He'd spent most of the time trailing around after Decker, exploring the farm and sleeping well at night after all the fresh air.

She loaded up a plate for him, passed him some water, then took the glass of wine Decker handed to her. 'Thanks.'

'Cheers.'

They clinked glasses, and Eva leaned back with a sigh. 'It's so peaceful here.'

'It is.'

'Nathan!'

Alex slid from his chair and tore across the terrace towards the figure that had appeared at the back door to the house. 'You're okay!'

Eva stood. 'Alex, careful – he's not well.'

She couldn't help smiling at Nathan's face as Alex hugged him. His hair dishevelled, he wore one of Decker's shirts and a pair of jeans. His feet were bare.

'Found the clothes, then?' asked Decker as Nathan approached the table, Alex in tow.

'Yes, thanks.' His gaze drifted to Eva.

'Hey, Sleeping Beauty,' she said, keeping her tone light. 'How are you feeling?'

'Like I've been shot.' His jaw dropped as he took in the landscape. 'Wait – are we in Italy?'

Eva smiled. 'You slept most of the way.'

'You snore,' said Alex, before running off to play with a black and white cat that had appeared at the far end of the terrace.

Eva covered her mouth with her hand, but couldn't prevent the laugh that escaped her.

Nathan's eyes found hers once more, and she knew she'd have to tell him, soon. Decker was right – she owed him.

'I need to thank you,' she said, reaching across for his hand as he sat down. 'For saving Alex.'

He shrugged, then winced as the stitches in his shoulder pulled. 'It's okay,' he murmured. 'It was instinctive. I didn't think.'

Eva squeezed his hand, then let go. She could see if she made too much of a fuss, he'd begin to analyse the events too closely, and delayed shock might set in. She'd helped Decker dress his wounds when he'd been unconscious, and had been surprised how quickly he was healing.

'He's fit, for a nerd,' Decker had said. 'It'll help him recover faster.'

Now, Nathan waited until Decker had guided Alex away

from the cat and back to his chair. 'How long was I asleep for?'

'Three days,' said Decker.

Nathan's eyebrows shot up. 'Three days?'

'I gave you some extra morphine,' explained Decker. 'You needed to rest, to heal.'

'Oh.' He took a sip of the wine Eva poured for him. 'Oh, that's good. What happened? How did we get here?'

Eva glanced at Decker, and he nodded. Maybe it wouldn't do any harm to help fill in some of the gaps in his memory.

'Decker knew someone on the outskirts of Prague who helped us. He patched you up, and we left soon after that.'

'What is this place?'

She shook her head. 'I didn't know about it. Decker brought us here.'

'This is the first time anyone's been here as a guest,' said Decker. 'I like my privacy.'

'I'm sorry, I didn't mean to sound ungrateful,' said Nathan. 'I didn't realise it was your home.'

Decker shrugged. 'No offence taken. We needed somewhere safe to hide. It made sense to come here.'

He stood, walked over to the low wall that bordered the terrace and peered into the distance, squinting at the sunset that had begun to fill the horizon.

'How do you know it's safe here?' asked Nathan.

Decker used his wine glass to point at a cypress tree on top of a low hill halfway between the house and the road. 'Because that's as close as the last uninvited guest got.'

Nathan's eyes opened wide. 'What happened to him?'

'He's buried under the tree,' said Decker, before wandering back to the table. He drained his glass and reached for the bottle.

Nathan spun to face Eva. 'He's kidding, right?'

## TWENTY-SEVEN

Decker topped up their glasses, checked over his shoulder that Alex was busy playing with the cat once more, then turned his attention back to Eva.

'Now would be a good time to tell him.'

'Tell me what?'

Eva sighed. 'I should've told you this at the beginning. I'm sorry. I thought because you were the one tasked with monitoring me and Alex, you'd know.'

'Know what?' Nathan's brow furrowed and he leaned closer, his eyes full of concern.

Decker cleared his throat, pushed away his chair, and sauntered over to the side of the house, returning with a broom with which he began to brush leaves away from the paving stones, camouflaging their voices further from Alex.

Eva was struck by how quiet the terrace had become as

the sun dropped over the horizon. She took a deep breath. There could be no turning back now.

'Douglas wasn't my fiancé,' she said, then raised her gaze to meet Nathan's eyes.

He sat, a stunned expression crossing his face, before his mouth opened, then closed once more.

'I'm sorry. I realise that's probably come as a bit of a shock to you,' said Eva. She reached out for Nathan's hand, but he snatched it away.

'I thought you trusted me,' he said.

'I do,' said Eva. 'Please believe me, I do, but I thought they would have told you everything when you were assigned to the case.'

'No. They didn't.' Nathan leaned back, a hiss of breath escaping his lips as he closed his eyes and ran his fingers through his hair.

He stayed that way for a moment, his fingers massaging his scalp.

Eva swallowed. 'I was assigned to Doug as his close protection officer,' she said, her voice low. She sensed Decker moving behind her, and shook her head. 'It's okay.'

Decker sank back into his chair and picked up his wine glass, his brown eyes unfathomable.

'Anyway, like I was saying, I was assigned to the embassy to protect Doug,' she said.

'Miles told me you were an assassin,' said Nathan, opening his eyes. He leaned forward. 'Is that true?'

'Yes.' Eva began drawing circles with her forefinger across the table. 'The last job I did for them was particularly... bad.' She blinked to clear the memory. 'So, Petersen – my handler at the Section – assigned me to the embassy. They needed one of their diplomats looking after, and I needed the break.' She stopped drawing and peered across at Nathan through her fringe.

'I'd only been at the embassy a month, but Doug and I, we – we just *connected*. One day we were working as usual, and — I don't know, it was like we both realised at exactly the same time how we felt about each other.' Eva looked down at her hands. 'We couldn't stop ourselves, even if we wanted to.'

She sniffed, and wiped her eyes. 'So, no, he wasn't my fiancé,' she said, waving away Decker's offer of a handkerchief, 'but we were very close. We tried to keep it a secret, but I think the Section knew something was going on, which is why they did what they did.'

'What do you mean?'

'Douglas was working with the Section on something. At first I wasn't made privy to what it was, but then things changed.' She held up her hand to stop Nathan interrupting. 'There was an engineer, a genius apparently, who had been working on a new bioweapon for a private contractor in Poland. The private contractor was supplying the Russian military with state-of-the-art technology, and the engineer began to get worried that the system was so advanced, there would be no stopping it if it was deployed.'

'So, he decided to jump ship?'

Eva nodded. 'He approached Douglas at a software convention in Prague, completely out of the blue, on my watch. Douglas was there as one of the special guests. He was always keen on bringing like-minded people together, so the software convention was a perfect vehicle for him to invite brilliant minds from all over the European continent. The engineer was one of the guest speakers.'

She leaned across the table, picked up a fresh glass and filled it from the jug of water. She swallowed half its contents without coming up for air, then refilled it.

'The engineer requested a private audience with Doug, and when they were alone, told him about the weapon and that he wanted to defect,' she said. 'Of course, Doug alerted the UK intelligence services as soon as we got back to the embassy, and the Section took over from there, telling him how to make contact with the engineer at his hotel without arousing suspicion, and arranging to meet up with him again.'

Nathan frowned. 'They'd need proof that the bioweapon existed, wouldn't they?'

'Right,' said Eva. 'At first, the engineer refused – said it was too dangerous, but Doug persisted, and they arranged to meet the following day. I went with him.'

'Did he get the proof?'

'Yes. He turned up with a memory stick with photographs and a couple of design drawings,' said Eva. 'The problem was, he brought something else with him, too.'

'What? A tail, you mean?'

'No,' said Eva. 'Alex.'

Continue the story in *Assassins: Vengeance...*

# PART TWO
# ASSASSINS VENGEANCE

# ONE

*Italian/French border*

Eva shifted gear and powered the four-wheel drive through a tight bend before flooring the accelerator once the narrow lane straightened.

They'd been travelling for the past five hours, Decker driving first before he swapped places with her at a small roadside café on the Italian side of the Alps.

He remained alert though, constantly checking the mirrors, his fingers tapping on his knee as they travelled in silence through the night, then slid his hand around the armrest set into the door and hung on tight as Eva shot round the next bend in the road.

'If we'd been a couple of weeks later, all of this would've been covered with snow,' Decker had explained.

Now they'd been travelling for nearly two hours over relatively flat terrain, open fields bare since harvesting, with only an occasional dwelling to indicate any signs of life in the area.

Coupled with the grey skies that glowered above as the sun had set, Eva found the landscaping depressing, and the threat of rain ominous.

As soon as Nathan had found out Alex's true origins the day before, he'd shoved his chair back and begun to pace the terrace of Decker's villa.

'We have to do something,' he'd urged. 'This is no place to be dragging a kid around – what if he gets hurt?'

'I'll think of something,' Eva insisted.

'Like what? Put him into the local kindergarten?'

'Stop it.'

'No.' Nathan had checked over his shoulder and lowered his voice. 'Eva, he's six years old, for crying out loud.'

'We're here,' said Decker, interrupting Eva's thoughts.

She slowed the vehicle as a pair of old concrete gate posts came into view.

'Keep going,' said Decker. 'We're not stopping yet.' He pointed through the windscreen. 'There's a turning half a mile ahead.'

Eva sped up and found the junction with ease, an unsignposted track that led from the lane and disappeared into the woodland.

Overgrown tree branches slapped at the windows and doors of the four-wheel drive as she steered it through deep ruts and pot-holes. She reached for the lights and dimmed them as she brought the vehicle to a halt.

'Now what?'

'Wait here.'

Decker slipped from his seat, closed the door quietly behind him, and disappeared into the night.

'What's he doing?' Nathan leaned between the front seats. 'Where's he going?'

'I presume he knows this place,' said Eva. 'But given the state of the front gates, I doubt he's been here for a while, so he'll be checking it out.'

They peered through the window after Decker, but his silhouette was soon swallowed up by darkness as the moon disappeared behind a cloud.

'Why are we here? Why couldn't we stay at the villa?'

Eva ignored the questions, and instead shuffled in her seat until she could see past Nathan. 'How's Alex holding up?'

'Great – he's fast asleep.'

'Okay.'

'Are you going to tell me how the hell you ended up with him?'

She nodded, and reached out to squeeze his hand. 'I will. Let's make sure we're somewhere safe first though.'

They both jumped at a tap on her driver's window.

She opened the door. 'Well?'

'All clear,' Decker said. 'A bit run down, but we're only

going to be here for a few hours, so it'll do. Bring the supplies. Leave the car where it is.'

Eva climbed out, inhaling the crisp countryside air. A breeze whipped her hair around her face, and she tied it back, stretching as she waited for Decker to lift Alex from his seat, the boy still fast asleep, exhausted.

Nathan handed her one of the boxes of provisions they'd stopped to buy on the way, and lifted the other from the vehicle.

'How far is the border?' asked Nathan.

Decker jerked his chin towards the lane. 'Another couple of miles.'

He locked the vehicle and began to lead the way.

They followed him through the undergrowth towards the hulk of a house that bobbed in and out of view through the trees, the wind rustling leaves above their heads.

Eva let the two men go ahead of her. The surroundings filled her with trepidation after the events of the past few days, and she strained her ears for the sound of other vehicles on the lane.

After a while, she began to relax, trusting that Decker's uncanny knowledge of the area would mean another safe sanctuary.

As if echoing her thoughts, Nathan cleared his throat.

'Is this another home of yours?'

Decker didn't answer until they were out in the open once more and standing at the edge of an abandoned farmyard.

'Not exactly,' he said. 'But I've been here before. A long time ago. We should be fine.'

Eva's eyes had begun to adjust to the murky light, and as the moon scuttled between clouds, she realised they were approaching the property from the rear, away from the prying eyes of anyone travelling along the lane.

To her left, the ruins of a barn stood stark and bare, the timber framework and part of the corrugated iron roof the only indication that there had ever been a building there in the first place. A jagged pile of rocks lay discarded next to it, evidently the remnants of what once had been the walls.

Rusted and broken machinery lay scattered across the yard, and Eva wondered how long it had been since the farm had actually produced anything. She hurried to catch up with Decker and Nathan, careful not to trip over any discarded wire or metalwork.

The farmhouse itself had been made of the same sturdy stonework as the barn, and even in the poor light afforded by the moon, looked as if it had stood in the same place for centuries. Small windows looked out onto the yard they'd crossed, deep sills cut into the stonework a clue to the thickness of the walls.

As she approached, Decker handed Alex to her, taking the box from her instead, and pushed open the door.

'I'll get a fire lit,' he said. 'There should be some dry timber around here somewhere.'

'Won't people see the smoke from the chimney?' asked Nathan.

Decker shook his head and put the box on the floor. 'Ski season doesn't start for a few weeks yet, and the only houses around here are owned by tourists,' he said. He nodded towards Alex. 'I want to make sure he keeps warm. At least then he'll sleep better.'

Eva shifted Alex's weight onto her hip. 'Kitchen?'

'Through there.' Decker handed over a flashlight to Nathan. 'You'll need this.'

She followed Nathan as Decker disappeared out into the yard, the torch beam bouncing off the walls of a flagstone-paved passageway until it opened out into a large kitchen.

A long table filled the centre of the space, with an old wood-burner stove and range off to the right, and windows that faced the rear of the property.

Pushing the box he carried onto a granite counter, Nathan handed her the torch and began to rummage through the contents until he pulled out a thick blanket. 'Here,' he said. 'Let's find somewhere he can sleep for a bit.'

By the time they'd settled Alex, Decker had returned with enough timber to keep a small fire going through the night. Eva pulled three chairs closer to the hearth and soon they were drinking hot soup from some chipped mugs Decker found in one of the cupboards.

'So,' said Nathan, setting his empty mug on the floor. 'Tell me why we're here. I thought we were safe in Italy?'

Eva wrapped her hands round the empty mug, its surface still holding some warmth from the soup it had contained, and stared into the fire, while she sought the right words. Eventually, she spoke.

'You can imagine how shocked we were at finding a small kid in tow with the engineer,' she said. 'It threw us completely – you'd have thought he would have mentioned Alex when he first spoke with Doug about defecting, but he hadn't.'

'Is Alex his real name?'

'Yes.' Her eyes found the sleeping bundle near Decker's chair, the firelight casting shadows over the boy's face as he slept. She exhaled and leaned back. 'The Section had to act fast – here was an engineer that had evidence of a significant threat to the power balance in Europe, wanting to defect, and under instructions from his government to call in every three hours while he was in Prague. We had one hour of that timeframe left to make a decision.'

'So Doug offered to help him defect?'

Eva nodded. 'Immediately. We took him and his boy back to the embassy with us.' A wave of sickness threatened to consume her. 'In all the confusion, no-one had the sense to ask the engineer if there was anyone else with him.'

Nathan's face paled. 'What happened?'

Eva put her empty mug on the floor and balanced her elbows on her knees, watching Decker who had moved across to the fireplace to stoke the logs.

Embers shot up the chimney, before the fire settled once more into a steady burn.

'We'd put them into one of the guest suites at the embassy

while the Section spoke with London. Doug had just ordered food for them, and then the engineer asked what he was going to do about his wife.' She sighed. 'For a supposed genius, he sure as hell had a way of keeping important information close to his chest. Of course, everyone panicked. It turned out that his wife was still at the hotel he'd been staying at while the conference was on. The Section sent two agents there – the deadline for the engineer to call his superiors had passed fifteen minutes earlier. I couldn't go – I was still under orders to protect Doug, and there was no way they were going to let him go to the hotel.'

Nathan glanced at the sleeping boy and lowered his voice. 'She was dead, wasn't she?'

'Yes,' said Eva, her voice dull. 'We think they posed as hotel security, so she opened the door to them, not suspecting anything. Knowing the engineer, he probably hadn't even told her about his plans to defect – or that he'd passed on state secrets to the British. We think he took Alex to the meeting point as a cover, in case his handlers stopped and asked where he was going.'

'Jesus.' Nathan ran a hand over his face. 'How did they manage to get to the engineer if he was staying at the embassy?'

'Simple. He disobeyed orders.' Eva sighed. 'He left the embassy to go and buy cigarettes; told the agent that was tasked with minding him that he was off to the toilet, and instead left the building. They shot him as he was leaving the tobacconist.'

'They knew he was at the embassy already?'

'It was an obvious place to look,' said Decker. 'All they had to do was wait, and see if anyone made a mistake.'

'It makes you wonder what he was like to work with, if he disobeyed instructions not to leave the building,' said Nathan. 'I mean, surely after finding out his wife had been killed, he'd be a bit more careful.'

'Unless he was having second thoughts about helping the British,' said Eva. 'It's something that I've been spending a lot of time thinking about recently.'

'Suicide by assassin?' Nathan said. 'Really?'

'It worked,' said Eva.

She saw Nathan's eyes fall to the small boy that lay curled up, oblivious to the conversation about him. 'So, how did you end up with him?'

Eva glanced at Decker.

He'd positioned himself with his back to the fire, eyeing her warily, his hands clasped behind his back. There were some things even he didn't know about her mission for the Section, and she wasn't sure how he was going to react when he found out.

She took a deep breath.

'When Doug finally managed to tell him about his mother and father, the first thing Alex did was ask where his twin sister was.'

# TWO

*Berlin*

When his mobile phone buzzed on the counter-top, Miles reached for it without taking his eyes from the laptop screen in front of him.

'Hello?'

'If you can meet me at Mauerpark in fifteen minutes, I've got something you might be interested in.'

Miles snapped the laptop shut, his full attention on the caller.

Since leaving the office, he'd put a subtle request out to each of his contacts in other agencies, telling them Knox had given him strict instructions to get results, or suffer the consequences.

Most had sympathised with him – Knox had a reputation

for being difficult to work with and burning through people that reported to him, so no-one was surprised another member of his staff was disgruntled at being put in the firing line.

Alan Greene was one such contact; he worked for Interpol and so had access to most of the alerts circulating the continent in relation to counter-terrorism measures. Requests from the Section would naturally cross his desk. After twenty years working in the organisation, he was well-versed in subversive trade craft, especially when it was being applied within the very organisations created to counteract threats to national security.

'Care to elaborate?' Miles asked, testing the water.

'An old friend of ours appears to be on the warpath,' said Greene. 'In fact, given the location of where he's been seen, and who he's been seen with, I'd wager he had something to do with the shootout in Prague nine days ago.'

'I'll be there,' said Miles, and hung up.

He shrugged on his jacket, locked the apartment door and, seeing the displays for both elevators stuck on lower levels, pushed his way through a fire exit door and ran down the service stairs two at a time.

After discarding the idea of taking his car and trying to find a space in the tight time frame Greene had given him, he opted to take the tram instead.

As the tram jostled along Bernauer Street, conveying its passengers towards the Christmas markets, he mulled over

Greene's call and tried to tune out the incessant chatter from the tourists around him.

There were only a few people that would fit the loose description he'd provided. Agents came and went, moved on, got promoted, but to come out of retirement – and so publicly – would be risky. Working as a field agent for the Section wasn't exactly the sort of job people retired from.

Not unless they left permanently.

In a wooden box.

Miles jerked his head up as the tram slid to a halt, realising he'd already reached his stop. He jumped onto the kerb and hurried towards the park entrance, checked his watch and realised he was already two minutes late.

He could only hope Greene would wait.

Miles entered the park and circled the walking paths until he saw a figure huddled on one of the benches. As he drew closer, the figure stood and extended his hand, vapour escaping his lips into the cold air.

'Glad you could make it. Thought you were going to bail out on me.'

'Not a chance,' said Miles. 'I appreciated the call. What have you got?'

'I've got evidence to suggest that the Caretaker is active again.'

Miles's heart lurched. Of all the agents whose names had run through his head, he'd missed that one. 'I thought he quit after his brother was killed? What's he doing?'

Greene passed him a photograph.

In it, a car had driven under the camera location, the man they were discussing at the wheel.

Miles felt his jaw slacken as he recognised the passenger. *Eva.*

'Where was this taken?'

'On the border with Austria and Italy.'

'How on earth did you get this?'

'The Schengen Agreement isn't what it once was,' said Greene. 'Even if the border crossings aren't manned, we have to photograph every vehicle that passes through.'

'When was this taken?'

'Eight days ago.'

'Any idea where they are now?'

Greene shook his head. 'We believe Decker has a house in Italy somewhere. So far, he's managed to evade us whenever we've tried to track him. Keeps off the grid most of the time.' He took the photograph back. 'You were lucky. I only spotted this because of the alert out on her.' He tucked the photo into his jacket pocket. 'Are you going to tell me what's going on?'

Miles tried to ignore the prickling sensation at the nape of his neck. 'Alan, I'm not sure *I* even know what's going on.'

The two men began to walk back towards the park entrance.

'So, when will Knox move you off the case?' asked Greene. 'Is he worried you'll steal his glory?'

Miles snorted. Knox did have a habit of waiting until investigations were almost concluded, then moving his managers to one side and taking over just at the critical point. However, this time, he wasn't sure that was the case. As far as he was concerned, he was no closer to working out what was going on, and had no idea how long it was going to take.

Unless Knox had information that Miles hadn't been made privy to?

'I don't think so,' he said eventually, weighing his words with care. 'You know what it's like – there are so many threats out there, most of us are juggling several different investigations at once.' He shrugged. 'This one intrigues me though.'

'I'll bet.' Greene didn't look convinced, but at least had the professional decency to keep his thoughts to himself.

As they drew closer to the gates, Miles shook hands with him. They'd split up, make sure they hadn't been followed, before Miles would make his way back to the apartment.

'You'll let me know if you come across anything else?'

'Sure. And make sure you get in touch if you need help,' said Greene. 'I'm not sure what's going on, Miles, but it must be big if this guy has decided early retirement didn't suit him.'

'That's what I'm afraid of.'

# THREE

Decker cursed under his breath, and stomped away from the fireplace.

Eva could hear him pacing behind her, and closed her eyes. 'I'm sorry, Decker. I was sworn to secrecy. I couldn't tell you.'

She held her breath, waiting for him to respond.

'It's a shock, that's all.'

A strong hand was placed on her shoulder, and squeezed.

'Thank you,' she said. She opened her eyes to find Nathan staring at her.

He was silent for a moment and Eva held her breath, wondering what secrets from her past would have to be divulged if they were ever going to work out what was going on, and still not sure how the analyst would be able to help, despite his determination.

Eventually he spoke.

'How on earth did you get involved in all this?'

'I was approached by the Section about a month after graduating university. They told me they'd been watching me for a while, which isn't as creepy as it sounds,' she said. 'I was always good at sports, and I was on the university's pistol shooting team. I loved it. I won some competitions – that's how they spotted me.'

'So, they asked you to become an assassin, and you said "yes", is that it?'

Eva winced at the sarcasm in Nathan's voice.

How could he ever understand?

'I went to university as a way to escape my life,' she said. 'Working for the Section guaranteed I'd never return to the way things were before. Ever. My childhood was shit,' she said. 'Both my parents died before I was Alex's age, and I was put into foster care. There are a lot of good people who foster kids. Unfortunately, the people I was sent to weren't.'

Out the corner of her eye, she noticed Decker shift uncomfortably.

'Of course,' Eva said, 'the Section knew all of this. Every single recruit on that pilot programme had the same messed-up background as me. And the Section used that to their advantage.'

'I can't imagine how hard it must've been for you,' said Nathan. 'I'm sorry.'

She shrugged. 'It's only while I've been in hiding these past three years I've had time to think about it,' she said. 'At the time, I was too excited to worry about the ethics of it. Of course, being an orphan and from a foster family who couldn't care less, it meant I had no family to explain myself to – or that the Section would have to deal with if something went wrong.' Her jaw tightened. 'It'd save them any complications if people start asking awkward questions at funerals, that's for sure.'

'The Section's psychologists knew how to tap into that fear and turn it into anger,' she added. 'That's how they trained us. They'd wear us down with questions about our past and our lives as kids, and then unleashed it on the training grounds. It worked.'

Eva noticed Decker's jaw clench, then saw Nathan's complexion pale moments later, and she swallowed.

'I thought you knew all this,' she said, bewildered. 'You were the analyst assigned to my case, right?'

'I wasn't told about your history,' Nathan spluttered. 'I mean – Jesus – what sort of person does that?' He shook his head. 'No wonder you were at breaking point when the Section put you on close protection duty at the embassy.'

Eva glanced down at her hands. 'At the time I joined the Section, it was a challenge,' she said. 'A way to prove myself – to me, if no-one else.' She glanced over her shoulder and met Nathan's eyes. 'Up to that point, no-one gave a shit what happened to me.'

Nathan exhaled; she could see him try to keep his calm. 'How many of you were recruited by the Section?'

'There were four of us at the end,' said Eva. 'Sixteen of us started the course. One died two weeks after we finished training.' She shivered. 'It was an accident, but it was a wake-up call to me. Another was killed on active service. I don't know where. We weren't privy to each other's missions.' She shivered. 'I knew then that I had to be the best I could be, if I was going to survive. And now, I might be the only one left.'

'None of this was on your file.'

'It was deemed to be too sensitive.'

'What happened to Alex's sister?'

'Three years ago, the Section radioed the team that were still dealing with the aftermath at the engineer's hotel room. They'd managed to lock the scene down to prevent the hotel staff from finding out and calling in the local police,' she said. 'They began to search the room again. Remember, they thought they were dealing with the murder of the engineer's wife,' she added. 'They had no reason to know there was potentially someone else in the room with her at the time.'

Nathan's eyes widened. 'She didn't witness her mother's murder, did she?'

'We don't think so,' said Eva. 'We think her mother hid her before she answered the door to the room; I don't know – call it maternal instinct if you like – but her actions saved her daughter's life. The Section's team found her hiding in the wardrobe behind the panelling at the back.'

'Was – was she okay? I mean, she must've have been traumatised,' said Nathan.

'I don't know. I never met her. Sorry,' she said, standing up, 'I need a drink of water.'

'Wait,' said Decker. 'I've got something stronger. You sound like you need it.'

He disappeared into the shadows, and returned with three plastic beakers and a bottle of red wine. 'I think we all need this.'

Eva took her cup from him and paced in front of the fire. Now that she'd made a start, she didn't want to stop in her narrative of the events of three years ago. Desperate, she knew deep down she wanted Decker and Nathan to hear the whole story, to see if they could shed any light on what was happening to her.

She may have been one of the best assassins ever recruited by the Section, but her abilities didn't extend to information analysis, and she knew she needed help.

She took a sip of the Tuscan wine before continuing. 'Before he died, the engineer told Doug that Alex was the key to the information he'd passed on as part of his defection deal with the British. Of course, then the engineer was assassinated before he could tell us any more.'

'What happened?'

'The Section brought in a team of psychologists – they decided the only way to find out what Alex knew about the people who killed his father was to place him in a softer environment,' said Eva. 'So, they sent Doug, Alex and me to a house in the suburbs. We had to pretend we were a family.' She broke off and wiped at her eyes, then held up a hand as both men moved towards her. 'It's okay. You need to hear this. I need you to hear it – we've got to work this out somehow.'

She sniffed, then carried on. 'There were two psychologists – a male and a female – who took it in turns to visit the house for a couple of hours every day. They spent a week with Alex, trying to work out what he might know, but it was no good – he'd either forgotten it, or was too traumatised to want to recall it. Apparently, the team talking to his sister had the same problem. She wouldn't – or couldn't – tell them anything.'

Eva took another sip of her wine, ignoring the trembling in her fingers and hoping Decker wouldn't notice. 'They had just left on the fifth day, when Doug was murdered.'

She wiped her eyes once more, then sat down in her seat, clutching the beaker between her hands as she stared into the fire. 'Everything happened so quickly after that. The Section moved me out of the house with Alex, and that's when I found out what my new mission was.' She managed a smile as her eyes found the sleeping boy. 'I was tasked with keeping Alex safe, for as long as it took for him to remember what his father might have told him.'

'I'm presuming he hasn't remembered?'

'No. He hasn't,' said Eva. 'The psychologists showed me a few exercises to do with him a couple of times a week, to see if it jogged his memory. There's been nothing.'

'Why did you insist on bringing him to France?' demanded Decker. 'He was safe in Italy. *We* were safe in Italy.'

Eva glanced down at her glass and realised it was empty. She walked across to where Decker sat, and picked up the bottle of red, refilled her glass, and then took a sip.

'Alex's twin is here.'

'Where?'

'At a place south of Toulouse,' said Eva. 'The Section decided to split up the twins for their own safety. I was tasked with looking after Alex. There's another woman from the same training programme as me, looking after his twin sister.'

'How do you know where to find her?' said Nathan, peering over his wine glass.

Eva sighed. 'Unknown to the Section, when Alex got placed with me and his sister was sent to France, I kept in touch with my colleague. We felt we had to, for the sake of the twins. We used none of our Section-sanctioned protocols, though – I think we both knew there was more to what happened to the engineer than we were being told, and we had to protect the twins at all costs.'

'When the bloody hell were you going to tell me all of this?' Decker managed to keep his voice low to avoid waking the sleeping boy, but the menace still cut through. 'After all we've been through?'

'I couldn't,' snapped Eva. 'If anyone found out the kids were still alive, there was a very high chance of them becoming targets.' She sighed and put her wine glass on the floor next to Decker's chair. 'And that's why we're here. I've never met his twin. She was kept away from us. What if she panics? At least if she sees Alex, she might remember him. She won't trust us, but she might trust him.' She peered over her shoulder at the sleeping boy. 'Besides,' she said, 'he's got nowhere else to go.'

'When was the last time you spoke to your counterpart?' said Nathan.

'Six months ago.'

'So, she might not even be there.'

'I have to find out for sure.'

'This is crazy,' snapped Decker. 'They were split up for a reason, Eva. And yet, you want to take Alex straight back to the person you've been keeping him away from?'

'No,' she said. 'To *save* her. If they found Alex and me eleven days ago, I'm presuming they know where his twin is as well.' She glared at Decker. 'I'm trying to get to her before they do.'

# FOUR

*France*

A cold breeze enveloped Eva as she climbed from the vehicle.

The surrounding countryside was quiet, the silence broken only by the squawk of a lone crow wheeling above a field at the back of the property.

Footsteps crunched on gravel before Decker joined her.

'Looks abandoned. No vehicles. No smoke from the chimney.'

'Looks can be deceptive.'

'What are you thinking?'

'Feels like we're being watched.'

'Agreed.' The wind changed direction, and he sniffed. 'Better have them wait in the car.'

Eva frowned, then turned her head and caught his meaning.

There was definitely something in the air.

She glanced over her shoulder to where Nathan and Alex stood next to the car. 'Wait there,' she called.

Decker tossed the car keys to Nathan, who caught them one-handed and clutched them to his chest.

'Stay in the car,' said Decker. 'Keep warm.'

'It'll give them some protection from attack, too,' murmured Eva as they began to walk towards the side of the house, looking for a way in.

'I know. But there's no need to tell him that and cause alarm.'

Eva swept her gaze over the house.

It looked solid, with the same no-nonsense build as the house they'd stayed in overnight. Its brick exterior had been rendered once, a long time ago, but now bore the tell-tale traces of accidental neglect. The owner obviously had more pressing business to attend to.

The curtains had been drawn closed, and no windows were open.

'Look,' she said, and pointed at the wall above one of the lintels. 'Bullet holes.'

Wary, they stepped closer, weapons raised.

'Someone lost their element of surprise,' said Decker.

Eva checked over her shoulder. 'There's no cover, that's why,' she said. 'Whether they came across the fields or along the road, they would've been spotted a mile away.'

Decker squinted into the distance. 'If she saw them coming, why didn't she run?'

Eva turned back to the house and took a step back, assessing its build once more with a critical eye. 'Panic room – same as me.'

'I don't think she made it.'

Eva fought down the wave of sickness that threatened to engulf her. What had happened here could have happened to her. To Alex.

Only Stefano's death had saved them.

'Come on,' she said. 'One way to find out.'

They reached the corner of the building and followed it round to a back door that faced the field.

Cropped stalks of what had once been barley poked out from the dark earth, and a fresh wind blew in their faces.

Eva took several deep gulps before facing the door.

Two more bullets had obliterated the lock, and on leaving, the intruders had simply pulled the door back into its frame to trick anyone giving the property a fleeting glance.

'Wait here,' said Eva. 'Give me five minutes. If I don't come out, take the car and go.'

'Copy that.' Decker took up position with his back to the house, his eyes sweeping the landscape. 'Make sure you're back before then.'

'Will do.'

Eva took a step back, then kicked the door open, raising her weapon at the same time.

A black void appeared, a gloomy space that, once Eva stepped over the threshold, revealed a kitchen.

Eva swept her gun back and forth as she waited for her eyes to adjust, taking in the crockery that remained stacked in the sink, the water long since drained away.

And still, that smell that permeated the air through the whole house.

Decker's shadow crossed the door as Eva moved through the room, yet she knew he wouldn't follow – not unless she asked.

They'd worked together before, once, and he'd treated her as an equal then, never questioning her judgement. Now, they knew even more was at stake and their trust in each other was implicit.

With Decker guarding the rear of the property, Eva edged her way through a doorway that led into a living area. She swept her gun around the space, but no-one shot at her; no-one emerged from the darkened recesses of the room.

She crouched, reached out and flicked back the faded crimson rug that covered the floor, to reveal wide flagstones, their surface pockmarked with over a century's wear.

She bit back an exasperated curse. She'd been hoping to uncover a trapdoor, a place for Alex's twin to hide.

Instead, the solid floor stretched away to all four walls uninterrupted.

Eva straightened, glanced at the front door, and noticed that four heavy bolts still hung in place. Her gun wavered as her eyes found the soft toy discarded on the two-seater settee against one wall. In four paces, she'd crossed the room and picked it up, turning it in her hands.

The blue rabbit had been an apparent favourite, evidenced by the worn fur, patched up body parts and a button for an eye.

She propped it against one of the cushions, and began to climb the wooden stairs built into the opposite wall. In her mind, she ran through several scenarios, all of which were discarded – Alex's sister was nowhere to be found downstairs; there was simply nowhere to hide.

The smell grew stronger as Eva reached the top step, and she used her sleeve to cover her mouth and nose in an attempt to mask the stench.

She could hear it now, a muted buzzing from the direction of the front of the house. Years of training dictated she check the other rooms first, so she did so, quickly discounting the small shared bathroom and child's bedroom, a lump forming in her throat at the ordinary signs of two lives brutally interrupted.

She opened cupboard doors, pulled back rugs from timber floors, but there was no trace.

Eva squared her shoulders, tested the weight of the gun in her hand through habit, and pushed open the door to the main bedroom.

She gagged, took a step back, and swore.

She was no stranger to violence, but the manner in which her colleague had been tied up and systematically tortured left little to the imagination.

The thought that the women had surely screamed her last breath within earshot of a six-year-old girl was almost unbearable.

Eva blinked back tears as she leaned against the bedroom wall.

There was no need to search the room; it had been pulled apart with brute force, a gaping hole in the opposite wall revealing a shallow recess.

Eva stifled a sob and fled the room, ran down the stairs and almost barrelled into Decker as she burst through the back door.

His strong arms caught her, his voice calm.

'Steady.'

He unwound her fingers from the grip on her weapon, flicked the safety and waited while she gulped at the fresh air.

'Well?'

'She's dead.'

'The girl?'

'Gone. There was a recess in the wall. Whoever did this tore it apart to get to her.'

Eva moved away from the house, crossing the back yard until she reached the stubbly perimeter of the field. She wrapped her arms over her chest and kicked at the loose stones at her feet.

'What do you want to do?'

Decker joined her, his gaze on the woodland beyond the field, his grip on his weapon light, but ready.

'Find whoever did this to her,' said Eva. 'And make them pay.' She turned her back on the field and stared at the house. 'Somewhere out there is a very frightened little girl.'

'She might be frightened,' said Decker. 'But she's clever, too.'

'What?'

'Look.'

Eva spun on her heel as Decker pointed towards the thicket of trees.

'One o'clock position. Watch.'

Eva shielded her eyes and focused on the spot Decker indicated. 'What am I looking for?'

'Wait.'

Eva held her breath and tried to calm her racing heartbeat.

What had Decker seen? Was it possible Alex's sister was still alive?

Then she saw it.

A glint of light that flickered on and off.

'Morse code?' Eva stepped forward in surprise.

'E. V. A.' Decker smiled. 'I think someone was expecting you.'

'But how? How does she know my name?' How does she know what I look like?' Eva frowned. 'How did she know I'd come?'

Decker peered over his shoulder at the house, then back to the woods. 'I guess despite everything, there's always hope.'

# FIVE

Decker held out Eva's gun to her. 'I'll wait here.'

'Hang on to that. I don't want to frighten her.'

Decker grabbed her arm. 'It could be a trap.'

'I know.'

'We don't know if anyone else is out there.'

Eva bit her lip. 'If there was anyone else around, I don't think she'd have signalled.'

'Don't be long.'

The grey afternoon sun was beginning to fade as she made her way across the barren field towards the location of the flickering light.

She tried to keep her gait relaxed, despite her eyes darting left and right, seeking out any dangers that might be lurking.

She didn't doubt that Decker could shoot an assailant from his position nearer the house, but she'd be dead before he'd get a chance to fire.

She shivered at the sheer desolation of the bleak landscape, and wondered how long her counterpart had had to endure such loneliness. At least in Cyprus, Eva had hidden in plain sight.

Mud started to cake her boots, slowing her pace, and she silently thanked her counterpart for training the girl to wait and remain hidden. As she drew closer to the woodland, she brought her hand up to her brow to shade her eyes from the dull light and peered into the gloom.

A face appeared from behind a tree trunk, pale with wide blue eyes, and then a girl of Alex's age stepped out, dressed in a pair of grubby jeans and a hooded sweatshirt.

'Hello. I'm Eva.'

'I know,' said the girl. She lifted her hand, and held out a scrap of paper.

Eva frowned, then stepped forward and took it from her. She almost dropped it when she turned it over to reveal an old photograph cut from a newspaper showing her and Douglas at the electronics conference the twins' father had attended.

'Where did you get this from?' she murmured.

'Sally,' said the girl. 'She made me keep it safe. "Just in case", she said. I'm Grace.'

Eva blinked, and let her eyes wander around the wooded area. 'Where have you been hiding, Grace?'

'I'll show you.'

Eva noted the pride in the girl's response, and in that moment realised the little girl was a lot tougher than her tiny physique first led her to believe. She felt a wave of sadness consume her at the thought that the girl's childhood had been ripped away from her, thanks to her father's actions, which was quickly replaced by a rage that she battened down, refocusing on the task at hand.

There would be opportunity for revenge in time. She had to ensure the twins were safe first.

She pushed a low-lying branch out of the way and froze.

Grace was standing next to a raised platform, its surface camouflaged by leaves and twigs, so that when dropped, it would blend effortlessly into its surroundings.

She recalled that Sally's training had been in jungle warfare; she'd started her career in the British Army and had trained extensively in the jungles of Belize before growing bored with regimental life and looking for a new challenge.

She shuddered at the memory of the torn apart body in the house, and shook her head to try to clear the thought.

Eva wandered over and peered under the trapdoor. A ladder led down to a space that had been built specifically to house Grace's small frame.

'Have a look,' said Grace. She handed over a torch.

'Okay.' Eva swung herself onto the ladder and climbed down the rungs until her feet touched a solid floor.

The walls and floor had been sealed professionally to keep its single occupant warm and dry. Two shelves had been set into the wall, laden with foodstuff more suited to camping, while four large containers of water stood next to the foot of the ladder. A canvas camp bed had been placed against one wall, complete with sleeping bag and pillow. An assortment of books and games littered the rest of the space.

Eva ran some calculations in her head. There was still plenty of food; probably another two weeks' worth, and the same for the water supplies.

She climbed the ladder to find Grace eyeing the woodland around them, her eyes constantly moving.

'What happened?'

The girl turned to her, tears in her eyes. 'I was playing in the house when Sally ran downstairs and told me to run. She said there were some men that would be coming, and that I mustn't ever go back to the house.' She screwed up her fists. 'Ever.'

'Come here.'

Eva crouched down and scooped up the girl into her arms, then straightened and began to walk back the way they'd come. 'We're not going to go back into the house,' she said. 'I'm here with some friends, and we're going to take you somewhere very safe, okay?'

She could hear her own voice shaking and cursed the men that had done this. She stomped across the field, Decker's figure growing closer, and tried to keep her focus.

If she fell to pieces, he'd never believe her capable of completing the mission she'd set herself, and he'd try to talk her out of it.

She had to hold it together a little longer.

'Alex!'

Grace kicked out and slipped from Eva's arms before tearing towards the car.

Eva's throat constricted as the twins embraced, and exploded into a torrent of excited chatter.

Nathan wandered over. 'Do I ask about her foster carer?'

Eva shook her head. 'I was too late.'

'We need to move,' said Decker. 'We've spent too long here already.'

# SIX

They'd travelled in silence for the past hour or more, each lost in thought.

Eva wracked her memory, replaying snatches of conversation she'd had with Douglas, Petersen – anyone who was remotely connected to the engineer.

She rested her head against the cool glass of the window and let the vibration from the vehicle dull her senses.

There was so much to understand, yet she sensed she was running out of time.

The violence of the attacks; the sheer brutality inflicted upon Sally indicated a sense of desperation.

Were her enemies working to a deadline she had yet to uncover?

What if she was too late?

'This will have to do.'

Decker's voice cut through her thoughts and she jerked upright, instantly alert. 'Where are we?'

'East of Grenoble.'

Eva rubbed at her eyes.

Decker turned the car into the forecourt of a cheap motel and killed the engine. He leaned on the steering wheel and twisted in his seat to face her.

'We need to rest. I'll get a room on my own. The two of you book a room with the kids. Make sure it's next to mine. Knock on the wall when you get there and I'll join you. Give me fifteen minutes.'

He slipped from the car and stalked towards the front of the motel, entering through double doors that faced the main road.

Nathan extracted himself from the passenger seat and moved behind the steering wheel before twisting around to face Eva.

'What's the plan from here?'

She ran her hand through her hair, and yawned.

'We need to rest first. We can't plan anything effectively if we're exhausted.'

An hour before, they'd stopped at a convenience store on the outskirts of a small town, and Nathan had insisted he be the one to dash inside and buy enough provisions to last them a few days.

'There will be cameras everywhere,' he'd said. 'At least if someone sees me, I'll be considered less of a threat than you two. I'm just a nerd, right?'

Eva had begun to protest, worried for his safety, but Decker had silenced her and sent him on his way.

'He wants to help,' he'd explained as they watched him enter the store. 'Let him – and he's right about the cameras.'

He'd returned without incident twenty minutes later, and they had powered away, keen to put as much distance as they could between themselves and the town.

Now, she pointed through the windscreen as Decker re-emerged from the motel's reception area and made his way towards a room on the far right of the sprawling accommodation block.

Eva noted the number of the room painted on the wall next to his, and motioned to Alex to let her climb out.

'Back in a minute.'

It didn't take long to check in.

Thankfully, the motel wasn't part of a branded chain, and the proprietor was keen to fill rooms that would otherwise remain empty until ski season began. Cash up front with no identification was accepted with a sly smile, and a derogatory remark about the tax department.

Eva smiled conspiratorially and hurried outside, holding up the keys as she turned and walked towards the room.

Nathan moved the car so it was parked outside the unit she'd rented, and after checking her surroundings, Eva opened the door and ushered Alex and Grace inside.

Decker joined them half an hour later, freshly showered and demanding food as loudly as the twins.

The small kitchenette turned into a hive of activity, and

as Eva sipped from a bottle of water, she was struck by the normality of the moment.

After they'd cleared away the pots and crockery, the children sat on a worn rug in front of the television watching a cartoon, busy chattering in their native language.

'It's amazing they still talk to each other in Russian after being so long apart,' said Nathan as he sank onto one of the armchairs. 'You wouldn't think they'd remember.'

Eva laughed. 'You need to get out more. It's not Russian. It's Polish.'

Nathan frowned. 'Polish? I thought you said the engineer was Russian?'

'No – he was working for a Polish contractor supplying to the Russians,' said Eva. 'Why?'

Nathan ran a hand over his face, his skin pale.

'What's wrong?'

'Two months ago, the Section received an alert that Maxim Kowalski had escaped from prison,' he said.

'Who the hell is Maxim Kowalski?' growled Decker.

'He's a Polish scientist who the Russians accused of plotting a terrorist attack against them. He's a madman,' said Nathan. 'And if he's the one who's after these kids, you're in serious trouble.'

'Why?' said Eva.

'He'd been charged with fraud, but everyone knew that was a trumped-up charge,' said Nathan. 'The Russians arrested him to keep him quiet.'

'Quiet about what?' said Decker. 'What did he do?'

Nathan made sure the twins were still watching the television, and lowered his voice. 'Maxim Kowalski was the owner of a bio-engineering company. He'd grown up in the Soviet era, of course, but once the Communists withdrew from most of the country, he started a very lucrative business in weapons design,' he said. 'Except there were rumours he was experimenting with biological weapons.' He swallowed. 'We heard from the Russians that he'd been testing the viruses he created on people his thugs had kidnapped. They always used homeless people, or illegal immigrants – people that wouldn't ever be reported missing.'

'Jesus,' Decker murmured.

'What was the name of the company he set up?' asked Eva.

'MK Future Bio-engineering,' said Nathan. 'Why?'

'That's who the engineer was working for when he defected.'

# SEVEN

Eva pulled the curtains across the window.

'We're clear,' she said. 'No-one's been in or out of this car park since we arrived.'

Decker switched on one of the lamps next to the bed, draped a cloth over it to dull the light, and crept back to where Eva and Nathan sat once he'd checked the sleeping forms of the twins hadn't been disturbed.

'We'll take it in shifts to stay awake and keep a look-out,' he said. 'That way, everyone gets their head down for a couple of hours at a time.'

'Works for me,' said Nathan. 'I'll take the first shift. You've been driving all day.'

Decker nodded, pulled spare linen out of the wardrobe and made a makeshift bed on the floor before turning his back to the room. He was asleep in minutes, his soft snores reaching Eva's ears.

She smiled, then glanced up as Nathan passed her a steaming mug of coffee. It was a powdered mixture, but she inhaled the burnt aroma, glad of its warmth.

Nathan lowered himself into the chair next to hers under the window, lifted the hem of one of the curtains, then took a sip from his drink.

'Any thoughts on this Maxim Kowalski?' he asked, keeping his voice low.

Eva shook her head. 'No. I was trying to remember if the engineer mentioned his name at any point, and I don't think he did.'

'Probably too scared.'

'But Maxim obviously had a vested interest in what the engineer was developing.'

'Maybe. It doesn't explain how he found out about you and Sally though.'

Eva tapped her fingernail against the surface of the mug. 'I wonder how he's funding all this,' she said. 'I mean, just the surveillance to locate us must've cost a fortune – he must be using mercenaries, but how can he afford them?'

'People trafficking,' said Nathan. 'Interpol have had him on their "most wanted" list for months, but he's rarely seen in public, and he delegates most of the dirty work from what I could gather.'

'What was his last known location?'

'After the prison?' Nathan shrugged. 'Some suspect he returned to Eastern Europe. Nothing's been substantiated.'

Eva leaned over to the small coffee table near the far wall and tugged the folded European road map towards her.

They'd purchased it earlier. Although the scale meant smaller villages had been missed off, Decker had been reluctant to buy anything more specific.

'Just in case we're being followed,' he'd said as they'd paid for the fuel in cash. 'With this, we could be anywhere.'

Now, Eva unfolded the map until the furthest eastern reaches of the continent were visible. She spread it on the table between her and Nathan, whose eyes flickered away from the window before returning to his view of the car park.

'What are you doing?'

'Trying to get a feel for where he might be,' said Eva. 'Can you remember the names of any of the old communist weapons testing facilities?'

She grabbed a pencil left with some notepaper next to the room phone and circled the rough areas on the map as Crowe rattled off the names before tapping the pencil against her chin. 'Too big,' she murmured. 'Too much risk of being spotted.'

'Where was the facility he and the engineer worked at?' asked Nathan. 'I've seen it mentioned in a report back at the Section a while back.'

'A forest, the other side of the Sudeten mountains on the Polish and Czech border.'

'Isn't it more likely he'd return to the one place he knows?'

'Again, too risky,' argued Eva. 'The Russian authorities and the Polish police would be watching that place – it's too obvious.'

'I disagree,' said Nathan, a smile on his lips. 'That facility was abandoned two years ago after a virus was rumoured to have escaped the laboratory.'

Eva dropped the pencil onto the map and leaned back. 'You mean to tell me Maxim would knowingly go back to a place where a biohazard is on the loose?'

Nathan shrugged. 'It'd be a perfect cover. Look.' He pointed at the map. 'The nearest large town is a good ten kilometres away. Far enough to ensure no prying eyes. Close enough to ensure the rumour about the virus continues to circulate.'

'Hiding in plain sight,' said Eva. She frowned. 'So how come the authorities haven't checked it out?'

Nathan shook his head. 'I don't know. Maybe they believe the rumours, too.'

'Or,' said Eva, sitting upright. 'It *is* true. They know about it – maybe were even responsible for it – and by staying away, they can avoid any awkward questions about their involvement.'

'What if Maxim somehow arranged for the accident to occur while he was in prison – so that he'd have a safe haven once he escaped?'

'Jesus,' said Eva. 'He's never stopped, has he? All this time, he's been planning, preparing – so once he got out of prison, he could continue his work on the weapon and locate the twins.'

'We need to get access to the internet,' said Nathan. He flicked the curtain and checked the car park once more. 'We have to find out more about that accident. Do you know if there was anything on the public record about the project the engineer was working on?'

'I don't think so. But it'd be on the Section database, surely?'

Their eyes met.

'It'd be risky,' said Nathan. 'If we access that, they're going to know our location.'

'So, we keep moving,' said Eva. 'We'll find an internet café – how long do you think you'll need?'

'Well, if we're going to send up a flag where we are, I might as well use my own login,' sighed Nathan. 'So without having to hack into the system, all we need is the time to find the information we're after.'

'How long?'

'Twenty minutes?'

'No. Too long. Ten.'

'Fifteen.'

'Deal.' Eva grinned. 'Although I don't think Decker is going to be too happy when we tell him.'

'You're right, I'm not,' a muffled voice grumbled from the floor.

# EIGHT

*South-east Poland*

Maxim slammed the cheap glass tumbler onto the table.

The homemade alcohol burned his guts, and served as a reminder that no matter what he told his men, he was a ghost – an outsider, desperate and unpredictable.

He glanced over his shoulder at the form of a young woman stretched out on his bed; his thoughts turned momentarily to the wife and daughter he'd left behind three years ago, the memory of them consigned to the labyrinth of memories that threatened to resurface.

He eyed the bottle of pills. When he was in prison, they'd fed him the drug intravenously. Not for his benefit, but to ensure he remained docile enough that the various guards and doctors could go anywhere near him.

For two years, he'd been variously strapped to a gurney or chained to a bare wall, raving as the drugs took their toll on him while the state-employed psychiatrists conducted their tests upon his wretched body.

He'd survived though, once he'd worked out the routines and subtle nuances of the doctors' characters; he'd bribed guards, used his outside network to threaten and influence until one blessed night, an orderly had entered his room at three in the morning, unlocked the straps that held him to his bed, and left without a word, the door wide open.

Maxim had wasted no time.

He'd ripped the straps from his body and padded barefoot after the orderly, slipping into the shadows as a guard had passed the far end of the corridor, before edging towards a fire escape the orderly pointed to.

'Wait forty seconds. No more, no less,' he'd hissed. 'I'll deactivate the alarm. When you push this door open, you'll have five minutes to leave the complex.' He'd pressed a hand-drawn map into Maxim's hand. 'Follow this. No deviations.' He'd lifted his eyes to Maxim's, his face full of hope. 'This will guarantee my wife's safety, yes?'

Maxim had given an almost reverent nod of his head, but hadn't said a word. As far as he was concerned, promises had to be spoken aloud in order to be kept.

'Good luck.' The orderly had spun on his heel and disappeared around the corner of the corridor. Thirty-four seconds later, Maxim had heard the door mechanism release with a click, and he was gone.

Now, the pills worked to his advantage. They allowed him to concentrate, to maintain control over his empire deep in the forest.

He knew the state still hunted for him; but he ruled by fear, and this ensured his safety.

For now.

He pushed himself up from his chair, stalked across the room and swung the door open, squinting at the bright sunlight that dappled the treetops.

The cabin had been built by one of the occupying forces two generations ago, and served as his private lodgings away from the dilapidated facility. He relished the warmth on his skin as he shoved his hands in his pockets and tried to calm the nerves his memories evoked. During the colder months, his joints ached as a permanent reminder of the damage his torturers inflicted upon him, and as soon as the days began to lengthen he planned to emerge from a painful hibernation spent beside the wood-burning stove in the cabin.

'Maxim?'

The familiar voice called to him from the edge of the clearing, and he turned on his heel to see a man who stubbed out a cigarette before stalking towards him.

'Samuel. When did you arrive?'

'In the early hours of this morning. I was informed you shouldn't be disturbed.'

'I have been busy.'

Maxim shook hands with the man and averted his eyes to conceal the lie. There was no need for his men to know the truth about how much rest he required in order to function properly. Weakness wasn't an option, not now.

'Did you find her?'

'We found the woman. Despite my best efforts, she would not talk.'

'That's disappointing. You must be losing your touch.'

'I doubt it. Two of my men passed out; they couldn't stand to watch.'

'Where is the child?'

'We never found her. We tore the house apart, but there was no sign of her. The building was surrounded by fallow fields – we would have seen her in an instant if she was still there.'

Maxim growled and turned away. 'You have failed me, Samuel.'

'I am sorry, Maxim,' said the man and hurried to follow. 'I have my men monitoring all communications. We will redouble our efforts to find the other woman and the boy.'

'She has help, you know that?'

'The man is nothing but a Section analyst. He will be of no use to her.'

'I'm not talking about the analyst. The Caretaker has been sighted.'

Samuel's eyes widened. 'He's meant to be dead.'

'So are you.'

The assassin's jaw clenched. 'I will have my revenge on her.'

Maxim placed his hand on Samuel's arm. 'Make sure you do.'

He left the man standing in the clearing and pushed his way through the bracken and trees, moving deeper into the woods.

After the engineer had betrayed him by trying to sell their secrets to the British, he had despaired. All their plans, all that money and power – gone.

Their former masters had hunted him down, taking out their anger on his mind, on his body.

Soon, however, he would have to return to the outside world, to the very place that had set out to destroy him. And, once there, he would take his vengeance.

And ensure the blame was laid firmly at the doorstep of the British government, and those who betrayed him.

Reaching the entrance to the bunker that German occupying forces had forced slaves to carve out of the hillside over sixty years ago before the Russians took over, Maxim stalked through the open door of the once-abandoned laboratory and made his way towards the small group of men working at the far end.

They'd positioned themselves to take advantage of the lights set up around them and powered by an old diesel generator. The electricity had been cut off two years ago by the authorities before the complex had been forgotten, left to rot.

One of the men was crouched next to an array of

equipment, a screwdriver in his hands as he murmured instructions to the two men beside him.

Maxim's footsteps echoed off the walls, and as he drew closer, the man peered over his shoulder at him, then stopped his work and stood as Maxim approached.

'It's not ready yet,' he began.

Maxim held up his hand. 'I know. You said it would take a while.' He squinted in the fading light to better see what the man had been working on. 'How much longer though, Vadir?'

The engineer shrugged. 'Two days should do it.'

'Good.'

Maxim circled the equipment, ignoring the other two men that moved away. 'You're sure it will work?'

'Yes. Can you prevent the antidote being administered?'

Maxim recalled his conversation with Parkes, and clenched his fists. The children would have to be located, and soon.

'Yes. I can stop the antidote.'

# NINE

*Berlin, Germany*

Miles cursed under his breath and stabbed at the laptop keyboard once more.

A different combination, a different file path, and—

He swore again, and not for the first time aimed his frustration towards Knox and the man's decision to send Nathan with Eva to the hotel.

The only person that had up-to-date information about Eva's work – however sparse that information might be – was now a hostage, taken by one of their own.

A creeping paranoia threatened to overwhelm him.

Since his meeting with Knox, he hadn't been able to shake the feeling that he was being used.

The Section chief had seemed reticent about the Code

One that had been issued – essentially a kill order to eliminate Eva and anyone close to her.

The Codes – three levels of discipline that varied in severity – only applied to the Section. They were a way to provide the British government with a level of comfort that should one of their covert operators cross the line – however tenuous the definition of that line was, and often depending on what the government's agenda was – there was a way to eliminate the problem.

Only a Code One resulted in a kill order though.

He'd spent the afternoon wading through reports on the database, stretching his security access to its limits while he hunted for more information.

After several hours, he'd reached a conclusion.

Only one operative had ever escaped a Code One before.

The Caretaker.

Although Knox had been reluctant to pass on the file, he'd eventually acquiesced, and now Miles sat thumbing through the pages, a mixture of awe and dread sending a shiver across his shoulders.

He hadn't heard about the Caretaker before, likely because when the man had been most active, Miles had been busy working behind the scenes in Central and South America trying to slow down the CIA's involvement in several countries before they wrecked the whole of the southern hemisphere's stake in OPEC and caused an even bigger headache for the British government and its interests.

The assassin had a formidable history, peppered with

Special Forces training, an Egyptian prison record, and a breath-taking escape from enemy territory in a country whose details had been redacted – even at the level of access that Miles had been granted.

Reading between the lines, it appeared that the Caretaker had some scruples though.

Upon being tasked with the "tactical assassination" of a low-ranking official in a Middle Eastern opposition political party, the Caretaker had called foul.

And then immediately dropped off the Section's radar.

As Miles turned the page, the reports turned from praise for the Caretaker's work to anger at his betrayal, with several interviews conducted behind closed doors with anyone at the Section who had crossed paths with the man as Knox and his team tried desperately to control the situation.

He dropped the file to the table surface and ran a hand over his face, his mind racing.

What if Knox had anticipated that he'd want to try to save Eva?

What if the Section chief was using him to draw both her and the Caretaker out into the open so they could be eliminated at the same time?

Miles exhaled, leaned back, and glared at the laptop screen, then shook his head and turned his attention to the passing pedestrian traffic through the window.

A light dusting of snow had fallen on the pavement, and a couple walked past laughing as they slipped and slid across the icy pavement.

He groaned, and realised he'd forgotten to call his wife.

Then he wondered if he'd still have a wife by the time the whole Eva Delacourt debacle had been solved.

He'd escaped the confines of his subterranean office three hours ago, desperate for sunlight and had found a quiet corner of the embassy's private café within which to work.

Darkness had fallen while he worked, and now he stared at his reflection for a moment, wondering what to do.

A waitress passed his table, and he signalled for more coffee before returning his attention to the computer as a new email message flashed up on the screen.

His phone buzzed at his elbow a split second later.

'Alan?'

'You got the email I just sent?'

'Yes.'

'Got a trace on one of our missing friends. CCTV image taken from a place outside Grenoble.'

'Thanks.'

'There's something else. How quickly can you get to France?'

Miles checked his watch and made a quick calculation. 'Seven hours perhaps?'

'I'll meet you at Bellgarde. It's about fifty miles south of their last known position.'

'Why?'

'We've got another one. Similar to yours, except she didn't get away.'

Miles ended the call and opened the email attachment.

The image depicted Nathan in a supermarket, his head lowered in a vain attempt to hide his face from a camera on the other side of the aisle, a basket in his grip.

Miles frowned.

*What the hell were they doing in France?*

# TEN

*France*

Miles scratched at the stubble on his chin and tried to ignore the red-eyed stranger that stared back in the rear-view mirror.

He was tired; exhausted if he were honest with himself, but a second phone call with Alan Greene had put paid to any notion of pulling over to the side of the road and taking a nap.

Instead, he'd driven through the night, crossed borders without incident, and now sped through French lanes, dreading what he would find.

Until Greene had told him while he navigated his way across the border, he'd had no idea there was a second version of Eva hidden in the French countryside. He'd phoned Knox afterwards, demanding to know why he hadn't been told about the female agent who hadn't been as lucky as Eva.

Knox had been cagey, citing operational procedures, and Miles had cursed in frustration.

'Dammit, Gerald. It would've been useful to have known about this before the attack in Berlin,' he'd said.

'Calm down,' said Knox. 'You know now. We were hoping to get in contact with her before anything happened.' He'd paused. 'Miles? There was a child staying with her, a little girl. Find out what's happened to them. I'll need a report from the scene, understand?'

Miles had tasted bile. *Another child?* He'd cleared his throat, confirmed he'd phone back, and had ended the call, his thoughts clouded.

Now, Miles cursed and swerved, narrowly avoided a deep rut in the side of the road, then lowered his window and let the cool air blow through his hair.

The cold breeze invigorated him, and helped him to concentrate.

He needed the help from Greene – since the phone call with his supervisor, his mind had been awash with conflicting thoughts. Mostly about what other secrets Knox was keeping from him. And, eating away in the background, the realisation that he might find a dead child waiting for him. His hands tightened on the wheel as he ran through the conversations he'd had with Knox in Berlin before he was dispatched on the hunt for Eva. Knox must've known that there was another agent like Eva in deep cover.

Why the hell, then, hadn't he said something at the time?

And why hadn't Eva?

Miles clenched his jaw at the realisation that if Knox had told him there was another agent like Eva, then he might have been able to warn her, to save her life.

He jerked upright in his seat, sending the car into the opposite side of the lane before correcting the swerve, his pulse racing.

He swallowed, trying to slow down the facts that churned in his head.

Eva had been attacked in Cyprus because of Alex. Because Alex knew something, or represented something to someone.

Her counterpart had then been attacked in France, and now a little girl was missing.

Never a religious man, Miles now found himself praying they found the girl, and that she wasn't dead.

Taken where, then?

By whom?

And, why? Why were the children so important?

He hit the brakes and slowed as bright blue lights strobed a few hundred metres away, then crawled to a standstill and lowered his window as he approached. He reached into his breast pocket for his identification and held it out to the gendarme that approached the car, his breath turning to vapour in the chill morning air.

'*Bonsoir*,' Miles mumbled, slightly embarrassed at the state of his school-level French.

'Good morning, sir.' The gendarme smirked, his English perfect.

*Strike one*, thought Miles. 'Alan Greene is expecting me.'

'*Bon*.' The gendarme swept his arm towards a gated track. 'Drive down there. You'll see the vehicles at the end. Forensics will provide the necessary clothing.'

'Thank you.'

Miles buzzed his window up and set off down the track, the car rocking violently over the ruts and potholes in the pitted surface.

A group of vehicles was parked outside the demarcated crime scene, the tone sombre as he climbed from his car. Greene strode towards him and shook his hand.

'Thanks for coming.'

'I got here as soon as I could.' He peered up at the two-storey building and squinted. 'Bullet holes?'

'It's worse inside. They tortured her, Miles.'

Miles dug his fingernails into his palms. The pain numbed the other images that were threatening to engulf him.

'It's one of the worst I've ever seen,' said Greene. 'And I've seen some bad ones in my time.'

'Who would do such a thing?' said Miles.

'A madman,' said Greene, and shrugged. 'I've got no other explanation.'

'He must've had help.'

'Agreed.' Greene swept his hand across the tyre tracks in the mud. 'Forensics have found four different treads so far. One set belongs to the woman's car over there. Two more are slightly older – there was a rainstorm two nights ago so the tracks have faded a bit; we think maybe those two vehicles came together. And there's a fresh set here. No more than twenty-four hours old, given the rainfall prior to that.'

Miles bit down on the thought that entered his mind.

Two vehicles, probably used by the woman's attackers. Then, maybe, a different car, one to two days later. Could Eva have been here? Had she tried to reach the woman before the attackers could find her?

'Any sign of the girl that was living here?' he said instead.

'Yes, but we haven't found her,' said Greene.

Miles's shoulders sagged.

'Come with me,' Greene said, and led Miles towards the boundary with the field. He pointed towards the trees on the opposite boundary. 'We found a hide about fifty metres into the woods,' he said. 'And it was professionally built. Not a kids' plaything. It's been dug into the ground, with very effective camouflage.'

'If it's so well camouflaged, how did you find it?'

'Because the trapdoor is raised, and it's empty.'

'Shit.' Miles turned to face the house and squinted in the sunlight that was beginning to crest the roof. 'Do you think whoever murdered the woman found the girl?'

Greene sighed. 'I don't know.' He shrugged when Miles raised an eyebrow. 'Look, it's just a gut feel, but I think the woman saw them coming and got the girl to run to the hide and stay there.'

'Then why would she leave it?'

'Maybe she saw someone she knew. She wouldn't leave if she didn't feel safe.'

'No-one in the area has seen her?'

'She's not with any of the neighbours, no. The woman kept to herself, didn't socialise with anyone. You've seen the distance between the properties out here. The local gendarmes have spent all night door-knocking, but I don't think they're going to find anything.'

Miles shoved his hands in his pockets. 'Can I take a look at the hide?'

'Of course.' Greene pointed towards a line of tape sectioning off part of the woods. 'Head in that direction. There's another forensic team working there. Jean Carre is running the site; just let him know you're with me.'

'Thanks.'

Five minutes later, having traipsed across the field and made himself known to the chief forensics officer, Miles glanced over his shoulder at the house in the distance, then back at the hole, and realised he was looking at the woman's own version of Eva's panic room.

With the floors of the house being solid flagstones laid on bare earth several decades ago, there was no way a panic room would ever be able to be installed. So, she'd improvised, using her training to build the girl a safe haven.

He withdrew his phone and speed-dialled Knox.

'The woman is dead,' he confirmed. 'And there's no sign of the girl that was with her.'

'Shit.'

Miles could hear the other man pacing, and then a door slammed before the sound of Knox sinking into his leather office chair reached his ears.

'What else?'

'There was a hide built in the woods. Looks like the girl was there when the murder happened, thank God,' said Miles. 'But she's not there now. If she was trained to run to the hide in case of danger, then she would have been trained to stay there until she saw someone she knew or recognised.'

'What are you thinking?'

Miles stepped over a puddle and began stalking back across the field towards his car.

'I think Eva beat us here. So, do you want to tell me what's really going on, Gerald?'

# ELEVEN

Eva had spent an hour trying to persuade Decker to stay at the motel with the twins, ready to move as soon as she and Nathan returned from the internet café.

They'd found one a mile away, and despite Eva's initial insistence that they travel to a larger town before raising a flag about their whereabouts, Decker had pointed out that their current location was perfect.

'Look,' he said patiently, and showed her the map. He stabbed his finger on the road they'd left to find the motel. 'We're in the middle of a series of highways going in all directions. By the time they lock on to your signal, we could be anywhere.'

Nathan had agreed, his analytical background rising to the challenge. 'It's true,' he said. 'They'll be watching the system in case I log in, but they still have to trace the IP address of the computer we're using, and then get someone there. The Section only has so many assets – chances are, we'll have a couple of hours' head start on any of them.'

Now, Eva sat next to him in a smoky café, peering over his shoulder as he used a Virtual Private Network to log into the Section's database, while Decker sat in the car one block down, the twins on the back seat playing I Spy. The irony wasn't lost on Eva, even if she'd lost the argument with Decker.

'We stick together,' he'd growled, ending the discussion.

Eva shifted in her seat, already growing impatient. 'Will it help, using a VPN?'

'I hope so,' said Nathan. 'The Section has software that can unmask it, but it'll slow them down.'

They'd made a list of what they wanted to search for before he'd entered his login details, and had narrowed down their search to specific names and dates to try to avoid wasting precious minutes.

In addition, Nathan set a stopwatch app in the top right hand corner of the computer screen. They'd agreed they'd shut down everything and wipe the browsing history with two minutes in hand, in case anything went wrong.

His finger hovered over the "enter" button and he glanced at Eva. 'Ready?'

'Do it.'

He pressed the key and the Section's logo appeared, together with a "search" icon in the middle of the screen.

'Okay. Let's see what's in the system about Maxim Kowalski,' said Eva, and leaned forward. Her eyes flickered over the screen as the results of the search string began to appear.

'Only three?' Nathan frowned, then tapped the keyboard.

'Three at your level, perhaps?'

'I'm assigned as your watching brief. I should be able to see everything. I've got the clearances.'

Eva chewed her lip. 'All right – there's not a lot we can do about it now. Let's take a look at what we've got.'

The first search result linked to a Russian news report, and although her language skills were rusty, Eva got the gist of the article quickly.

'It's about Maxim's trial,' she said. 'It says that the man arrested by Russian authorities two months before had been found guilty of conspiracy towards the Russian government and sentenced to life imprisonment.'

'No photo though.'

'Try the next one.'

The second search string was from an English language news agency based in Poland, and reported the arrest of Maxim.

Eva sat back in her seat. 'Look at the date. Maxim was arrested the same day Douglas was killed.'

'No such thing as coincidence.'

'Exactly. Can you print this off?'

'Are you kidding me? This is a level seventeen database. You can't just log in and print off whatever you like, or take a screengrab – that's the whole point!'

Eva shrugged. 'Sorry. I don't really do computer stuff.

What's the next article about?'

Nathan shook his head, then turned his attention back to the computer and clicked on the final search result.

Eva ignored the hiss that escaped his teeth, too absorbed in the text on the screen.

From an official Section report, the document set out the events of an accident at a secure laboratory in Poland, six months after Maxim's imprisonment. A satellite photo had been appended to the report, depicting a thick wooded area with three red circles marks on the image.

She peered closer. 'This looks like an old facility from the Cold War. Look – the report alludes to the main facility being cut into the hillside here. The trees help disguise any outbuildings. The only reason the Section located this was because of all these emergency vehicles parked in this clearing.'

Nathan enlarged the photo on the screen. 'Those aren't normal emergency vehicles. That's the logo of their military biohazard team.'

Eva frowned. 'Where are all the people? The workers? I'd expect to see decontamination tents.'

'Hang on.'

Nathan closed the photo file and pulled up the accompanying report once more, then began to scroll down the page. His finger froze above the mouse when he reached the penultimate paragraph.

'Oh, my God.'

Eva swallowed, then began to read, her voice barely above a whisper. "'It is believed that the accident that occurred here was deemed too secret in nature and would cause embarrassment to the authorities. It is alleged that, rather than treat the workers at the facility, a decision was made to terminate all employees with immediate effect and close off the area as a contaminated zone for at least fifty years".'

Nathan clicked on another link, and a second satellite photo appeared.

A circle had been drawn around a small clearing amongst the trees, a lone figure walking away from the area with what appeared to be an automatic rifle slung over his shoulder.

'What am I looking for?' said Nathan at Eva's sharp intake of breath.

She tapped the screen, her finger on the new earth beside the figure.

'This. It's a mass grave.'

'Jesus.'

They sat for a moment, stunned, before Eva's eyes caught sight of the digital stopwatch on the screen blink to the next minute.

She slapped Nathan's arm to shake him from his thoughts.

'Back to the search screen. Is there anything about the attack on the embassy in Prague?'

Nathan's fingers swept over the keyboard, and then he pressed "enter".

'One document.'

'That can't be right,' said Eva.

He shrugged. 'You saw what I typed in. This is all it's got.'

'Open it.'

Eva rested her chin in her hand as she leaned closer to read the text while Nathan scrolled down the screen.

Her interest turned to growing horror as she read the content, the report clinical in its analytical detail of a mission gone wrong, and of a treachery that went to the core of British government diplomacy.

She ignored Nathan's sharp intake of breath as he caught up with her in the text.

'Skip the rest, 'she said, ignoring the tremor in her voice. 'Go to the executive summary.'

A sickness twisted her stomach as Nathan whispered the final words of the report.

'"After careful investigation, and once both children had been successfully taken away, our findings conclude that the engineer had been the victim of a treasonable act made by persons within the government's diplomatic corps, who had sought to use the information offered by the engineer to further his own interests".'

'Stop.'

Nathan paused, and glanced at her. 'What?'

'Who authored this report?'

He hit a button and peered at the screen once more.

'Philip Petersen wrote it. Miles Newcombe uploaded it four days ago.'

'Go back to the report about the accident. Who authored that one?'

Nathan brought up the report and scrolled to the end. 'Huh. Well, what d'you know?'

'Gerald Knox.'

'I'm surprised they haven't blocked any of my access to this. You'd have thought they would know I'd be tempted to take a look.'

Eva hissed through her teeth, her eyes darting to the door. 'Shut it down.'

'What? We've still got seven minutes.'

'Shut it down *now*.'

Nathan logged out, cleared the browsing history as agreed, and shut the computer down.

Eva was already standing, her heart racing.

'What's wrong?'

'It's a trap,' she said. 'Decker was right. I should've listened to him, but I was too interested in finding out about Maxim.' She leaned down and grabbed his arm. 'We need to go. Now.'

She pulled him through the café, ignoring the startled glance from the owner, and stopped when she reached the door, Nathan barrelling into her.

'Wait,' she commanded.

She peered between the posters that plastered the surface of the door, dirt smeared over the glass, and craned her neck left and right.

The street was quiet, save for the occasional car that passed without slowing, and no pedestrians loitered on the pavements either side of the narrow thoroughfare.

Ahead, she saw Decker sit up and lean forward in the driver's seat of the waiting car, and heard the engine rev.

'Come on,' she said. 'We need to be quick.'

They ran, Eva discarding any notion to keep calm and not draw attention to themselves. They needed to get away from the café, and fast.

If she was right, someone in the Section was a lot closer to finding out where she'd been and where she was, and she had no intention of hanging around to see if her assumption was correct.

# TWELVE

*London*

Knox replaced the phone into its cradle on his desk and smiled.

Eva and Nathan had been located in a town outside Grenoble, based upon Miles's own assertion that keeping Crowe's access codes operational would prove too tempting to the fugitives.

And, if Eva and Nathan were in Grenoble, then Decker and the twins couldn't be far away.

Eva would never let the boy out of her sight for long – it was against her programmed protocols.

For all the good the black ops team Eva had belonged to had done, the fact remained that it left them predictable, and therefore vulnerable.

It was why she was the only one left.

Three years on her own had evidently resulted in Eva's boredom leading to her educating herself in tactical manoeuvres that had never been taught to the close-knit team, and he suspected Decker was responsible.

He allowed himself one consolation. At least he'd had the foresight to erase all information about the operation from three years ago from Nathan's access rights, leaving only the reports that would pique Eva's interest while allowing him to remain in control of the situation.

He had to.

If he believed for one moment that the whole project was unravelling, or showed his hand too soon, everything he had worked for would be destroyed.

Knox made his way across to a small cabinet next to the bombproof safe in the corner of the room, slid open the door, and extracted the crystal tumbler and a bottle of thirty-year-old single malt.

Pouring a generous measure, he returned to his chair and sank into it, a sigh escaping his lips.

He savoured the first taste of the amber liquid, enjoying the gentle burn that enveloped his throat, then placed the glass on the desk and rubbed a hand over tired eyes.

He'd thought that by keeping the team small, he'd be able to avoid the problems normally associated with such a clandestine operation.

The shooting in Berlin had been an unwelcome reminder that, in this job, nothing was ever certain.

Thankfully, the Section's media relations team had worked tirelessly behind the scenes, and now ninety per cent of the world's media outlets were reporting it as one of many lone terrorist cell incidents that was sweeping the continent.

On the other media reports, he kept a close watch.

Conspiracy theorists were often laughed at, but if the general public knew how close those stories were to the truth, it could feasibly destroy the British government and its allies.

He picked up a report from the set of trays next to his computer monitor, and leafed through the contents.

Miles Newcombe was a diligent analyst, brought in-house to train a select group of graduates Knox had hand-picked to work in the Section and fresh out of university.

After intensive training, Miles had been sent out into the field, first in Europe and then as a lone operative looking after the Section's Venezuelan interests. In recent years, when things had started to heat up there and rumours abounded about CIA involvement as the regime began to collapse, Miles had been brought back to London.

The Section couldn't afford for the Americans to discover their existence, and luckily for Knox, Miles had seemed content to return to England, get married, and settle into a desk-based job.

Until now.

The fact that Miles had made contact with Interpol troubled him.

He knew it was only a matter of time before the

European authorities began to question British intelligence services about the incident in Berlin. At least the explosion in Cyprus could be legitimately based on faulty gas appliances, even if they had received a helping hand from Eva.

In the meantime, he had to control the information provided to Miles. It had to be done in such a way that it wouldn't interfere with his extracurricular activities.

That was why he'd insisted Miles catch a plane from Toulouse that deposited him at Heathrow in the early hours of that morning.

Knox wanted him back within his control, so he could monitor his every move from here on. It was simply too risky having him running around Europe after Eva, given his past.

One wrong move on Knox's part, and he knew he'd lose him for good, especially if Eva got to him first and told him what she knew.

No, he needed Miles where he could see him, and hoped the man's tradecraft was as rusty as he'd been led to believe.

After a debrief that had reached into the late afternoon, Knox had dismissed him, confident the man hadn't suspected anything and sent him on his way, tasking him to run the operation to bring Eva and Nathan back to London to the safety of the Section's headquarters, and preferably delivering them in one piece, despite the Code One.

Neither of them had mentioned Decker.

He reached out for the glass, and turned the crystal

tumbler so the light from the desk lamp cast miniature rainbows over the paperwork in front of him.

The speed at which Eva was working worried him.

As did the fact that Nathan appeared to be helping her. He wondered what lies she had told him, and whether the man could be trusted after all this was over.

He sighed. He suspected not.

The man simply had too much information already, and was unlikely to remain loyal to the Section for much longer.

Especially if Eva continued to chip away at the truth.

He took another sip of the whisky before his thoughts turned to Samuel Parkes.

The fact that the assassin – one he'd trained – was still alive scared him more than he'd ever admit to anyone else.

The man was meant to be dead, eliminated by a kill order Knox himself had signed.

A chill crossed his shoulders, and he wondered who the lone gunman worked for these days.

The alternative was something he didn't wish to contemplate too closely.

If Parkes was working alone, that could mean only one thing. The man had a vendetta against Eva, and wouldn't stop until she was dead.

# THIRTEEN

Miles pushed open the fire escape door, and stepped out into the crisp city night.

He didn't worry about alarms; the smokers within the office had disarmed them years ago, and so he was reasonably confident he could spend some time alone with his thoughts, uninterrupted.

He shoved his hands in the pockets of his trousers, closed his eyes and inhaled the cold air. It invigorated him, helped make sense of some of what he was witnessing, what he was learning about the secret service that had been his employer for the past ten years.

He walked over to where the reinforced roof met the top floor of the building, and perched on its surface, his mind in turmoil as his breathing produced a fine mist in front of his face.

He wondered why Eva hadn't told him more when he'd

interviewed her, before instantly berating himself for contemplating the question.

She'd known their conversation was being recorded, and unknown to him, was aware her enemies may well have been in the building with her.

Miles exhaled as his gaze swept over the city landscape.

A full moon bathed the city, the occasional cloud scuttling overhead. Car horns echoed off the buildings here and there, and a jet engine roared in the distance. On the horizon, the tumbling lights of the sprawling boroughs were laid out in a patchwork, the metropolis pock-marked by dark areas of parkland here and there.

All those people, safe in their homes, safe in their jobs – did they really have any idea what went on behind the scenes to maintain the illusion of safety?

Sure, they heard or read in the news whenever the media got a hold of a red alert; a bomb threat that had been thwarted, a passenger jet safely landed that could have otherwise been blown out of the sky; but did they ever stop to contemplate the cat and mouse one-upmanship that played upon the paranoia of the country's leaders and their cronies, fuelled by the ever-present media?

Miles didn't kid himself – he may have joined the secret service with the intention of serving Queen and country, but it had been drilled into him from early on in his training that there was a bigger mechanism in charge – that of Great Britain Limited. You either worked for the firm, or you were considered a threat to the firm.

And Eva was most definitely considered a threat for a time, if not still.

His earlier briefing with Knox churned his thoughts.

The man had seemed genuinely concerned about the revelation that Eva's counterpart had been found dead, the young girl missing, but there had been an underlying impatience about the man's demeanour during the whole conversation – as if there were more to the situation than Miles was being told.

By the time he'd been dismissed, he'd made up his mind.

He no longer trusted Knox, and would have to strike out on his own if he was going to find out what was really going on within the Section.

His hand shook as he reached inside his jacket and withdrew a folded sheet of paper.

Some would call him old-fashioned, but he'd insisted his contact at the hospital fax it to him rather than use email. He regarded his increasing paranoia as a healthy way to stay alive. The fewer people that knew about his own investigation, the better. If Eva had reason to believe her life was endangered, then he had no doubt that his own could be cut short very quickly if he alerted the wrong people.

He unfolded the page and angled it until the typed text could be read with the aid of the light from the moon.

It had taken an hour of wrangling and subterfuge to obtain the report on Petersen. It hadn't helped that the doctor's office had sent him on a wild goose chase earlier that day, directing him to the wrong specialist before realising their error. In between running Knox's operation to locate Eva, he'd missed calls from the hospital department, and it had been late by the time he'd slipped out of the office for coffee and phoned them back from a pay phone at the back of a twenty-four-hour kebab shop.

After what he was finding out about the Section, he wasn't taking any chances by using his own mobile phone.

He ran his fingers down the side of the page as his eyes swept over the text once more.

The summary stated that there were several contributing factors that may have caused Petersen's memory to fail, but the man had no prior medical issues on his record, and there was no sign of a similar condition in his family history.

Miles slipped a second sheet out from under the first. It was a copy of the email Knox had sent to all Section personnel upon Petersen's retirement, and one which Miles recalled with clarity.

*I regret to announce that our colleague, Philip Petersen, will be retiring due to personal reasons.*

Miles remembered the hushed conversations he'd had with colleagues in the days after Knox's announcement; everyone had simply accepted that the poor old man had left it too long before he'd retired and the stress of the job had burned him out.

Now, however, the fact that Petersen's diagnosis had been announced just days after the botched defection of the engineer and the assassination of Douglas Bolton, Miles wasn't so sure.

What if it was simply a convenience for the Section to have Petersen removed to hide their embarrassment?

Had the old man put up much of a fight? Did they drug him, to give the impression of dementia?

And how deeply did Knox's involvement run? He'd certainly benefitted from Petersen's sudden removal, taking over as Section chief – the youngest in the department's history.

Miles began to shred the pages between his fingers until the sentences and words were illegible, then edged to the side of the building and looked over the side.

Twenty-seven storeys down.

He swallowed, took a step back, and glanced over his shoulder.

If someone had followed him and wanted him dead, now was their chance.

He turned back, opened his fist, and let the pieces of paper tumble into the breeze, cast adrift over the streets below.

He watched for a moment as they fluttered away, then spun on his heel and stalked towards the fire exit door.

Whatever was going on was bigger than Eva's cover being blown, he was sure.

And someone in the Section sure as hell knew about it.

# FOURTEEN

*France*

Eva drummed her fingers on the steering wheel, and tried not to let the *swoosh* of the tyres on the wet asphalt lull her to sleep.

She had taken over from Nathan three hours before, his snores now emanating from the back seat while the twins rested against each of his shoulders, their mouths open in slumber.

Decker unfolded the map across his lap and grunted.

'Our best bet is to skirt around the north of Grenoble,' he said. 'We can't avoid all the main roads, but we can stay away from the cities.'

Eva checked her watch. 'We need to stop soon. Keep a lookout for somewhere to stay.'

Decker held the map closer and peered at the contours across the page. 'There's a campsite or something about five miles up the road from here. Maybe they have cabins we can stay in.'

Eva shook her head. 'Too risky. It's pretty open country out here – is there anything like a picnic area or wildlife refuge around?'

'Yeah. It will take us another half an hour or so to reach it, but it looks like a waterfowl sanctuary or something.'

'Perfect. All we need is a roof over our heads. We've got plenty of food and water, and the kids can sleep on our coats.'

She blinked, and rubbed at her eyes.

Within minutes, a sign on the side of the road pointed out directions to the sanctuary, and she turned onto a narrow lane that wound its way through the darkening countryside.

The pale winter sun began to chase towards the horizon, and she could feel the air temperature drop despite the old car's heating system.

They had dumped Decker's four-wheel-drive outside of Grenoble, and she and Nathan had hidden with the twins at the fringes of a park while he sourced another vehicle for them.

The area was rundown, and Eva had spent the time pacing the pavement as Nathan kept the twins occupied on a swing set that they'd found in one corner of the recreation area. She'd hoped they appeared like any other family on an unplanned afternoon outing, and tried to keep her shoulders relaxed, while all the time her eyes scanned the nearby apartment block for any sign they were being watched.

When the small four-door white vehicle had turned the corner, she knew he'd found the perfect one for them. A common make and model, its rust-filled wheel arches and weary exterior would ensure they would go unnoticed – at least until the owner reported it stolen.

They'd hastily transferred all their supplies to the car, then left the doors to the four-wheel drive open and drove away.

'With any luck, the local kids will steal it and do us all a favour,' said Decker.

Now, she braked to navigate round a sharp bend in the road, the camber shifting under the vehicle.

A sweep of trees gave way to a panoramic view of a lake surrounded by long rushes and grass, and Eva drew up to a wooden bird-watching platform as a flock of geese swept gracefully across the water's edge before landing in the middle.

'Stay here while I check it out,' said Decker as Nathan stirred on the back seat.

He climbed out, extracted his gun from his jacket, and slammed the door shut.

Eva watched in her mirrors as he paced back up the road, then swept round in a wide arc and made his way towards the wooden hide.

'Where are we?' said Nathan, leaning forward.

'Sixty miles north-east of Belley,' said Eva. 'We'll rest here tonight. We need to come up with a strategy, especially given what you and I found out at the internet café.'

She waited until Decker had given the all clear, and then she and Nathan began to unload the provisions from the back of the car and followed him across to the observation hut next to the water's edge.

The twins ran ahead, excited by the wind that tugged at their hair and clothes and for a moment, she let herself pretend that they were a normal family.

She wasn't prepared to admit it to Nathan or Decker, but she knew in her heart that she would lay down her life for the two children that were pointing and shouting with glee as the geese took off once more from the water, startled by their cries.

The observation hut looked to be only a few years old, and she was grateful that hunting season had ended the previous month so there was little risk of them being found.

A toilet block stood some way from the hut and Eva spotted the tell-tale equipment above ground signifying a buried septic tank.

In the fading light, she spotted animal tracks in the mud – deer, foxes, and rabbits.

The outside of the hut had been weatherproofed, and had been raised off the ground on stilts. A short flight of steps led up to a covered porch and the door, which Decker held open for her.

'It had been left unlocked,' he said. 'I've already checked inside. It's safe.'

She cast her eyes around the space, noting the mouse droppings in one corner and the dead flies that littered the sill of the observation window. She brushed them away before wiping her hands on her jeans.

A chill draught punched through the gaps between the wooden slats of the hut's walls, and she was glad that they had brought the camping stove with them so the children wouldn't catch a cold.

Eva turned in the doorway and called to the twins. She needed them to eat and settle down for the night, so that she could sit and discuss tactics with the others.

There was too much to take in, too much she didn't understand, too much she didn't want to believe.

Half an hour later, they had a camp fire burning on a low heat on the outside steps, and the twins were becoming sleepy.

Eva made up a rough bed for them to curl up on before handing them a mug of soup each.

'Here. Have that before you go to sleep. It'll help to keep you warm.'

'So, are you two going to tell me what happened at the internet café?'

Decker refilled his mug, then moved across the hut and sat with his back to the wall.

Eva glanced across at Nathan as she sat next to the stove, but he refused to meet her eyes.

Instead, he leaned forward and turn down the gas flame a little, sending shadows scurrying into the corners of the porch.

She sighed and moved across to the box of documents she'd brought in from the car, and pulled out the files she'd retrieved from the safe in Prague.

She cast her eyes over the content of each file, desperately trying to locate a document she'd put away when she and Douglas had arrived at the flat after the engineer's defection, one that set out the terms of his agreement with the British government.

It wasn't there.

Only one other person had had access to the safe, and he'd been shot on the doorstep of his home three years ago.

'What are you looking for?'

She shifted on the floor until she could face Decker and quickly explained about the laboratory incident and subsequent cover-up by the Polish and Russian authorities, no doubt bribed by Maxim Kowalski.

Decker listened with apparent interest, and then took a gulp of soup before placing the mug on the floor next to him.

'What else did you find?'

Eva swallowed.

There was no easy way to tell him. No way she could break the news gently.

She ran her eyes over the man who had sworn to protect her, who she could always rely upon to help her, no questions asked, and dreaded what her revelation would do to their friendship.

It was why she'd ordered Nathan not to bring it up until they were far away from Grenoble.

She knew what Decker's temper could be like, and she didn't want him cooped up in a small vehicle with her when he found out.

'Eva? What's going on?'

His voice had taken the dangerous tone she'd only ever heard once before, a long time ago when they had worked together.

The man who Decker had been talking to at the time hadn't survived the night.

She could hear the danger simmering under his words, and took a deep breath before responding.

'There was a document. On the system. Together with the report about the laboratory. It was a communiqué from the Section chief at the time—'

'Petersen?'

She nodded.

'What did it say?'

'It was dated six weeks after the engineer tried to defect. Some sort of internal audit finding. I didn't know about it at the time – I had already been sent into hiding with Alex, as you know, I didn't have any day-to-day contact with the Section after that. They only contacted me when it was time to move on again.'

'What did it say?' Decker growled.

Eva dropped her gaze and cleared her throat, angry at the sudden stinging sensation at the corner of her eyes.

'It blames the assassination of the engineer and his wife on Douglas. It said that he was a double agent, and that although he'd encouraged the engineer to defect, he'd done a deal with the Russians to ensure the engineer's knowledge was never shared with British or American intelligence.'

Decker was on his feet in one fluid movement, his eyes blazing.

'That's a lie,' he snarled.

'It's in Petersen's report,' said Eva, craning her neck to look up at him.

He bent down, picked up the mug, and threw it against the opposite wall.

At the back of the room, Grace began to wail, the panic in her voice evident.

Eva rose from the floor and glared at Decker before he stormed across the hut, wrested the door open, and stalked out into the night, slamming the door hard enough in his wake to shake the wooden walls.

Eva hurried over to Alex and Grace and hugged them.

'Shh. Shh. It's okay. Decker is okay. He's just had some bad news.'

Eventually, Grace's cries subsided, and the two children curled up, their fear giving way to exhaustion.

Eva made her way back to the camp stove, and took the cup Nathan handed to her.

'I took the liberty of replacing the soup with some wine,' he said. 'Figured you might need it after that.'

'Thanks.'

'What's his problem? He seemed to take that news a lot worse than I expected. Were he and Douglas friends?'

Eva sighed, and ran a hand through her hair.

'Douglas was John Decker's brother.'

# FIFTEEN

Decker returned an hour later, slipping through the door amongst a gust of wind and leaves, and hunkered down next to the camp stove, flattening his hands out to the flames.

'I'm sorry,' he said.

'You've had a shock. It's okay,' said Eva. She reached out and patted his arm. 'I'm glad you came back.'

'He wasn't a traitor.'

Eva bit her lip. She had no idea what to believe anymore.

'Eva, I'm cold.'

She looked up at the pitiful voice, to see Alex shivering, rubbing his hands up his arms to try to get some warmth into his limbs.

'Hang on. You need some more layers to put on.'

She moved to the door, extracting some of the clothes she'd brought from Decker's villa out of a bag and then made her way over to the makeshift bed.

Handing a blanket to Grace, she pulled an old sweater over Alex's head, then ruffled his hair.

'It suits you.'

'It smells.'

'The alternative is being cold, or having a hard wooden floor to sleep on.'

He stuck out his bottom lip, then reached for one of the mugs of hot chocolate she passed to him and Grace. 'I suppose I'll wear it, then.'

She turned back to the camp stove, the smile on her lips dying as she saw Nathan's expression.

'What's wrong?'

He had paled, his eyes troubled as he stared at Alex.

'Nathan?'

He blinked and turned his attention to her, then pointed at the boy. 'What's the story about the tattoo on his arm?'

'We never found out. He won't talk about it.' She moved closer to him and lowered her voice. 'The psychiatrists who interviewed him when he was at the embassy three years ago tried, but he got too upset by their questions. The thought was that as he got older, he might open up to me about it, and I'd be able to pass the information on.'

'What about Grace?'

'What about her?'

'Does she have a tattoo like it?'

'I don't know. I haven't looked.'

'You need to.'

'What's going on?' Decker moved from his position at the gap cut into the side of the observation hut.

'I'll explain in a minute.' Nathan turned back to Eva. 'Can you ask her to roll her sleeve up?'

Eva straightened and wandered over to where the twins sat, then knelt and tucked her hair behind her ear.

'Grace? Alex has a secret drawing on his arm that he likes to keep hidden, haven't you Alex?'

The boy lowered his cup from his face, and nodded, his eyes widening.

'Do you mind showing it to Grace?'

He held out his cup to Eva, then rolled up the sleeve of the baggy sweater and turned his arm until the soft inner skin was showing. Near his elbow, a short red sequence of numbers had been cruelly engraved, and as she always did when she was forced to look at it, Eva shuddered.

'Have you got one like that, Grace?'

The little girl nodded.

'Please could I see it?'

Eva handed Alex's mug back to him, and sat back on her heels as Grace placed her cup on the wooden floor and pushed back her sleeve.

Eva gasped, and called over her shoulder to Nathan.

'You need to explain yourself.'

He joined her, and gently took the twins' hands in his. 'Do you mind if I look?'

Alex shook his head.

'It's ugly,' said Grace. 'Sally always told me to hide it so people wouldn't see.'

Eva watched as Nathan gently moved the twins' arms closer until they were touching, the row of numbers now joined together.

'What does it mean? It's just a load of zeros and ones.'

'It's binary code.'

'Binary code? Meaning what?'

Nathan let go of the twins' hands. 'Thank you,' he said, and moved back to the camp stove.

Eva gestured to the twins to roll down their sleeves and finish their hot drinks, and then joined him.

'Binary code for what?' she demanded.

Nathan took a sip of water from a bottle before recapping it and setting it on the floor.

'Unless I'm mistaken – which I don't think I am – it translates into the chemical formula for smallpox, or a variant of it, at least.'

Eva glanced over her shoulder.

The twins had fallen asleep, their soft snores filling the hut.

She turned back to the others. 'The engineer – I always assumed he was a civil engineer, or something like that. He wasn't, was he? He was a biological engineer. He was testing the smallpox he'd developed on *people* – including his own kids. Except they obviously developed a natural immunity to it.'

'That's why Maxim arranged for the story about the

accident at the laboratory to take place while he was in prison,' said Nathan. 'He eliminated any possibility of a vaccine being made available once he'd escaped and unleashed his bioweapon. Everyone at the facility who'd been inoculated or developed an immunity during the time the engineer was conducting his experiments there was massacred. The engineer was already dead—'

'Which leaves Alex and Grace,' said Decker. 'They're the only ones who have immunity.'

Eva frowned. 'But the British government already has the antidote to smallpox, at the secure facility at Porton Down in Hampshire.'

'No, they don't. Not anymore.'

She spun round to face Nathan. 'What do you mean?'

'It was never made public, because the government didn't want to cause a panic about contamination at the time,' he said. 'There was a fire there five years ago, and unknown to the British public or the world's healthcare organisations, there isn't a smallpox vaccine anymore. Not in Britain, or – as far as we know – in Europe. It was completely destroyed. They'd never get an antidote out of the United States in time, either – it takes too long to create the bacteria needed.'

'Maxim obviously found out about the fire,' said Eva.

'That's why he wants to kill Alex and Grace,' said Decker, keeping his voice low so as not to wake the twins. 'They're the antidote to whatever he's got planned.'

# SIXTEEN

*London*

Miles checked over his shoulder before holding up his hand to the bus driver that had eased to a standstill at the zebra crossing.

He jogged between two young mothers pushing toddlers in pushchairs, then slowed his pace and turned right down a narrow cobbled street lined with tourists.

He was soon lost within the throng, grateful for the cover the hordes provided.

Since he'd arrived back in the capital that morning, his thoughts had plagued him. During a meeting with his two analysts to bring them up to date on events since they'd left Berlin and reconvened at head office, it had taken all his resolve not to leave the room and storm into Knox's office to demand an explanation.

The fact that the whole team had returned to England spoke volumes about the level of involvement from higher up in the establishment.

The issue of Eva's disappearance, the attack at the hotel in Berlin, and the subsequent murder of Eva's colleague in France dictated that the Section be locked down until the matter could be resolved and the twins' location detected.

Except, no-one seemed to want to return to the events of three years ago.

*Why?*

He moved to one side, made sure he hadn't been followed, and pushed open the door to the old pub.

The musty air filled his senses as his eyes adjusted to the gloom.

Dust motes danced next to the windows, and he paused for a moment to watch the passing pedestrians.

No-one followed.

'Can I help you?'

Miles turned at the voice from the bar.

A young woman stood behind four pumps, her right hand resting on an open newspaper, a ballpoint pen twirling between her fingers.

'Just a half of bitter, please,' said Miles.

She smiled, a silver hoop pierced through her lower lip shining under the spotlights set into the ceiling above her head. 'No problem.'

Miles reached for his wallet and extracted a five-pound note. 'Do you have a phone I could use? The damn battery on my mobile's gone flat.'

The woman pushed his full glass towards him, took his money and pushed some buttons on the cash register. She handed him his change and signalled towards the rear of the building.

'Out near the gents,' she said. 'You'd be amazed how many people ask to use it.'

'Really?'

She grinned, and lowered her voice. 'Since all the phone boxes were removed from around here, the owner makes good money on it,' she said. 'Pays for his annual ski holiday.'

He smiled in return, the story no doubt one told on a regular basis. He took a sip from his drink, and placed his glass on the bar.

'I'd better top up his savings, then.'

Despite the real ale, his mouth felt dry as he wove his way past tables and chairs, his eyes seeking out the sign for the toilets.

Leaving the office, the questions he wanted to ask seemed well-rehearsed and to the point. Now, his heart beat painfully and for a fleeting moment he wondered whether he should simply turn back.

Except he couldn't.

His thoughts turned to Alex and his sister.

The boy's face upon arriving at the Section with Eva was one filled with terror. The lad had narrowly escaped being executed by a team of highly-trained terrorists in his own home before being bundled without ceremony onto an emergency RAF flight and taken to a sombre room while his mother was debriefed.

Only to be forced to go on the run once more when the hotel had been compromised.

Miles clenched his fists.

He exhaled as he reached the pay phone on the wall, rummaged in his pocket for some loose change, and dialled the number he'd committed to memory.

'Ashburn Care Facility,' a chirpy female voice answered.

Miles fed coins into the slot, and gripped the receiver. 'Hi, I'm trying to find out if you have a resident by the name of Philip Petersen.'

The voice at the other end hardened. 'I'm sorry, sir, but we don't give out residents' names over the phone. Can you tell me the nature of your call?'

'I understand,' said Miles. 'It's just that I live in Canada. I'm only in London on business for a few days, and I haven't seen my uncle since I was a boy. I'd like to see him, if that's okay?'

'And what's your name, sir?'

'Miles Newcombe. Would it be possible to get an appointment to see him this afternoon? I'm only up the road.'

He calculated the journey time in his head, and reckoned it'd be a two-hour round trip.

'One moment.'

The opening bars of *Greensleeves* cut in, and Miles turned to lean against the wall while he waited.

He ran a hand over his face, and glanced towards the bar area. The pub was still deserted, and he checked his watch. It'd be at least another twenty minutes before the place got busy with lunchtime regulars and hungry tourists looking for authentic English pub food.

He hoped to hell that despite the onset of dementia, the old Section chief remembered his name and would agree to see him.

He was running out of options, and Petersen was his last chance.

The music stopped.

'He's not available this morning, but you can see him later. Visiting times are from two o'clock,' said the woman, her tone brisk. 'Would that suit?'

'Perfect,' said Miles. 'I'll see you then.'

He ended the call, pocketed the change that ejected itself from the pay phone, and returned to his drink.

The barmaid had her chin in her hand, her face a mask of concentration as she stared at her crossword puzzle. She glanced up as he lowered himself onto one of the bar stools.

'I don't know why I do these,' she grumbled. 'Wednesdays are the worst. I always get stuck on at least one.'

He smiled. 'Go on – what's the clue?'

'"Spy planted in advance",' she said. 'And it's not "sleeper". Last letter's definitely an "r" though.'

Miles realised his hands were shaking and he lowered his glass onto the bar before it could slip from his fingers.

'Traitor,' he murmured.

# SEVENTEEN

*South-east Poland*

Maxim ignored the chill in the air, and paced the moss-covered concrete façade of the bunker.

A breeze swept through the forest, chasing the remnants of leaves from branches and scattering their remains at his feet.

A deathly silence encased the place, almost as if the wildlife knew the building was too dangerous to be near. He couldn't remember the last time he had seen a rabbit or a fox near the facility, and recalled a story from one of the older workers of a time when wolves lived in the area.

The old man had pointed to a ridge line in the distance. 'You could hear them howling at night – the loneliest sound in the world.'

Maxim had snorted at the man's sentiments, seconds before putting a gun to his head and pulling the trigger.

At night, sometimes, he wondered if the old hunters continued to prowl the forest. If they did, they did so in silence, unseen.

He still carried a knife with him at all times though, the old man's words echoing in his thoughts.

He hated the way the wind caused the trees to sway back and forth, and masking the sound of any approaching adversary. He knew his men patrolled the boundary and wouldn't hesitate to kill anyone that came too near, or ask too many questions, but being outside unnerved him.

He narrowed his eyes and peered into the forest, half expecting to be cut down by gunfire. He knew his men thought him paranoid, but it was what had kept him alive for this long.

Despite the natural camouflage from its surroundings, the entrance to the bunker was still covered in netting into which leaves and thin branches had been woven.

He forbade any electronic equipment outside the bunker, and none of the men were allowed to congregate in case the images were picked up by his enemies' satellites.

He squinted in the pale sunlight and lowered his gaze to the bunker entrance four metres below him.

The heavy steel door had been left ajar, but it didn't concern him. Only moments before he had watched as two men in biohazard suits moved their way through the gap, ready to begin their shift.

The top of the bunker was misleading and resembled one of the concrete pillboxes that scattered the forest north of his position.

Inside the steel door, leaves and forest debris had been left to rot, blown in by the wind over time and serving as a natural disguise to give the effect the place was abandoned, like so many other Cold War sites dotted throughout the country. It had been purposefully left alone to look deserted on the very rare off-chance any lost hikers got past Maxim's security measures and stumbled into the building by mistake.

Of course, if they did enter the building, there was no way out.

Not alive, in any event.

Underneath the first level was a different matter.

Two further levels stretched below the forest floor, each the size of a football pitch. The upper level was where Vadir worked with his team, perfecting the weapon that would deliver the gift he wished to bestow upon his enemies.

The lower level was where the biohazard team worked, and he had no intention of returning to that room.

He and the engineer had worked there together three years ago, on what he had thought had been a joint venture, and one that would make them both rich.

He ground the cigarette out with his heel, and inhaled the dank forest air before striding across the roof of the bunker and making his way down an incline covered in leaf litter. He slowed to navigate the gnarled tree roots that protruded from the hillside, and then nodded at the guard who stood to attention to greet him.

At the entrance to the bunker sat the rusting hulk of a tractor, a large fallen oak tree, and a number of rocks that all contributed to an impression of abandonment over several years.

The staged setting had the added advantage of slowing down any enemy who tried to storm the bunker before Maxim had a chance to destroy the evidence within.

The vehicles that his men did use were hidden a mile and half away, camouflaged under netting and tarpaulin when not in use.

He slipped through the gap in the door, inhaling the aroma of oil and grease that clung to the walls, left over from the underground factory and years of machinery working within the confined space.

Water was precious, and only used for drinking, so an underlying stench of body odour assaulted his senses the further he moved away from the fresh air coming through the bunker door.

He pushed open a second steel door, and blinked to let his eyes adjust to the gloom.

The narrow corridor opened out onto a steel gantry from which a flight of steps descended to a concrete floor. Beige paint covered the floors and ceilings, peeling away as the damp and cold began to worm its way through the building over the years since being constructed.

Ventilation pipes ran the length of the long narrow room, while exposed wiring protruded from the walls.

At the bottom of the stairs he turned and walked under the steel gantry into a second room, his boots echoing off the cavernous ceiling. He marvelled at the Soviet engineering, and then caught himself and cursed.

The Russians had no use for him anymore, and he knew that he had become an embarrassment to them.

The sort of embarrassment that had to be taken care of – permanently.

And it wasn't just the Russians he had to worry about. The Americans were still smarting from their treatment by the British government, and the fact that the engineer hadn't been delivered into their hands as promised.

A thin smile crossed his lips.

The Cold War continued behind the scenes and away from prying eyes. The rivalry between the Russians, British, and American governments had never gone away.

It was both a blessing, and a curse.

Vast sums of money and power could be gained, but the consequences of crossing the wrong people could be catastrophic.

He had made a mistake, trusted the wrong people, and paid the price.

Now, however, it was his chance for revenge.

He clenched his fist. The irony hadn't escaped him that the only things standing in his way were six-year-old twins and the legacy that their father had left them with.

Descending a second flight of stairs, he reached a steel door and hammered upon its surface.

It swung open, the guard inside the room standing to one side to let him pass.

At this level, the biohazard suits weren't required. Maxim refused to visit the lower levels, understanding all too well the dangers that lurked there. He had seen the after-effects, which had made his decision to hide all the evidence more pressing once he had been sent to prison.

He also had no qualms about sealing the two reinforced doors that separated the upper levels from the scientists' work, even if it meant handing them a fate worse than death. There were only so many counter-measures available to him to ensure the bioweapon wasn't released by accident before its true purpose could be realised.

He wasn't prepared to share the weapon with the very people who had imprisoned him, either.

No, instead he'd use it to teach them all a lesson.

As he stalked across the concrete floor towards the small team of engineers who worked tirelessly to realise his dream, he allowed himself a smile.

He would release a plague upon the cities of Europe, and watch as the Russian, American, and British governments blamed each other, while millions of their citizens died in agony.

# EIGHTEEN

Miles switched off the engine and rested his hands on the steering wheel while he stared at the glass double doors that led into the care facility.

After an uneventful hour's journey out of the city, he'd turned into the private estate, passed through open wrought iron gates and adhered to the five miles per hour speed limit depicted on signs that lined the winding driveway.

The red-bricked building had been carefully shielded from prying eyes by a growth of mature trees, although glimpses of its Victorian structure could be seen through the foliage. As the tree line retreated, the driveway swept through manicured gardens around which ornamental shrubs lined smooth concrete paths. Here and there, some of the more mobile residents could be seen walking with relatives or care home workers, making the most of the thin sunshine that bathed the grounds.

He tried to calm his nerves.

He wondered how bad the old spy master's condition was, and whether his health had deteriorated further since his retirement three years ago. He wasn't well versed in the vagaries of dementia, but knew that the symptoms varied from person to person.

He just hoped Petersen retained some knowledge of events from three years ago – anything to help him fathom what was hidden in Eva's past that would explain why her life was in danger, and why one – probably two – assassins were now active once more.

He shoved open the car door and clambered out, stretching his back before he turned towards the reception doors, and aimed the key fob over his shoulder at the vehicle.

The dull clunk of its locking mechanism reached his ears as he stepped to one side to let a middle-aged couple pass before him and followed them into the facility.

The reception area had been carved from the parlour of the original Victorian building, with white walls hosting a selection of requisite landscape photographs. A wide wooden staircase intersected the space, its balustrades polished to within an inch of their life. A navy blue carpet swept up the treads, levelling out onto a first floor landing that Miles could see from his position at the front door.

Near the reception desk, a range of framed certificates extolled the facility's management capabilities. Piped music played softly in the background, adding to the relaxed ambiance so obviously aspired to by the building's owners.

Four black leather chairs had been placed against one wall, and for a fleeting moment Miles was reminded of his dentist's waiting room.

The couple signed in, and seemed well-known to the man who sat behind the reception desk.

Miles waited while they exchanged pleasantries, and then waited as they finally turned and made their way up the staircase.

'Good afternoon,' said the receptionist as Miles approached the desk.

'Afternoon,' said Miles. 'I'm here to see Philip Petersen. My name's Miles.'

'Ah, that's right. My colleague said she'd spoken to you this morning.' The man pushed a leather-bound visitor book towards Miles. 'Sign in here, please.'

Miles scribbled a hasty signature.

He listened while the receptionist ran through the building's fire emergency procedures with a patient smile, and then took the visitor pass handed out to him.

'Which room is his?'

'Twelve. Up the stairs, turn right, then follow the corridor to the end.' The receptionist paused. 'If you need one of my colleagues for anything, just pick up the phone in the room and dial zero. Pull one of the red cords in the room if it's an emergency.'

'Okay.'

Miles thanked the man and climbed up the stairs, his gaze drifting towards the oil paintings that lined the wall directly in front of him while ahead, the hum of a vacuum cleaner reached his ears. A murmur from behind him carried through the piped music, and he glanced down to see the receptionist with a mobile phone to his ear, watching him.

The man raised his hand, smiled, and turned his attention to the documents on his desk, his voice muted.

Miles exhaled as he reached the landing and turned right as directed.

He hoped to hell the use of Petersen's name hadn't raised an alert, but resolved to question the old man and be out of the facility as soon as possible.

A man wearing blue overalls tugged a vacuum cleaner across the navy-coloured carpet, his head bowed as he pushed and pulled the hose attachment across the fabric. He stopped as Miles approached and pulled the machine out of the way so he could pass, and Miles nodded his thanks.

The door to Petersen's room was the third beyond the cleaner.

Miles took a breath, knocked twice, and reached down for the handle.

The door opened under his touch, and a face only known to him through photographs in the Section's archives stared out at him.

Taken by surprise, it was several moments before he could speak. He cleared this throat.

'You're looking well, Mr Petersen.'

'Come in. Close the door behind you.'

Confused, Miles did as he was told, then turned to face

the previous Section chief. All the questions he'd planned to ask flew from his mind as new ones formed.

He'd expected to find the man in a chair by the window looking wistfully out at the gardens, perhaps bundled in blankets with a vacant expression on his face.

Instead, he was face-to-face with a man nearly his own height, casually dressed in trousers and a pale blue polo shirt as if he was about to leave to play a game of golf. A full head of grey hair flecked with white had been carefully combed into place, and a gold watch hung on his left wrist.

'I don't understand,' he managed. 'I thought—'

Petersen smiled and gestured to one of the chairs next to the window. 'Shall we sit? You look like you've had a bit of a shock.'

Miles mumbled his thanks. As he moved towards the seating arrangement, he noted the layout of the room was much larger than the impression given from the hallway.

The door had opened into the main living area; to one side a fully equipped kitchenette had been built, while to his left a doorway led through to what Miles presumed was Petersen's bedroom.

The floor-to-ceiling windows opened out onto a balcony, although the panes were closed to the elements.

His brow furrowed, Miles took the seat indicated, and tried to order his thoughts.

'The records say you have dementia,' he blurted.

Petersen chuckled. 'They do, don't they?'

'But, you're well?'

'Never better.'

'You were expecting me?'

Petersen steepled his fingers under his chin, his pale blue eyes studying Miles for a moment. 'Those records haven't been touched in three years,' he said. 'An alert is raised if anyone requests them.'

Miles swore under his breath. 'I should've expected that.'

Petersen inclined his head.

'Why?'

'Sometimes it's easier to fade away than retire in plain sight,' said Petersen. He shrugged. 'I never did like the political wrangling. If I'd stayed anywhere in public view, I'd never been left alone.'

'But is it safe here? What about your protection detail?'

Petersen's mouth twitched. 'You've met them both.'

'Ah.'

Miles berated himself. He'd spent too long in an office, and should have realised both the receptionist and cleaner looked out of place. Now he recalled the receptionist's phone call as he was climbing the stairs.

'You were expecting me.'

'Yes.' Petersen leaned back in his chair, his gaze drifting to the manicured gardens beyond the glass. 'So, what did you want to talk to me about?'

'Eva Delacourt.'

The old man's Adam's apple bobbed in his throat before he spoke. His eyes hardened.

'What about her?'

'She's on the run. Her last safe house in Cyprus was compromised, and then someone tried to kill her at a hotel in Berlin. Five of our agents are dead.'

'Who's leading the investigation?'

'Knox.'

Petersen grunted.

Miles understood. It would have been unexpected if Knox hadn't taken charge of such a large operation, especially one with the potential to expose the Section – and all its secrets.

Petersen ran a hand over his mouth. 'Last known whereabouts?'

'France. A small village outside Grenoble.'

Petersen banged his fist on the arm rest.

'What's going on, sir?'

Petersen held his gaze. 'That's what I'd like to know.'

# NINETEEN

*France*

Decker had insisted on waking the twins and leaving the hut before the first weak rays of winter sun began to stretch over the furthest reaches of the lake the next morning.

He loaded the car in silence, a reticence both Alex and Grace took to be a foul temper, and they kept their distance from him.

Eva had sipped at the cheap, bitter instant coffee Nathan had handed to her, and tried to make them smile while they wandered alongside the lake's edge, stretching their legs before the next long drive.

At Aix-les-Bains, Decker had ejected them all from the car with their belongings, leaving them hiding in a copse of trees while he dumped the car and sought another.

'No point leaving them a trail of bloody breadcrumbs,' he'd said as he reappeared with a different car, its back windows covered with stickers and grime.

Eva had taken the last shift as lookout at the hut, and now sat in the passenger seat as he drove, tuning out the sound of Nathan talking to the twins, trying to coax them into their favourite game of I Spy as the countryside flashed past the windows.

They'd spent the last moments of darkness poring over their map, seeking out an escape route from France, bickering and discarding ideas until Decker had stabbed his forefinger on an area north-west of Geneva.

'This is where we'll go first. We need to lose the kids before we can go any further.'

'What's there?'

'Somewhere safe.'

Eva had rocked back on her heels. 'Are you sure?'

'Yes.'

She bit her lip.

'He's right,' said Nathan. 'It's too dangerous for them. Look what happened in Prague.'

Now, she sat upright as they approached the junction in the road, her senses alert.

It was one of two locations on the planned dash across the country where their route intersected a main road, and she and Decker were both alert instantly.

The first time, they'd had to zig-zag their way past a railway station on the outskirts of a town, and her heartbeat had accelerated painfully as she imagined sirens in the distance.

They'd made it past the built-up area without incident though.

Thankfully, the early start had meant they'd beaten any commuter traffic on the highway too, but she wouldn't relax, not yet.

Despite her misgivings about leaving the twins with someone she'd never met before, she knew that she had no other choice than to trust Decker.

She had been shattered by Petersen's assertion that Douglas was responsible for the engineer's assassination, and couldn't imagine what was going through Decker's mind.

She could only hope that, somehow, they'd be able to work out what the hell had been going on within the Section in their absence from London all these years, and discover Douglas's reasons for betraying his country.

Decker's jaw clenched. 'Clear your way?'

'Yeah. Go.'

He floored the accelerator, sending the vehicle shooting over the crossroads and back onto the minor road, putting as much distance between them and the highway as he could in a short space of time.

Eventually, his shoulders relaxed, and he slowed to the speed limit.

'We should talk about what we can do next,' he said.

Nathan leaned forward. 'Seems to me that we need to work out who the leak is in the Section first. After all,

Maxim's men didn't find Eva or Sally's safe houses by accident, did they? Who had knowledge about those?'

'It has to be Knox,' said Eva, twisting in her seat so she could face them both. 'You were only given enough access to find things out piecemeal, and in retrospect.'

Decker glanced away from the road at Nathan, then back.

'Are you sure *he* can be trusted?'

Nathan paled, and she reached out for his hand.

'Yes, I trust him. He saved Alex's life.'

Decker growled a response under his breath, but she ignored him.

'Miles was the one who suggested we stay in a hotel,' she said. 'And Knox agreed easily enough, so they could be working together, trying to box us in.'

'What about Petersen?' said Nathan. He squeezed Eva's hand before releasing it. 'How much involvement do you think he had at the beginning?'

Eva shook her head. 'Reading that report of his makes me think he was brought in afterwards, to clean up. Maybe with the onset of his dementia though, Knox saw an opportunity. He obviously knew about the laboratory accident and Maxim's escape from prison, and decided to use that information to his advantage.'

'Try to track down the twins, you mean?'

Eva nodded.

'I still say Douglas was innocent,' said Decker.

'I want to believe that too.'

'Is not a case of *wanting* to believe, Eva – I know he's innocent. He was my brother. He'd never betray his country.'

Eva sank back into her seat and flipped the sun visor down over the windscreen as the car crested the hill. 'Then I guess we have to find some way of proving that.'

She fell silent. Despite her assurances to Decker, she'd spent the past twenty-four hours replaying her time with Douglas in her mind, trying to work out if she'd been wrong about him three years ago, and whether she'd really known the man who had been her lover.

Was he really the suave diplomat she had been led to believe, or was there a darker side to him that she had failed to recognise?

She had been so exhausted at the time, overwrought from her last mission, and looking back, she wouldn't be surprised if she had overlooked some vital clue.

Had he used her to disguise his true motives?

When Alex had asked where his mother was, had Douglas signed her death warrant by telling someone where she could be found? Had he known then about Grace, and hoped she would be killed?

She shook her head to clear the thoughts.

Like Decker, she couldn't imagine Douglas betraying them all, so why was Petersen so sure that he had? What had the old Section chief known before his health deteriorated?

She beat her fist on the door frame in frustration. Now the man had retired and become a victim of his illness she would never know.

More worryingly, if she suspected he knew more than he had put in his report, then so would others.

And, if their enemies considered him a threat, then his life would be in danger, too.

'What about Maxim?' said Nathan. 'I mean, just because Decker thinks he's got somewhere safe to hide the kids, doesn't help you, does it? He'll still be looking for you.'

Decker swung the car to the side of the road and into a lay-by.

'He makes a fair point,' he said.

'I'll think of something,' said Eva.

They eased themselves out of the vehicle, stretching their legs.

'Need a wee,' said Grace.

Eva smiled. 'Me too. Come on – behind the hedge.'

They scrambled over a nearby steel gate and into a muddy field, a rough grassy verge saving their footwear from becoming sodden, and Eva stood guard as Grace wandered off a little way.

By the time they had returned to the vehicle, Decker and Nathan were leaning against the radiator grille, Alex perched on Decker's shoulders while he pointed to the valley below.

'What are you looking at?' said Eva as she approached, shading her eyes.

'Switzerland,' said Decker.

# TWENTY

*London*

Knox ran a hand over tired eyes before leaning back in his chair, and stared at the ceiling.

If he'd known Miles had planned to meet with the old Section chief, he'd have been more careful.

Now, the ambitious case officer had ruined everything.

He'd known Miles wouldn't be able to resist continuing his own investigation, despite being stood down from the official operation, and so he'd assigned two of his most trusted operatives to shadow the man.

He had assumed Miles would use his contacts to find out where Eva had taken the boy – and the boy's sister, if the reports he was receiving were correct.

All Knox could do was hope he'd manage to salvage

something from the mess that Miles had created by visiting Petersen.

Unable to sit still for long, Knox pushed the chair back and began to pace the carpet. The bulletproof window to his office let in a modicum of light, its darkened glass designed to add privacy as well as protect the building's inhabitants.

He stopped and glared out at the muted tones of the cityscape before him, and clenched his fists at his sides.

There had to be a way to save the operation.

He glanced over his shoulder at the communiqué that had been received only an hour before.

As he suspected, Eva had used Nathan to access the files and was no doubt by now acting on information he'd fed to her, on the run in unknown territory, and not knowing who she could trust.

The children would become a hindrance to her now, slowing her down and increasing her paranoia. She'd begin to make mistakes, and doubt her own ability.

He'd always wondered if she had been closer to Douglas than she admitted under questioning following his assassination, despite her assertions to the contrary.

They'd all been shocked, of course, but he'd watched Eva with interest, trying to fathom if she would collapse under the pressure of interrogation before he got to the truth.

It hadn't worked, of course – Petersen had stepped in and taken over within twenty-four hours of the whole debacle, scattering the remnants of his female team across the continent, and ensuring they remained hidden.

And then the old Section chief had been spectacularly removed from office, their masters citing ill health and a confused mind.

Everything had been proceeding according to plan.

Until now.

Dread consumed him.

His instincts screamed that there was something else, something he'd missed, but the moment the thought crossed his mind and he tried to grasp it, it flitted away once more.

He moved back to his desk and picked up the photograph of Samuel Parkes.

So far, there had been no sign of the lone gunman since the attack at the hotel in Berlin, and he half wondered if perhaps he'd returned to the shadows, his mission failed.

He discarded the thought a moment later.

Samuel Parkes wasn't the type to give up – that was the problem.

Once he was set loose, there was no way to recall him.

He wouldn't stop until his target was dead.

Except, there had been no more sightings of him, which could only mean that he or his masters – if he wasn't working alone – didn't know of Eva's whereabouts, either.

His head snapped up at a knock on his door, and he swept the photograph and reports into his briefcase before sliding it under his desk.

'Come in.'

One of the analysts who worked for Miles peered in, his hair awry, and bags under his eyes.

'Miles asked me to let you know we've got a trace on Eva.'

Knox felt the knot in his stomach tighten, and he locked his computer before striding across the carpet towards the door.

'Show me.'

## TWENTY-ONE

Miles paced the floor as he waited for Knox to join him, his eardrums ringing with the pounding of his heartbeat.

Since returning from his clandestine meeting with Petersen, he'd been unable to rest, the old man's assertions that he would do all he could to help providing little comfort.

He'd been ushered from the man's room at the care home only half an hour after he'd arrived, and had turned at the door, confused.

'What should I do now, sir?'

Petersen had chuckled and patted him on the shoulder. 'Act normal, Miles. Carry on as usual, and don't tell anyone we've spoken.'

'What about you?'

'Oh, don't worry about me. Lots to do, m'boy. Lots to do.'

Despite everything, Miles knew he had to do as Petersen

said and carry on as if the conversation had never happened, so the current Section chief wouldn't suspect anything.

If Knox was indeed a traitor, then Miles knew he'd have to conceal his suspicions – or quite likely end up dead.

He shuddered at the memory of the house in France.

His two analysts had worked nonstop in his absence, piecing together every minute snippet of information to try and trace Eva.

The breakthrough, of course, had been when Nathan had accessed the Section's database.

Despite his suspicions about Knox, he had to admit the man understood his operatives well.

He hadn't understood the choice of information Knox had uploaded to the system though – hadn't even known of its existence until he'd read it himself forty-eight hours ago.

He held up the reports with a shaking hand as Knox had peered at him over his reading glasses.

'Is all of this true?'

'Myself and Petersen authored the reports, yes.'

'But – Douglas?'

Miles had dropped the papers onto the desk and run a hand over his head. 'What will Eva do when she learns of his involvement?'

A wolfish smile had passed Knox's lips. 'She'll follow the story like a trail of breadcrumbs, Miles. It will be too irresistible for her.'

A sense of uneasiness clawed at Miles now, and he

battened it down as the door to the small ops centre opened and Jason appeared, followed by Knox.

The Section chief hurried over to where he stood, his eyes scanning the rows of monitors lining one wall.

'You found her?'

'We've got a CCTV image of her here, in a car passing the railway station,' said Greg, and changed the images in front of them to show a large composite photograph. 'This image was extracted from the footage. It's the best one we've got.'

'When was this?' said Knox.

'An hour ago,' said Miles. 'We are just waiting for French police to confirm if the vehicle has been sighted within a fifty mile radius of that position.'

He watched the Section chief's reaction, but apart from a slight clenching of the jaw, the man seemed focused, and as composed as ever.

Knox peered at the image. 'Is that Nathan on the back seat?'

'Yes,' said Miles. 'We're assuming the blurred forms on either side of him are the twins.'

'And John Decker is driving,' said Knox. 'Interesting.'

The phone on Jason's desk began to ring, and the analyst answered it, his voice low. Miles held his breath, fighting down the adrenalin that threatened common sense.

The man's face went grey, and he ended the call before clearing his throat.

'That car has just been found abandoned thirty miles

from this position,' he said. 'There's no trace of the occupants. She's gone.'

'What do you mean, "she's gone"?' Miles glared at the analyst. 'Gone where?'

The analyst held up his hands, his eyes troubled. 'That's the problem,' he said. 'We don't know.'

## TWENTY-TWO

The aroma of pine needles and mud permeated the interior of the car as Decker steered the vehicle through the narrow alpine lanes.

Eva's eyes remained on the road in front of them, in case an ambush lay in wait.

She checked over her shoulder. The twins were asleep, Alex's head resting on his sister's shoulder.

Eva swore under her breath.

Nathan leaned forward and peered between the front seats.

'Penny for your thoughts?'

She exhaled. 'What sort of parent drags their two young kids into something like this?' she muttered. 'What on earth was he thinking?'

'Maybe he was desperate?' suggested Nathan. 'Maybe the alternative was worse?'

Eva shook her head and refocused on the passing scenery.

'Where are we taking them, anyway?' asked Nathan.

'It's a boarding school, a small one, outside Geneva,' explained Decker. 'I know the headmistress. It'll be a safe place for them.'

'Boarding school?' spluttered Nathan. 'How on earth are they going to be safe there?'

'Because, it's built like a fortress,' said Decker as he braked the car to a standstill. 'It has armed guards, no doubt due to the fact that several heirs to the Saudi throne are in attendance, and the grounds-keeper and catering staff are all ex-French Foreign Legion.'

'Oh. I see.'

Eva leaned across the central console and squeezed his hand. 'They'll be fine, Nathan. You're right – it's no place for them, being on the road.'

'Wait here.'

Decker got out, slammed the door shut and strode towards the man who'd emerged from the gap in the heavy steel door.

The man was taller than Decker, and enveloped him in a bear hug before jerking his head towards the car.

Eva bit her lip as the conversation continued, wondering what was being said.

'Do you know who he is?' Nathan leaned between the seats.

'No. But if Decker trusts him, so do I.'

'He doesn't have many friends, does he?'

'Most of them are dead.'

'Oh.'

They stopped talking as Decker shook hands with the man, and turned back to the car.

He opened the door and leaned in, smiling at Alex and Grace.

'Come on, then. Let's get you settled into your new home.'

The twins scrambled from the car, their necks craning to take in the enormous ramparts of the castle that soared above them.

Eva and Nathan joined Decker as the man approached.

'This is Simon,' said Decker, making the introductions. 'He'll be in charge of the twins' security while they're here.'

The tall man smiled. 'They'll be safe here. You've done the right thing. There are children their own age they can play with, and they can join in the lessons from tomorrow.'

Eva exhaled and glanced over her shoulder to where the twins were giggling at a gargoyle that protruded from one of the high windows.

'Come on, you two.'

They ambled over to where the adults stood, and Eva crouched down to them.

'Okay, listen to me,' she said, trying to keep the tremor from her voice. 'I need you to be really, really brave for a little longer. Can you do that?'

Alex nodded.

'Yes,' said Grace.

'Good.' Eva forced a smile. 'This is Simon, and he's going to look after you. You're both staying here together for a while, so look out for each other. And do as Simon tells you, understood?'

Both the twins nodded.

Eva cocked an eyebrow. 'I'll know, you know, if you're being naughty.'

The twins giggled.

Eva crouched, tucked the twins' coats around them and made sure all the buttons were fastened. The twins' breath fogged in the air between them as they waited patiently for her to finish fussing over them.

'Where are you going?' asked Grace, a frown creasing her brow.

Eva sighed as both of them stared at her, waiting for an answer.

'Sorting some things out,' she said, keeping her tone light.

Alex looked over his shoulder, at the imposing architecture of the castle. 'What do we do if we don't like it here?'

Eva swallowed. 'Tell you what,' she said, patting the front of his coat. 'If you get scared, pretend you're a wizard, and this is your school until the holidays.' She forced a smile. 'Like the books, remember? Can you do that?'

'Yes.'

Grace nodded. 'Yes.'

'And what do you do if you think something isn't right?'

She hated asking, but she had to hear it. She had to know they'd keep a lookout for each other.

'Tell Simon,' they chorused.

'Come here,' she croaked, tears hot behind her eyelids.

*Hold it together*, she thought. *Just a little longer.*

She closed her eyes, inhaling their perfume, running her hand over the texture of their hair, as long as she dared.

'We need to go,' murmured Decker, jangling the car keys before tossing them to Nathan.

She drew away from the children and stood, her legs shaking. 'I know.'

She forced a smile, waved, and hurried towards the waiting vehicle.

Eva climbed into the car, all her energy seeping from her as Nathan started the engine and pulled away from the gates. She turned, waving through the window to the twins until they grew too small to see, and the car began to weave its way back down the mountain towards the highway.

She looked down as a warm hand enveloped hers.

'They're great kids,' said Nathan. 'And they have a great person looking after them.'

'I know,' she said, wiping at her eyes. 'I know.'

'What are you going to do?'

Eva took a deep breath, reached into the backpack at her feet and withdrew a 9mm pistol. She slammed a fresh clip into the base of the gun with the heel of her hand.

'Finish this,' she said. 'Once and for all.'

Continue the story in *Assassins: Retribution*

# PART THREE
# ASSASSINS RETRIBUTION

# ONE

*Prague, Czech Republic*

'Why are we back here?'

Nathan shivered, shoved his hands into the pockets of his three-quarter-length wool coat, and turned to Eva.

She kept her eyes on the building across the river from where they stood, and tried to ignore the freezing wind that lifted off the water and assaulted her face.

'Because this is where it all began,' she said. 'Douglas's murder. Me, going into hiding. Everything.'

She squinted as a taxi boat shot past, the bright morning sunshine reflecting off its windows, then blinked to clear the temporary blindness.

'Isn't that dangerous? Look at what happened at the

gallery when we were here. Surely there are people waiting for you to return?'

She saw his hand reach to his shoulder as he spoke, and lowered her gaze. 'Yes.'

'Here. Hot drinks.'

Decker approached, his large hands clasped around three takeout cups from a café further up the street.

Eva took one of them gratefully, savouring the sweet taste of the hot chocolate as she continued her observation of the house that had once housed the head of the British government's science and innovation delegation in Prague, Douglas Bolton.

She hadn't heard of him when she was working for the Section – she simply hadn't been involved in politics, even if she *had* been used by the politicians, or at least the people that really ruled the British government.

Her life before Prague had been one of solitude, her path only crossing with Decker's six months before the debacle that had been the engineer's defection, and she hadn't known about his being Douglas's brother until the diplomat himself had ventured the information one night.

They had lain in bed, curled up together after their first passionate encounter, Douglas smoothing her hair away from her face and telling her that he knew who she was, *what* she was, and how his family was connected to her.

She'd sat bolt upright, clutching the sheets around her, horrified that the Caretaker had spoken about her so openly, and wondering who else he had brokered the information with.

Douglas had managed to calm her, smoothing his hands over her shoulders, coaxing her back to his pillow before telling her that Decker had only mentioned her because he'd seen her entering the embassy with his brother, and had an enormous amount of respect for the diminutive assassin.

And now, it seemed that Douglas had played them all, committing treason and selling secrets to the highest bidder.

She swallowed, pushing the thought to the back of her mind, and forced herself to focus.

'So, like I said, why come back?' said Nathan.

'I'm trying to view it from a killer's perspective. The engineer's assassination, I can understand.'

Nathan choked on his drink, and beat his fist against his chest.

She shrugged. 'Sorry. It's what I do. What I *used* to do.'

'I still haven't got used to the idea yet. Go on, though.'

'If I were Maxim, I'd definitely want the engineer silenced. And, as diabolical as you'll think it, I'd also have killed his wife, erring on the side of caution in case the engineer spoke about his work to her.'

'We also need to consider the possibility she was involved,' said Decker. 'Especially if we work on the assumption that the engineer was testing the antidote on their kids.'

'Good point.'

Nathan shivered. 'Some family they were. What a hellish

legacy to leave your kids.'

Eva turned her back on the river to face them. 'But I still don't understand why Douglas was killed. It doesn't make sense.'

'It does if he was sacrificed,' said Decker. He held up his hand to stop her interrupting. 'What if someone in the Section was doing a deal, and it went wrong?'

'What sort of deal?'

'To sell the engineer and his secrets to the highest bidder. Or back to his paymasters.'

'The Russians?'

Decker shrugged. 'The Cold War only ended on paper, Crowe. Don't kid yourself otherwise.'

'Who else would have wanted the antidote?' said Eva.

'Anyone and everyone,' said Decker. 'Especially here in Europe. The British, the Germans – the Americans would have a vested interest in anything that happens over here, too, especially if it'd threaten their own security. We even have to consider the Israelis – they're just as paranoid as the rest of them.'

Eva shook her head. 'Something doesn't fit. Why didn't the Section go after Maxim if they thought he was a threat?'

'Who's to say they didn't?' said Nathan. 'We know he was eventually caught and imprisoned by the Russians. What if the British provided them with the information to do so?'

Decker whistled through his teeth. 'That would explain why he's got a vendetta against the Brits. He holds them responsible.'

Nathan drained the rest of his hot chocolate and smacked his lips. 'What do you think his plans are?'

'It has to have something to do with whatever was going on at that testing laboratory in Poland,' said Eva, pacing the pavement. 'Otherwise, why would he go so far as to stage an infectious outbreak? I think he faked that, then worked on arranging his escape from prison. He's probably been redeveloping the virus since then.'

'You'd need money to do that,' said Decker.

'Not necessarily,' said Nathan. 'We had a whole department in London dedicated to tracing the equipment being bought and sold online that could weaponise a virus for under a hundred dollars. You'd need a very small laboratory to develop that.'

Eva frowned. 'If it's so cheap and easy to do, why would he need to return to the old laboratory facility?'

'Volume,' said Decker. 'If he and whoever is helping him have managed to produce this, then my guess is that they're doing it on a phenomenal scale. From what Nathan's told us about this guy, he's not the sort to do things by halves.'

'And distribution,' said Nathan. 'I have a feeling that Maxim Kowalski has something planned that will involve the manufacture and distribution of a weaponised smallpox virus on a scale no-one in this world has ever seen.'

Decker pulled up his collar and tossed his empty takeout cup into a nearby bin. 'All right. Enough sightseeing. We've got work to do.'

# TWO

*London*

Miles kept his head down as he hurried along the subterranean corridor.

He didn't want to be stopped. He didn't want to engage in conversation. He wanted to get to his office, close the door, and try to get his head around the fact that his Section chief could be the mole that had endangered Eva in Berlin, and likely arranged the armed ambush that had led to Nathan Crowe being shot in Prague.

He had had his suspicions, but the CCTV images of Crowe at the French supermarket confirmed them – the man held his shoulder differently. Miles had spent enough time in some of the most dangerous places in South America to recognise when someone was recovering from a gunshot wound.

It seemed that Knox was prepared to sacrifice anyone that got in his way.

In the meantime, Miles knew he'd have to look like he was carrying on as normal, while all the time trying to fathom how he could keep Petersen up to date about the situation without exposing their arrangement.

The old spymaster had been adamant that no-one else be involved.

'Too risky,' he had said at their last covert meeting. 'You can't trust anyone, Miles. Use them, yes, but don't trust them.'

Miles could see the sense in the man's words.

As it was, he'd managed to keep his two analysts away from his clandestine project, tasking them instead with keeping a lookout for when Eva next made an appearance.

Her return to Prague had been unexpected, though.

And worrying.

His two analysts had confirmed that the twins had completely disappeared, and that the grainy images taken from the building next door to Douglas Bolton's old home only depicted the three adults.

An involuntary shiver crossed his neck.

He'd never worked with the Caretaker, but his reputation had been formidable – not least because he'd defied Section orders and survived to tell the tale. The man had simply dropped off the grid – until the shooting in Berlin had sent Eva on the run.

What did he know that would see him risk his life for Eva?

His hand shook as he punched in the code for the door to his office.

Shutting it behind him, he rested against it for a moment, his eyes closed.

He'd forgotten what the adrenalin rush had been like.

In South America, he'd been a shadowy operator, brokering deals across borders that supported the Section's nefarious activities while all the time convincing himself it was for a greater good. He didn't ask questions, obeyed his orders, and had, in his younger days, enjoyed the power that came with the position, however tenuous the persona he adopted had been.

His top lip curled upwards.

He'd grown soft in the years since leaving the field and acquiring a desk – and a wife. He boxed regularly to keep the paunch off his gut, and had started to add interval training to his morning routine after catching sight of himself in the mirror in the bedroom one night and wondering what had happened to the hardened agent he'd once been.

Now, however, the thrill of the chase was accompanied by a gnawing paranoia that crawled through his mind.

*Was he doing the right thing?*

*What if he was wrong?*

He opened his eyes and shook his head to clear the

thought, then paced across the room to his desk and dropped the manila folder from his hand.

The latest intelligence had been worrying.

Any normal person would run from danger, but it seemed Eva Delacourt was hell bent on digging away at the past and whatever it held with no regard for her own safety.

He simply couldn't understand why.

One of the photographs slipped from the folder as it skidded across the desk, and Miles tugged it free, spinning it around on the smooth surface so it faced him.

Crowe's features sported a new beard, trimmed and neat. He held his takeout cup in his left hand, still favouring the arm where the bullet had damaged his shoulder.

What interested Miles was that the man's stance had completely changed, and not simply from the injury.

He appeared hardened, surer of himself, and Miles wondered what damage the man was capable of if Knox hadn't arranged to take over Crowe's security access to the database the moment the operation in France had failed to capture them at the internet café.

Instead, they'd withdrawn the hit team and regrouped, watching and waiting to see what Eva would do next.

Miles replaced the photograph and moved around the desk, sinking into a leather chair behind it and logging into his computer.

His instructions had been clear, but didn't make it any easier.

He opened the encrypted email software, and began to type.

# THREE

*Prague*

Decker had argued against returning to the Czech capital when Eva had first suggested it some days ago, but she had insisted – the flat above the bookshop provided the only safe haven she'd ever had.

In the end, they had left Nathan in a café half a mile away and had conducted a recce of the streets around the bookshop over the course of a few hours. Satisfied that their whereabouts remained unknown, Decker had acquiesced.

It had taken another two days to source the equipment they needed.

Now, the living area was unrecognisable. With the money Eva had squirrelled away, which they hadn't used while on the run, Nathan had been able to procure the hard drives, screens, and cabling that now littered the dining table and rug beneath her feet.

When she had questioned the sense in accessing the internet once more, he had shaken his head.

'It's not like the internet café,' he said, sweeping his hand over the equipment. 'The way I've set this up, no-one will find us. What you see here is a fully functioning dark web ops room.'

Even Decker had been impressed.

Upon returning from the observation of the house near the river, they had settled into their research, to try and ascertain what Maxim's plans were for his bioweapon.

Eva leaned forward as the front page of the Section's database appeared on the screen nearest to her and the results of Nathan's search began to load. They had resolved to start at the beginning – locating the laboratory facility that had supposedly closed down after the devastating accident, and then work backwards and trying to find a link that would prove their suspicions about Maxim's plans.

Nathan had located a series of satellite images in the database from three years ago, evidence that the Section had attempted to correlate the engineer's story before agreeing to his defection. In the images, different aerial views of the densely-wooded area provided little information – any buildings were simply too well camouflaged by the tree canopies around them.

Decker had grabbed a pad of paper and a pen and, based

on what they could see from the images they had, begun to draw up a plan of the testing facility.

It was rudimentary, but at least provided them with an overview of the layout.

It was also evident that the facility had been built far enough away from any populated areas so it could also be easily guarded, as there were no other buildings to be seen in the photographs for miles around it.

'Okay,' said Nathan. 'These are old images. Let's see if we can find something more recent.'

His fingers flew over the keyboard, and then a second suite of satellite images began to load on the screen next to Decker.

The assassin's eyes narrowed. He reached out and tapped the screen.

'Can you zoom in here? This road here – it's only ten miles from the testing facility. What are these four trucks doing there?'

Nathan hit a button and the image enlarged.

Sure enough, four large heavy goods vehicles could be seen travelling along a single road. The lead vehicle had been setting a fast pace – the dust from the trucks' wheels rose into the air behind them, partially obscuring the image at close range.

'That's too much of a coincidence,' said Decker. 'Those are heading for the testing facility, aren't they?'

'When was this?' Eva cast her eyes over the satellite images, searching for a date.

Nathan stabbed his finger at the bottom of the screen. 'Here. Three days ago.'

'Are you able to zoom in close enough that we can get the licence plates of those trucks?' said Eva.

She waited while Nathan turned the angle of the images, and then leaned over as the back of the last truck in the convoy came into view.

The dust from the truck's wheels obliterated the last two digits on the licence plate; however she smiled when she saw the lettering stencilled onto the mud flaps.

The logo of a heavy goods vehicle rental agency could just be made out.

'Bingo,' said Decker.

Nathan was already typing in the name, and leaned back in his chair as the details downloaded.

'They're based in Prague,' he said.

'He's getting ready to mobilise,' said Decker, and folded his arms over his chest as he frowned at the screen. 'When those trucks reappear, they're going to be loaded and heading for their final destination.'

Eva swallowed. 'If those trucks were rented here, there's every chance that's where Maxim plans to release the weaponised smallpox.'

Nathan reduced the image on the screen and opened an internet browser before typing a rapid search string as he tried to extract more information from the images.

Decker huffed while the slow connection began to load, then strode over the threadbare rug towards the dining table, picked up a chair and set it down next to the coffee table.

As the page began to load, Eva nibbled at a fingernail. Dropping her hand to her lap, she frowned.

'Why is he mobilising now?'

'What do you mean?' said Decker.

'We haven't heard from your contact in Switzerland, so we can assume the twins are still safe. Until now, we've always believed he would try to locate them before releasing this bioweapon because they're the antidote.' She waved a hand at the screens. 'But this looks like someone planning an imminent attack. There's no way he'd risk having those trucks if he wasn't ready. So, what's changed?'

Decker launched himself from his chair, and reached out for one of the burner phones on the table. 'I'll phone my contact – we need to make sure the twins' location hasn't been compromised.'

Eva and Nathan remained silent as Decker made the call.

He spoke in hushed tones as he paced the floor next to the window, but as the conversation progressed, she saw his shoulders relax before he ended the call.

'They're safe. He reports that there's been no suspicious activity near the school or the surrounding villages.'

Eva exhaled, and sank back into her chair. 'At least that's something.'

She turned as Nathan emitted a curse under his breath.

'What's wrong?'

'This,' he said, and tapped the screen.

Eva gasped, and sat upright, the fine hairs on the back of her neck standing on end.

'What is it?' Decker moved away from the window and stalked over to where she sat at the table.

'Miles Newcombe has sent her a message via my email address,' said Nathan.

'How did he know I'd read it?'

'Law of averages,' said Decker. 'After the internet café, we'd obviously try to access the Section's system again as soon as we were able. All he had to do was wait.'

Eva ran a hand over her eyes. 'Am I that predictable?'

Decker shrugged. 'They trained you. What does he want?'

'To meet me and Nathan. In London.'

His eyes narrowed. 'Why drag you all the way there? Why not meet here, or somewhere else?'

'Perhaps he can't get away from London without raising suspicions.'

'It could be a trap.'

'I don't think so. Maybe he heard something about Maxim. I think he might help us.'

'You said that about Scott Lancaster,' said Nathan, his eyes troubled. 'That didn't end well.'

'It'll be different this time,' said Decker.

'Why?'

'I'll be there.'

# FOUR

*Poland*

Maxim prowled around the perimeter of the room, his eyes fixated upon the crates his men had stacked carefully on top of one another, ready to be filled once the weapon was ready.

'You're sure these will reach their destination safely?'

'They will,' said Vadir. 'We have four trucks that have been hired from different companies. The crates will be split up evenly, and the drivers aren't aware of each other's destinations.'

Maxim ran a hand over his chin.

He'd stayed away as the laboratory technicians had emerged from the floor below, cradling their creations before slipping each one into a small square box similar to a popular brand found in supermarkets across the continent.

When Vadir had first enquired how the weaponised smallpox could be delivered to its destination without being stopped, Maxim had grinned malevolently and pointed to the ceiling.

'Lightbulbs,' he'd said. 'The city will be awash with lights for the festive season, and it will be simple enough for the men to pose as council workers. All they have to do is replace a lightbulb here and there, and then walk away – no-one will be any wiser. No-one takes any notice of a man working in the street if he wears a high-visibility vest – despite the name, he becomes invisible.'

'But how will you trigger the pathogen?'

Maxim had shrugged. 'I won't. We wait. Only one of those bulbs needs to be broken – accidents happen. Maybe a street vendor will knock one while setting up his store for the day. Perhaps a council worker will wonder why the light is not working and will carelessly throw the bulb away when replacing it.' A smile crept over his features. 'Patience, Vadir. That is all we need.'

Now, he paced the floor, his own words echoing in his mind as Vadir urged the men to take care while the valuable cargo was prepared.

He didn't care if the trucks were stopped by the authorities at the border crossing; if the lightbulbs were damaged then, so be it.

There would be no escape for those around the vehicle,

and they would have no way of knowing what they had been exposed to until the first deadly symptoms began to show.

It would be the same for the citizens and tourists in the city.

A disease that had been officially confirmed as being eradicated in the late twentieth century would be unleashed, deadlier than ever before due to the genetic modifications Maxim's team had made to ensure haemorrhagic symptoms.

First, victims would sense a subcutaneous tingling, followed a day or so later by a rash that would quickly develop across their skin.

By this time, the victims would have already been in close proximity with family, friends, work colleagues, fellow commuters – spreading the virus as people inhaled the same air the victim expelled.

For the victim, the virus would progress quickly; the whites of their eyes would turn red, causing blindness while internal organs would haemorrhage and fail, leading to death.

Those who had been inoculated prior to the phasing-out of vaccination in the 1980s would still act as incubators for the fatal disease, while anyone born after then would be at risk.

'There is no-one in this world under the age of thirty who has immunity, except for the engineer's children,' said Maxim.

Vadir dropped his gaze and kicked at an invisible stone.

'We have not been able to locate them, Maxim. It is like they have disappeared off the face of the earth.'

'It is not good enough. What does our contact in the British secret service have to say?'

'He has been silent for two days now. His last communication to us was that he needed time to investigate further.'

Maxim gestured to the final disguised vials that were being slipped into place in the last crate. 'He is out of time.'

'What about the twins?'

'We will deal with them later. I want to have the maximum impact, to shake Europe to its core. The production has gone better than I expected, and it is too dangerous to store these vials for long. We have to do this soon.'

'As you wish, Maxim.' Vadir turned back to the men working at sealing the crates. 'What do you think will happen when the virus is released?'

'The Americans will blame the Russians,' said Maxim. 'Then, the English will do the same. The Russians and Americans will each point out that they only have the World Health Organisation's approved stock of the virus, despite several cases where old samples have been discovered in university laboratories. The British will eventually be forced to admit they lost the samples they had in a fire five years ago, and every government leader will do all they can to distance themselves from the accusations. The minute quantities of vaccine currently available is administered to military personnel travelling to the Middle East. They will spend too long arguing over whether to use this for their citizens, or inoculate all military personnel to protect themselves in the face of civil unrest. In the meantime, millions will die. Terrorists and rogue states spend billions of dollars developing nuclear capabilities, whereas we will demonstrate our ability to completely wipe out three quarters of the world's population with one simple masterstroke.'

Vadir frowned. 'So, where does that leave you?'

'As the richest man in the world, and the most powerful, when I announce that I have developed a vaccine that will protect the younger generation – which I will provide to them, for a price.'

'What if they say no?'

Maxim smiled. 'They won't. An ageing population cannot rebuild a devastated civilisation. If the governments of this world cannot inoculate their citizens against the further spread of this virus, there is no hope for them.'

# FIVE

*London*

Gerald Knox keyed in the last two digits for the combination to the safe behind his desk, then rose and moved across the room to where he'd installed a small coffee machine.

He tried to ignore the nagging sense of unease that had gripped him for the past forty-eight hours, but his gut twisted uncomfortably at the thought of the documents he'd placed in the safe.

He pulled a fresh coffee pod from a drawer under the machine and inserted it, the aroma of ground beans soon filling the space accompanied by the promise of a caffeine fix he'd been desperately in need of for the past five hours.

An emergency meeting had been called at the Foreign and Commonwealth Office, yet when he'd arrived and settled at the large conference table amongst the other delegates it had quickly transpired that the Minister's sense of urgency was several levels below what Knox and his colleagues considered a threat.

It had involved cricket, for a start.

After a heated discussion during which half-hearted threats about budget cuts had been made, the Minister had been pacified and hurriedly left for his office or wherever next he chose to wreak havoc.

Gerald had shoved his copy of the agenda and his notebook into his briefcase, keen to return to the Section, only to be waylaid in the corridor outside the secure meeting room by another departmental head who wanted to discuss "that ruckus in Berlin".

He'd had no choice but to join the man for drinks at the bar.

After an hour of enduring the man's whinnying tone and increasingly drunken state, Gerald had made his excuses and left, pleased that he'd managed to steer the conversation the whole time towards the other man's problems.

No further mention of Berlin had been made.

Which was just as well, because Gerald himself was still unsure what exactly had gone wrong.

He'd replayed the scenario over and over in his head since, only to return to the same conclusion each time.

Miles Newcombe had suggested the building, no-one else.

Knox blinked, his attention taken by the fact the machine had fallen silent, and raised the china cup to his lips.

The bitter liquid burned his mouth, but he savoured the flavours as he crossed the rug back to his desk.

Placing the cup on a mat near his computer screen, he lowered himself into the chair and ran a hand over tired eyes.

He'd thought that by restricting Miles's duties within the department that he'd be able to control him, but it seemed that he'd underestimated the agent.

He reminded himself of the successes the man had had in South America. Of course, he wasn't as cold-blooded as some of the people the Section employed, but he was ruthless and had maintained a reputation for doggedness.

He typed in his password and used his mouse to navigate around the screen until he found the files he wanted. Opening them, he cast his eyes over the content until he found the report that had chilled him upon reading it for the first time.

He'd been reluctant at first to let Miles manage the fallout from the Berlin incident and use his own contacts to trace Eva's whereabouts for the days following that, and had been pleased at the results to begin with, especially after he'd managed to track her to France.

The fact that the Caretaker had been mobilised in the meantime, and by Eva herself, was of concern.

As was Nathan Crowe's involvement.

Miles had reluctantly admitted they'd lost a good

resource there, but couldn't ascertain whether the man had accompanied her to France of his own volition or had been coerced – by force, or under false pretences.

Obviously, the man had escaped the Berlin hotel with her to save his own skin, but after that, they had no answers.

The Section simply couldn't work out whether Crowe was still one of theirs, or had opted to join Eva and the Caretaker.

And all because Miles had suggested the two stay together at the beginning.

And now, this.

Knox might have been Miles's immediate superior, but it didn't mean he had to trust him, and now it appeared his instincts had been right.

He'd tasked two of his most competent operatives to shadow the man and report his every movement on a daily basis – more frequently if the need arose.

He'd have congratulated himself for his foresight if the evidence hadn't been quite so terrifying.

The fact that Miles had actively pursued a meeting with the former Section chief, Philip Petersen, had surpassed even his own paranoia.

And to find out that the two men had maintained communication since left a hollow at the base of his stomach.

Petersen was meant to be ill; he was meant to be suffering from dementia.

That had been the official prognosis, and the one that had been broadcast to personnel three years ago.

It was the reason why the Prague incident had been managed such that the Section could clear up the mess left behind by Petersen, and still retain its standing within the intelligence community and, more importantly, the Foreign Office.

Knox closed the file on the screen, and reached out for the bottle of thirty-year-old malt whisky. He poured a generous measure into a tumbler on his desk, and then turned his attention to the manila folder at his elbow.

Flicking open the cover, he ran his eyes down a page of text that he'd learned by rote in the time since returning from the Foreign Office after it had been thrust into his hand by an aide who hurried alongside him before he'd reached the quiet confines of his office.

The Russians had tried to keep Maxim Kowalski's escape a secret, but in a world of cyber surveillance and subterfuge, there weren't many places left to hide such information.

It had been the Ukrainians who had first obtained the information, and had presented it to the British consulate in Kiev with ill-disguised glee six months after the event.

Knox strongly suspected they'd tried to find buyers prior to then, except no-one really understood the danger as well as the UK intelligence agency he now led, and by the time the deal had been brokered, the price had dropped considerably.

His hand trembled as he turned the page, and he took another sip of the whisky to steady his fraying nerves.

The only satellite images that had been available via the Ukrainians at the time had depicted the old testing laboratory after the accident reported by the Russians.

He'd spotted the ruse for what it was, of course. The Section had obtained other, more precise, images and these had been the ones he'd uploaded to the database for Crowe to find.

A murmured phone conversation with a contact at MI6 had resulted in the images he now ran his gaze over, and it made for chilling viewing.

He closed the folder, then logged out of the system and switched off the computer before turning his chair around to face the darkened city skyline, lost in thought.

Two things were very clear to him now.

Miles Newcombe could no longer be left to work alone, and Eva's growing knowledge of the operation was dangerously close to blowing three years of work skywards if he didn't intervene.

# SIX

*Hyde Park, London*

Eva shoved her gloved hands into her coat pockets and scowled at the grey clouds that covered the city.

The sombre weather aggravated her black mood, her thoughts tumbling over each other as she tried to piece together the events that had brought her here.

Nathan had reluctantly stayed away from the meeting place Miles had suggested and was safely ensconced within a basement flat Decker had led them to upon their arrival in the English capital the previous evening.

With increased border security at the Channel Tunnel and major airports, they'd elected to travel from the Continent by ferry instead, losing themselves within the crowds that returned from France laden with cheap alcohol and extravagant food choices ready for the Christmas festivities.

She had no idea how Decker had sourced the flat, and she knew better than to ask.

In their line of work, it was common to have several places to rest and recover – often spread around the world in case of compromise or simply the need to disappear for any length of time.

She wasn't surprised when, after ensuring they hadn't been followed, Decker had spent ten minutes loosening the floorboards in the living area before setting them to one side and reaching into the cavity.

A carefully curated collection of weaponry began to emerge before he'd replaced the boards, and then they had spent the next two hours cleaning and checking the arsenal of guns.

Eva had forgotten the festive holiday was almost upon them, but now she had a greater sense of urgency.

If Maxim was aiming for the ultimate impact with his plans, she had no doubt the following days would be crucial.

She had to find out what he was planning, and then stop him.

Nathan and Decker had spent the morning setting up the laptop and equipment they'd brought with them from Prague in their backpacks, creating a miniature operations room within the living area.

'It's not perfect, but it'll have to do,' said Nathan.

'Won't we be traced?' said Eva, nibbling at her thumbnail as she watched his fingers fly over the keyboard.

'I've used every trick in the book – and some others – to try to evade them,' he said. 'We're talking several layers of encryption, bouncing off different servers around the world. It's the best I can do in the circumstances.'

Now she sauntered along the ornamental lake's edge, casting her eyes over the statues that lined the path, and tried to look relaxed.

The irony that the English monarch, Henry VIII, had established the park as a hunting ground wasn't lost on her.

Right now she felt exposed, and she hated the sensation. Sure, she was armed, but as she watched a family of Asian tourists stroll by, their kids yelling excitedly at the swans that graced the water, she knew drawing her weapon would have to be a last resort.

Decker had arrived at the park fifteen minutes before her and undertaken a patrol of the area where Miles said he wanted to meet, his voice over her earpiece confirming she was clear to proceed.

He'd hidden himself away now, unseen to even her trained eye and despite her attempts to seek him out.

'Stop it,' his voice had commanded after less than a minute. 'Relax. You spot me, you'll give my position away to anyone watching you.'

'Sorry.'

'You're out of practice, Delacourt.'

Her top lip had curled at the insult, but she knew he was right.

She sighed and began another loop of the Serpentine's northern curve, crossing the bridge and turning right to follow the path alongside the Long Water.

A chill wind created choppy waves upon the lake's surface.

Her eyes swept the immediate area, taking in the two landscape gardeners who moved amongst the ornamental gardens, tidying up the detritus that had been cast aside by visitors.

Footsteps approaching from behind her snapped her out of her reverie and she spun around, ready to fight.

A man ran towards her dressed in a long-sleeved top and running shorts. He ignored her as he ran past, the music from the headphones in his ears emitting a slight rhythmic hiss.

She turned back to her route, exhaling. He was no threat – no professional assassin would run in headphones, let alone have the music turned up that loud. It simply deadened the senses, and didn't allow for evasive action.

A dog barked on the other side of the lake, closely followed by another higher pitched yelp.

She looked where the sound came from, and watched while the owners of the two mutts did their best to pull the dogs away from each other as they strained on their leads. When the attempted fight had been broken up, the lady with the larger dog raised her hand in apology and hurried away.

The path wound between the lake and small copses of trees – not ideal for surveillance, and she forced her shoulders to relax. A statue to her left evoked childhood memories of hiding in the school library as an eight-year-old, her head buried in a fantasy tale that helped dull the reality of her own life.

She saw Miles before he noticed her.

He looked much more worn down than when he'd interviewed her in Berlin after the attack on the compound in Cyprus.

He wore a dark woollen coat, but had left it unbuttoned so that his charcoal grey suit showed, and she wondered also if he'd purposefully done so to enable him to withdraw a gun.

She tried to recall whether he was left- or right-handed, and then forced herself to relax. Both she and Decker were armed, and if Miles tried anything she doubted whether he would survive to squeeze the trigger.

Lack of sleep was etched into his features and as he drew closer, she saw that his eyes were bloodshot.

'Eva.'

'Miles.'

She waited, unwilling to start the conversation, knowing her silence would unnerve him. If she spoke first, she would appear weak.

And despite Decker's comment that she was out of practice, she certainly wasn't weak.

'Thanks for coming.'

She acknowledged the comment with a snort. 'I don't think I had a lot of choice, did I?'

'There's a lot going on, Eva. I won't lie to you – I think there's a leak in the Section.'

'No shit.'

She brushed past him, then stopped as his hand wrapped around her arm. 'Eva, listen to me.'

She rounded on him. 'Why should I listen to you?'

'Because I might be the only friend you've got there at the moment.' He dropped his hand and gestured to the grass next to the path. 'Let's walk over here, away from other people.'

Eva glanced over her shoulder.

A woman was walking towards them, her hands laden with shopping bags, her mobile phone tucked under her ear.

In the other direction, the family with children were approaching, the kids' playfulness now tempered by an obvious tiredness caused by exuberant play, jet lag, or both.

She followed Miles into the shadows under the trees, letting him walk ahead of her.

His whole posture spoke of someone who expected to be under surveillance but he smiled as he stopped and turned to face her.

'Eva, you can trust me.'

'I don't believe you. You were the one who suggested Alex and I stay in the hotel in Berlin. Why was that?'

'It's the first place that came to mind. Where are the twins?'

'Somewhere safe.'

'They're six years old, Eva. They need to be cared for properly.'

'They are. Who's the leak in the Section?'

'I'm still trying to gather evidence.'

'That doesn't help me. Why did you want to meet?'

'I want us to stay in contact with each other. It's the only way I can guarantee your safety.'

She narrowed her eyes. 'I don't believe you. In fact, I think—'

The tree trunk next to her exploded a split second before Miles barrelled into her, knocking her to the ground.

'Get down!'

She tumbled underneath him, rolling away and covering her head with her hands as a second shot echoed over the landscape.

Someone cried out, and Eva lifted her head from the soft wet grass to see the woman with the shopping bags sprawled on the path, her purchases spilled around her, and a large pool of blood pulsing from her body.

The family were on the ground only metres away, the mother's face ashen as she held her son to her chest, her husband cradling their daughter.

'Are you injured?' Eva yelled.

The man shook his head.

'Stay down!'

The family did as they were told, a moment before a third shot rang out, and Eva buried her head in the grass, fuming.

She'd been set up, walking straight into a trap, and the man lying prone next to her had used himself as the bait.

She heard more gunfire, a different tone this time, and lifted her gaze to see what was going on.

Decker emerged from the shadows, firing his gun at a target on the boundary of Kensington Gardens to her left. He ran over to Eva, grabbed her by the arm and began to pull her away.

'Let's go,' he said. 'I winged the shooter. We don't have much time to follow his trail.'

She scrambled to her feet and allowed herself to be dragged back to the path.

'Wait!'

Eva glanced over her shoulder at Miles's shout.

He raised himself into a crouch, his face stricken.

'You said I could trust you,' she yelled, and then followed Decker.

# SEVEN

Decker led the way out of the park and across Bayswater Road, weaving through the traffic that coursed past, the drivers oblivious to the drama unfolding around them.

Eva gasped as she narrowly avoided colliding with a cyclist, and then picked up her pace, tucking her weapon into her belt and pulling down her sweatshirt to conceal it.

Safely on the other side of the road, her heart rate steadying, she matched Decker pace for pace.

Sirens blared as the emergency services converged on the park, pedestrians stopping in their tracks and turning to face the noise, a mixture of surprise and fear on their faces.

Eva pushed past them. She knew they had to get away, to put as much distance as possible between them and the police, but now wasn't the time.

Now, they had to find the person behind the shooting.

Decker pointed to the pavement under their feet.

'He's bleeding.'

Sure enough, a regular spatter of blood stains marked their adversary's escape route.

'He's heading towards Paddington Station,' she said.

'If he makes it, we've lost him forever. We have to find him before he gets there.'

Eva craned her neck until she could look over the heads of the people in front of her.

Ahead, she could see a figure staggering drunkenly, the pedestrians around him frowning and shaking their heads as they passed.

A couple walking towards Eva and Decker were laughing.

'Christ, if he can't handle his drink, he shouldn't have started so early,' the man said, before the rest of the conversation faded into the distance behind Eva.

'Samuel Parkes,' she muttered. 'You're right – we were set up.'

She surged forward, but Decker put a restraining hand on her arm.

'Easy. He's not going anywhere fast, and we don't want to draw attention to ourselves. We need to wait until we're off this main road.'

Eva slowed her pace, but had to agree with the older assassin.

They had to corner Parkes away from prying eyes.

As it was, the pavement was packed, and she checked her watch, surprised to see it was already noon.

A businessman jostled her as he passed, his once

impeccable suit crumpled as if he'd been sitting in a meeting all morning, and his phone pressed to his ear as he barked orders.

The aroma of perfume assaulted her senses as they passed a department store, and she slowed her pace to navigate around shoppers exiting the building with bulky purchases and heavy bags.

A squeal of brakes reached her ears as a bicycle courier swerved off the road and onto the pavement with little regard for the pedestrians, and she side-stepped to avoid colliding with him before ducking behind Decker and using his bulk to clear her way rather than take on the crowds by herself.

'Here we go,' he said, and picked up his pace once more.

They zigzagged through the crowd, Eva checking her watch periodically to give inquisitive bystanders the impression they were late for an appointment rather than in pursuit of one of the Section's most dangerous and unpredictable rogue assassins.

As they jostled passers-by, Eva peered around Decker to try to catch a glimpse of their quarry.

Parkes stumbled, clutching hold of his right thigh as he tried to put some distance between himself and his pursuers.

Eva glanced down at the pavement.

The spots of blood had fallen more closely together, and seemed heavier.

'He's dying.'

'Good,' said Decker.

'Not good. I want to talk to him first.'

'You could have told me that before.'

'Sorry,' she said, unable to hide the sarcasm in her voice. 'I had my head buried in some grass while two men were exchanging gunfire.'

He said nothing, but clenched his jaw and forged ahead, weaving between a section of scaffolding poles protruding from a building's façade while ignoring the warning signs for the construction works above their heads.

Parkes suddenly ducked to his right and disappeared from view.

'Shit.'

They began to run, quickly closing the distance, and found a narrow alleyway.

There was no sign of Parkes.

'He's managed to stem the blood flow.' Eva checked over her shoulder, but the crowd was moving fast and no-one looked to see what she and Decker were doing.

She withdrew her gun and edged further into the alley, Decker at her side.

A few yards in, the alleyway widened, and split into two.

Tall buildings either side cast shadows over each thoroughfare, while bins and abandoned junk obscured their view.

'Which one?' she hissed.

'Split up. You take the left one. I'll meet you at the other end.'

'Okay.'

She began to sidle towards the left-hand spur.

'Eva?'

'What?'

'Be careful, yeah? Answers aren't worth dying for.'

She nodded, then took a deep breath, set her shoulders, and entered the secondary alley.

A cloying stench of urine and rotten food struck her immediately, the narrow space not allowing much air from the thin strip of sky visible above.

Her feet scuffed through discarded food wrappers and cigarette packets, and she lowered her gaze to check where she was treading.

She couldn't afford to trip and land on a used hypodermic needle.

Every one of her senses were screaming at her to get out of the narrow space, to run.

She needed answers though, and despite Decker's advice, she didn't want to kill Parkes unless it was absolutely necessary.

A shuffling sound further along the alleyway reached her ears, and she froze.

The weight of the weapon in her hands gave her a sense of familiar comfort, but it didn't stop her heart ratcheting up a notch.

A rat crept out from behind one of the bins, nosed its way through a discarded crisp packet, and then scurried away with its find.

Eva breathed out, but didn't relax.

In the distance, the sirens stopped and she realised they were rapidly running out of time.

Once the police began to speak to witnesses, especially the family she had spoken to, the hunt would begin.

She wondered fleetingly whether Miles Newcombe had escaped the park before the emergency services had arrived. She quickly discarded the thought – he wasn't her problem right now. She'd worry about his treachery later.

The hairs on the back of her neck stood on end, and she slowed as she approached a rusting green-coloured bin on the left-hand side of the alleyway.

Its position created a problem.

The space between its outer edge and the right-hand side of the alleyway was such that she would have to squeeze past, and there was every chance she would be heard.

She swallowed.

Transferring the weight of the gun to her right hand, she crouched and tried to peer under the wheels of the bin, in case Parkes had hidden behind it.

It was no use – there was too much litter that had been shoved and kicked underneath the bin, and it blocked her view.

She checked over her shoulder to make sure Parkes hadn't doubled back and cornered her.

The alleyway behind her was deserted.

Realising that she had delayed enough, she moved to the right-hand side of the bin and began to sidle past it, careful not to let her clothing snag on the sharp edges.

As she reached the other end, she swung round and aimed the gun at the space behind it.

There was no-one there.

Movement behind her reached her ears, and she swung round, weapon raised.

Parkes emerged from a doorway, the deep recess a relic of Victorian architectural design.

The meagre light gave his features a grotesque mask-like effect, highlighting the manic grin he wore.

'Eva Delacourt.'

Eva edged backwards until her back was against the opposite wall. 'Stay where you are, Parkes.'

He chuckled. 'It's not like I'm going to run anywhere.'

'I'd rather not take chances, that's all.'

'Your days are numbered. You and me? We're literally a dying breed.'

'Unfortunately, Parkes, you have a tendency to return from the dead.'

He choked out a laugh. 'No thanks to you.'

'Is that what this is all about – revenge?'

He shrugged, before his face contorted and he clutched at his leg with both hands. When he recovered from the spasm of pain that wracked his body, he glared at her.

'You were lucky to escape in Berlin.'

'I wasn't lucky. You were careless. You were so busy trying to make sure your face wasn't picked up by the security cameras, you didn't take into account that I'd see you from the reception area.'

He cursed.

'Who told you I'd be there?'

He shook his head.

Eva took a step closer, angling the weapon until it was trained on his other leg.

'Who sent you? Was it Miles Newcombe?'

'Fuck you.'

She squeezed the trigger.

Parkes collapsed, screaming.

Eva watched dispassionately as he writhed on the floor, his hands moving from his right thigh to his shattered left knee.

She took a step closer, and aimed the gun at his head.

'Last chance, Parkes.'

He cackled, clutching his side, and then turned his head and spat onto the pavement before glaring at her.

'You don't know who you're dealing with, Delacourt.'

'Yes, I do.' Eva squeezed the trigger twice; a double tap to his head and chest, before she stared dispassionately at the man who had tried to kill Alex and his sister.

'And this time, Parkes, you can *stay* dead.'

# EIGHT

Miles ran over to the woman who lay spread-eagled on the ground, but it was no good.

She'd died instantly, the sweet scent of spilled orange juice permeating the air around her.

He turned and hurried over to the family who were starting to get to their feet, the mother hysterical.

Raising his hands, he spoke to the man in a calm voice.

'Are any of you hurt?'

The man shook his head. 'What is going on? Terrorist?'

'He's gone now.'

'Are you police?'

'No. I'm not with the police. They'll be here soon, though.' He gestured towards the park entrance. 'You should wait over there for them. Don't let the kids look back, okay?'

The man nodded, then gestured to his wife and they began to hurry away.

Miles watched them for a moment, then sprang into action.

He jogged away from the scene of the shooting, heading for the fountains that bisected the Basin at its northern end, then swerved left and headed towards a different exit than the tourists had taken, keen to avoid the armed police and military personnel that would no doubt be converging upon the park within minutes.

He lost himself within the throng and kept his head down, while all around him women screamed in terror, their cries blending in with those from the children who were being bundled away from the scene of the shooting by panicked parents.

He ignored the metal turnstile set into the ornamental hedgerow that acted as a boundary between the park and the street, and instead pushed past others escaping the park through the double wrought iron gates that had been flung open. As he burst through the entrance he dodged between the concrete bollards set onto the pavement, which prevented any vehicles from entering the park.

Congestion had set in on the two-way traffic that rumbled past as drivers slowed to gawk at the events happening before their eyes.

As he dashed across the first traffic lane, four police cars screeched to a halt at the kerb, the occupants spilling from the vehicles and converging on the green space.

Whoever the shooter was, he'd taken one hell of a risk. The city had been in lockdown for over a year now due to escalating terrorism alerts, and yet Eva was evidently deemed enough of a threat to carry out such an audacious attack in broad daylight.

It meant his fears were justified, and that her enemies were becoming more desperate.

But would she believe him?

He cursed under his breath at his own stupidity.

He'd been used, and he could only hope that he still had time to make amends, before somebody else was killed because of the political wrangling within the Section.

He'd been surprised at the appearance of Decker.

The way Knox spoke about the man, Miles had assumed the Caretaker would never set foot on British soil again.

Miles picked up his pace, knowing that if he was apprehended, the Section would disown him and the police wouldn't believe him.

The Section didn't exist as far as the law was concerned, and its affairs were conducted away from Parliamentary committees and the like.

It answered to no-one.

He knew he had to find Eva, to explain.

It was evident she was still in danger, and he held himself responsible.

If he hadn't insisted on running his own investigation behind Knox's back, none of this would have happened.

He could only hope she was telling the truth when she said the children were somewhere safe, far away from here.

He doubled back towards the entrance Eva and Decker

had left the park through, and quickly found a trail of bloodstains leading across the road.

Decker was right – he'd winged the shooter.

Miles paced the pavement, his eyes monitoring the traffic for a break in the constant stream of buses, taxis, and cyclists, then gave up and launched himself across the busy street, earning a torrent of abuse and almost colliding with a car travelling from the opposite direction.

He held up his hand in apology to the driver who glared through the windscreen, then took off along the street, following the trail of blood.

A stream of people was now running away from the park, the realisation that an armed man had been seen finally registering with them, the wave of panic palpable as confused bystanders stood stock-still on the pavement, wondering whether to run or watch.

Miles brushed past a man holding a mobile phone aloft, filming the exodus, and muttered under his breath at the stupidity.

Any sane person would seek shelter, and put as much distance between them and the sound of gunfire as they could.

A bus rumbled to a standstill behind him, belching out fumes while its passengers descended the back of the vehicle, only to take one look at the pedestrians pushing and shoving to board it before changing their minds and retreating back into the safety of the vehicle.

As it pulled away, Miles's gaze dropped to the pavement

once more and he frowned as he saw the increasing number of bloodstains he passed.

He began to run.

He had to reach the shooter before Eva and Decker caught up with the man – he needed answers, and he wasn't sure they'd ask the right questions.

There was no doubt in his mind that they would kill the man when they found him. That was what they did.

And, from looking at both their files, they did it very effectively.

Of course, now Eva wouldn't believe that he hadn't been the one to betray her, and that he hadn't set her up purposely for the meeting.

Miles prayed he would get a chance to explain himself before she or Decker decided he was one risk too many, and killed him. For that was what it would come down to, he had no doubt.

There was only one thing more dangerous than an assassin – a pissed off assassin.

# NINE

Eva thumbed the gun's safety on, and then leaned against the wall of the alleyway, breathing hard.

She swore under her breath.

She hadn't expected Parkes to reveal who he reported to, but at the same time was disappointed that she was no closer to finding out who was responsible for the events of the past few weeks.

She felt no remorse for killing the assassin.

After what he had done to Sally, he deserved what he got, and at least now one of the people trying to hunt her down had been eliminated.

Despite the suppressor fitted to the weapon, she knew the report had echoed off the walls of the buildings that hugged the narrow thoroughfare.

The sound of Parkes's scream would have carried even further.

Now, she needed to return to the basement flat as quickly as possible and arrange to leave the country with Decker and Nathan so that they could try to stop Maxim.

A faint *click* reached her ears, and she spun round, weapon raised.

'Forget it, Delacourt. You haven't got the angle.'

'Shit.'

She dropped the gun to her feet and raised her hands as Miles emerged from behind the bin.

'Was he the shooter?'

'Yes.'

He drew closer, keeping enough distance between them so she couldn't try to wrest his gun from him, and glanced down at the body at his feet.

'Same guy from Berlin?'

'Yes.'

His eyes flickered back to hers. 'I'm not a traitor, Eva. I'm simply trying to find some answers. I didn't know he would be in Berlin, and I didn't know he'd be there today.'

'Bullshit. Both locations were suggested by you.'

His gun wavered for a fraction of a second, but it was enough.

Decker loomed out of the shadow of a doorway behind Miles, and pressed his gun to Miles's head.

'Give me one reason not to shoot you.'

Miles handed over his weapon, a disgusted expression on his face. 'You need my help.'

Eva retrieved her gun from the ground, and made her way over to where the two men stood.

'Start talking. How can you help us?'

'Maxim's created a weaponised version of smallpox and is preparing to unleash it within the next week.'

'We know.'

'But you don't know what he's doing with it.'

Decker lowered the gun, but kept it trained on Miles.

Eva narrowed her eyes. 'What's going on, Miles? You could've told me this in the park. Or by email.'

He sighed, a defeated expression crossing his features. 'I didn't set you up, Eva. There's a leak. I had to talk to you face to face. It was a risk contacting Nathan as it was.'

'You could've come to us.'

He shook his head. 'You've seen what just happened. If I'd come to you, I might have been putting the twins in danger, too.'

Decker turned and kicked at an empty soft drink can, sending it spiralling through the air until it landed with a crash further down the alleyway.

'What makes you say that?' said Eva. 'And why should we believe you?'

'Because the moment you disappeared from Prague, Knox started to cut me out of the loop. I was left high and dry, Delacourt – just like you. Knox is up to something, and I can't work out what. In the end, I arranged to go and see Petersen.'

Eva snorted. 'What good did you think that would do? He's got dementia. He's no use to anyone anymore.'

'There's nothing wrong with him.'

Decker spun on his heel. 'What?'

'I know, I couldn't believe it either. That whole business of the Section telling everyone he'd been put out to pasture was a complete fabrication. Sure, he's in a nursing home, but I can assure you – he's as sharp as ever.'

Eva tilted her head at a sound, her senses alert.

'We need to move. We've been here too long.'

Decker placed a hand on Miles's shoulder. 'In front, where I can see you. No funny business, otherwise—'

'Yeah, yeah, I know.'

Miles shrugged off his hand and began to hurry along the alleyway, Decker at his heels.

Eva swept her eyes over the area to double check she had cleared it of spent casings, despite the weight in her pocket, and took off after them.

They sprinted to the end of the alleyway, then slowed their pace before bursting onto the main road once more.

Eva switched positions with Decker, and then looped her arm through Miles's and picked up her pace.

'Smile, dammit,' she hissed.

'Oh, yeah, this is just great,' he said out the corner of his mouth. 'Just me and two assassins out for a stroll on a fine winter's day.'

'Anyone ever told you sarcasm doesn't suit you?'

'They have now. Where are we going?'

Eva didn't respond.

As it was, the only safe haven they had was the basement flat, and right now she was trying to decide whether it was a good idea to lead Miles there.

Decker was obviously mulling over the same conundrum, as he caught up with them and nodded towards the end of the road.

'Turn left up here. We'll make our way back to the apartment via the cricket ground. I'll go on ahead to make sure it hasn't been compromised.'

'Copy that.'

Decision made, Eva watched as his tall figure loped away, and then glanced over her shoulder as a police car shot past, heading towards Paddington Station.

It was closely followed by a second and third vehicle.

The police and military response to terrorism threats in the city meant armed force was only minutes away, with personnel being stationed strategically throughout the metropolis.

If she wasn't careful, they'd be corralled into a security checkpoint, and that would be the end of it.

She checked her watch.

'We're going to miss our train,' she exclaimed.

Thankfully, Miles had spent enough time in the field to pick up on her cue instead of questioning her motives, and played right along.

'Run,' he said, raising his voice so it would carry over the pedestrians around them. 'We still might make it.'

They began to sprint, the people around them clearing a path, more than one person wearing a bemused expression at the couple that tore past bickering about whose fault it was that they were going to be late home.

'Down here.'

Eva pulled Miles with her into a side street to their right, then looped back to pick up their route in a zigzag pattern past the train station.

Once she was in sight of the large hotel at the end of the street, she finally slowed, then took a left and followed the main road as it crossed over the waters of the Paddington Basin.

She spotted a path leading down to the water's edge, and loosened her grip on Miles as they approached the first of a row of narrowboats moored against the concrete path that wound its way past a hospital.

'Wait.'

She stopped, and raised an eyebrow as Miles doubled over and rested his hands on his knees.

He raised his eyes to hers. 'I've been behind a desk for too long.'

'Don't you still work out?'

'Obviously not enough.'

A smile formed on her lips. 'There's a bench seat over there. Come on. Two-minute break. I can't have you dying on me, not yet.'

'Fabulous, thanks.'

He curled his lip before collapsing onto the wooden

structure with a sigh of relief, and after a moment checking they hadn't been followed, she joined him.

Decker was nowhere to be seen, but she knew he'd be watching.

Somewhere.

'So, are you going to kill me?'

'Not sure yet. Any reason why I shouldn't?'

'I meant what I said. I never gave up your location, Eva. I wouldn't do that to you. I certainly wouldn't do it to Alex. The poor kid had been through enough in his life.'

'You knew about Prague?'

'The engineer's defection?' He shook his head. 'Not at the time. Knox eventually let me have the information – piecemeal, mind. Probably trying to work out how to control this whole mess.'

'Who told them about Sally's location?'

He visibly shuddered. 'I don't know.'

'You went there?'

'I got a call from a contact at Interpol. Was Parkes responsible for her murder?'

She nodded.

'Then I'm glad you killed him.'

She turned her gaze back to the boats. 'Me too.'

'Decker doesn't trust me, does he?'

She laughed. 'Decker doesn't trust anyone. You shouldn't take it personally.'

'He cares about you though.'

She glanced down at her hands. 'Douglas was his brother.'

'Oh.'

She pushed herself up from the seat and turned back to him. 'You can stay there, or you can come with me.'

'What? No threats?'

'No threats. If the Section has a leak, which is what we suspected, then we're on our own. And we still have to stop Maxim. I think you might be one of the good guys. For some reason, I get the impression that our mole doesn't want him stopped, so we're going to need all the help we can get.'

'Any idea why someone in the Section is helping Maxim?'

'None whatsoever.'

Miles sighed, stood, and brushed his trousers down.

'I guess you *are* going to need my help, then.'

# TEN

Decker emerged from an alleyway close to the cricket ground as they approached and sprinted across the road to join them, barely out of breath.

'We're clear,' he said, shoving his hands into his pockets.

'Parkes must've been working alone, then.'

He grunted in response.

They walked in silence, Eva keeping a watchful eye on Miles.

She knew she didn't have a choice in bringing him with her, but despite her assurances to him, it made her uneasy.

She believed him when he said he didn't know he'd put her life in danger, but couldn't quite grasp the reason why the shooter knew she'd be there.

She stopped suddenly, and grabbed hold of his arm.

'Who else knew I'd be coming to London?'

Miles shrugged off her grip and held up his hands. 'I

thought Knox was the leak, especially when I was taken off your case after discovering you'd beaten us to France.'

'You got it wrong, didn't you?' said Decker, rounding on him.

'Yes.' Miles dropped his hands to his sides. 'I admit it, I made a huge mistake, but you have to understand – Knox had locked me out of the investigation. I suspected him of setting you up. After all, he admitted to me that he was the one who had recruited Samuel Parkes, so I thought he'd arranged for you to be killed. That's why I went to Petersen for help. Big mistake.'

'So, Petersen is the leak, not Knox? What makes you think it's him?'

Miles exhaled and shoved his hands in his pockets, then moved to one side and leaned against the high brick wall that bordered the cricket ground. 'Instinct, more than anything. I last saw him three days ago and he insisted that I speak with you in person. I pointed out that it was easy enough to email you via Crowe's contact details, but the old man wouldn't take no for an answer. Got quite agitated, actually. Said it was a matter of national security, and that I had to try to persuade you to meet with him.'

'So, what was your plan?'

'Originally, I believed him – I was going to meet you at the park, and then get you to come with me to see him. When Parkes attacked us I realised I was wrong.'

'How did Petersen find out I was in Prague?'

Miles shook his head. 'Not me. Who did you contact while you were there?'

Eva bit her lip. 'Scott Lancaster.'

Miles snorted. 'CIA informant. He must've told Petersen – for a price.'

'Give me one reason not to kill you now,' said Decker, advancing on him. 'Why the hell should we trust you?'

Miles slowly extracted his hand from his pocket. 'This.'

Decker snatched the USB stick from him and passed it to Eva.

'What's on it?' she said.

'The truth. Everything about what happened from three years ago. Everything about what's happened since.'

She frowned. 'Does Knox know you have this?'

'It was Knox who asked me to pass it on to you.'

---

Decker led the way down the short flight of narrow concrete steps towards the basement flat, the afternoon light fast receding over the horizon.

Eva kept an eye on where she trod, avoiding the lichen that clung to the concrete and made the surface slippery under her footsteps.

The basement flat had belonged to a contact of Decker's – someone who was out of the country "on business", he'd said.

Eva could guess what that meant.

She sighed.

If she survived the current situation, she realised she'd have to set up a whole new set of safe houses for herself, a decision tinged with sadness as she concluded the bookshop in Prague would have served its usefulness by then, and would have to be sold – or destroyed.

Nathan rose from his seat next to a small electric fire when they entered the room, and took a step backwards when he saw Miles.

'What's he doing here?'

'He's with us now,' said Eva. 'He can bring you up to speed with regard to the politics in the Section, but in the meantime, I need you to take a look at this.'

She handed him the USB stick, and he turned it in his hand.

'I can't wait to hear all about it,' he muttered. 'I suppose all the chatter I'm seeing in the forums about a shooting at Hyde Park is your doing, Decker?'

'The other guy shot first.' Decker stomped to the refrigerator that rattled in the corner and pulled out three cans of soft drink, tossing one to Miles and handing the other to Eva. He cracked his can open and took three long gulps. 'We need to get a move on. It sounds like we're the only ones who are taking the danger posed by Maxim seriously.'

'Fine,' said Nathan. He held up his hands. 'I can take a hint.'

He sat back down in front of his laptop, and inserted the

USB stick before starting to retrieve the documentation that had been saved to it.

As he worked, Eva cast her eyes around the room.

She didn't think the owner of the place was often there. It resembled a bedsit rather than a flat, with the main living area and kitchen encompassing one large space and a single bedroom leading off to the side of it. The bathroom was through another door.

Water stains covered the ceiling, and the whole place stank of cigarettes and mildew. When they had arrived the day before, there had been a baby crying in the flat two floors up, and a man and a woman arguing.

Towards the front of the basement flat, a single grimy window with yellowing net curtains provided the only way light could enter the property and there were no blinds, so Decker had torn up a cardboard box he'd carried their food purchases in and taped it to the windows at night.

He had then spent most of the evening complaining about the lack of a back door, and no means to escape if they were compromised. Eva shared his concerns, but pointed out there wasn't a lot they could do about it. As it was, they only intended to be there for a short time – especially now.

The belongings that they had brought from Prague with them comprised the computer equipment Nathan sat in front of, and a change of clothes but nothing more. Their three backpacks stood beside the wall next to the front door, ready to grab at a moment's notice if they needed to.

Crowe had set up a security camera further along the

street the previous night, attaching the small but powerful lens to a lamp post to act as an early warning system.

It was just as well; the old refrigerator clanged and hummed so loudly, they wouldn't hear anybody approaching down the steps.

She tore herself away from her thoughts at Nathan's voice.

'All right. Looks like it's all here, like Miles said. Let's make a start.'

# ELEVEN

Despite Nathan's assertions, it turned out that Knox had added a layer of security to the files in case the information fell into the wrong hands and, muttering, the IT expert began to strip away at the encryption while the others began to get listless.

Miles commandeered the single armchair next to the kitchen and picked at a loose thread on the arm of it.

Eva perched on the edge of one of the two inflatable mattresses they'd found in a cupboard the previous night, and nibbled at her thumbnail.

'We have to alert the authorities,' said Miles.

'Who, exactly?' Decker stopped pacing and crossed his arms over his chest. 'Knox has obviously given us this information because he knows more than he's letting on. And, I've got no doubt that he'll burn the lot of us if he needs to save his own skin.'

'It's not that,' said Eva, staring at the threadbare carpet while trying not to look too closely at the stains. 'It's because if this goes off, the entire European intelligence community will be pointing the finger at each other – and the Americans and Russians will get involved, too. By the time they sort out their differences and work out how they're going to deal with this situation, it'll be too late. We're the only hope Knox has got.'

'You mean it's a political hot potato?' said Miles.

She nodded. 'How much of this do you think the British government are aware of? They knew all about the engineer trying to defect three years ago; it's evident from the information Knox has given us that Petersen sold Maxim to the Russians. And someone tried to wipe that laboratory complex off the face of the earth, killing anyone that remained.'

'You think the British government did that?' said Miles, his tone incredulous.

'Wouldn't put it past them,' said Decker. 'Although it was probably done in such a way the Cabinet can say they knew nothing about it. I wouldn't be surprised if they contracted that job out to privateers. There's no way any of our special forces lot would've agree to it.'

'Here we go.' Nathan finished typing and turned the laptop to face them. 'Okay, I've been running some projections while you lot have been gossiping, and this is what I've got so far.'

He ignored the growl that Decker emitted, and changed the image on the screen to a satellite image.

'This is an aerial view of Prague. Based on risk calculations, and the number of people we'd expect Maxim will want to infect, it's the most likely target given his current location.'

'Why?' said Eva. 'Most people will be hibernating this time of year. Why not wait until the summer tourist season?'

'First, the virus is too unstable for him to store for that long,' said Nathan. 'Second, Prague experiences an influx of tourists in December because of the Christmas markets. You've got half a million people descending on places like Old Town Square and Wenceslas Square in the space of twenty days leading up to Christmas Eve.'

'That makes sense,' said Miles. 'Squash that many people into a built-up area, and any respiratory disease will spread easily.'

'Not to mention the fact it's cold and 'flu season, so people will be much more susceptible to infection,' said Nathan.

'How long do symptoms take to show up?' said Eva, her brow knitting.

'About two to three days, dependent upon which strain of the virus it is. Some are more aggressive than others.'

'It doesn't matter which variant it is if Maxim's weaponised it,' said Decker. 'You could start seeing casualties within an hour.'

'And a lot of people get cheap flights from the UK and the

rest of Europe to go to the markets,' said Nathan, 'so it'd be out of control pretty quickly. On top of that, you've got Americans who like to tack on the markets to the end of their European holidays before returning to the States, and the virus will spread from there.'

Eva cast her eyes over the display. 'What are the casualty projections?'

'We saw four trucks travelling to the facility,' said Nathan. 'Based on the fact those were all capable of carrying weight in excess of six tonnes each, this is what the projections look like.'

He hit a button and a counter in the middle of the screen began at one, and quickly escalated into seven figures.

It was still rising when Eva whistled through her teeth thirty seconds later.

'That's millions of people.'

'It's worse than nuclear fallout,' said Nathan. 'With a nuclear blast, at least only one area is affected. Okay, you'd get some radiation being carried into the atmosphere, but a weaponised virus such as smallpox? Think of it as a moving blast radius. Every person carrying that virus increases its reach. Globally.'

'Like Ebola or Marburg virus?' said Decker.

'Worse, in that those are usually contained within sub-Saharan Africa. This will wipe out three-quarters of the world's population within a month. It'll make the Spanish 'Flu look like a bad joke.'

Eva began to pace the floor. 'It'll be too risky to try and

stop them once they reach Prague. Four of us? We don't stand a chance. Even if we did manage to find the trucks, the areas around Wenceslas Square and the other market areas are serviced by bus and train routes.'

'What are you suggesting?' said Decker.

She stopped in front of him and raised her chin until she could look him in the eyes.

'We go to Poland. We stop the trucks before they leave the laboratory complex.'

He blinked. 'And how do you propose to do that? If we destroy them, there's still a risk of infection.'

'Not if we burn it.' She turned to Nathan. 'Right?'

He sighed. 'It's no guarantee. You'd have to make sure you destroyed it all, and at a very high temperature. We can't risk any of it remaining. You know what'll happen – the first government agency to reach the bunker after we go in will attempt to take the virus for itself. And, if we do this, it's going to send a bloody big flag up on the system. It won't just be our own people after that smallpox. You can bet everyone and their mother out of the Middle East will be keen to get their hands on it.'

'There's a way to burn it, all right,' said Miles from his chair next to the window.

Eva spun around to face him. 'Are you sure?'

'Yes, I'm sure. Let me make some calls.'

# TWELVE

Knox ended the call and tried to temper his anger and frustration.

There would be significant political fallout from the shooting in Hyde Park, and the Section would suffer for it.

He sank back against the soft leather of his chair and ran a hand over tired eyes.

He'd thought that by keeping Miles out of harm's way that he'd be able to better control the whole situation, especially after the debacle in Berlin so soon after Eva's hiding place in Cyprus had been compromised.

He berated himself; he should have known that Miles was too dogged to let it go so easily, and that he'd forge ahead with his own course of investigation.

He had suspected Petersen for some time; it had been the reason for him agreeing readily to the old spymaster's enforced retirement. Those at the top hoped the move would silence the former Section chief, but Knox knew better.

Petersen had always been too ambitious to agree to fade into the background and from people's memories. His ego simply wouldn't allow it.

Knox had argued at the time with his superiors that a more permanent solution was needed, but they'd quaked at the idea, arguing it was impossible.

Of course, that's how the Americans dealt with their dirty laundry, allegedly, but no. It simply wasn't *British*.

A knock at the door jerked him from his musings.

'Come in.'

His secretary peered around the oak frame, her wavy black hair swept up away from her face and her eyes worried behind the frames of her designer glasses.

'What is it, Jenny?'

'The Prime Minister's office called, sir. She wants to see you. Right away, they said.'

'Let them know I'll be there.'

She nodded and pulled the door closed behind her, and it was only then that Knox exhaled with frustration.

He'd told the PM's predecessor what would happen if they didn't nip the situation in the bud three years ago, and now it seemed it was back to bite him, exactly as he'd predicted at the time.

He eased himself from his chair, buttoned his jacket, and slipped his mobile phone into his pocket before leaving his office.

'Car's waiting for you downstairs,' said Jenny as he swept past her desk.

He acknowledged the information with a curt nod, and rode the elevator down the six storeys to the car park where his chauffeur was completing a last-minute check of the vehicle.

'Ready, Harris?'

'Sir.'

The back door was held open for him, and Knox settled into the plush upholstery as Harris slipped behind the wheel and powered the vehicle out from the subterranean space and into the busy street beyond.

As he watched the city pass by through shaded bulletproof glass, Knox mulled over the facts known to date, wondering how much of the situation the PM should be briefed about.

---

'The Prime Minister will see you now, Mr Knox. In the study.'

'Thank you.'

Knox straightened his tie, a frisson of adrenalin shooting through his veins as he stood and approached the double doors through to the Prime Minister's domain.

It was imperative he set out his arguments for his team, before the Secretary of State arrived and began to spin a tale of woe with embattled heads of the other security agencies.

He clenched his fist.

There was absolutely no way in hell he was handing over the operation to MI6. Not after everything he'd sacrificed over the past three years.

He knocked twice, and waited.

'Enter.'

He buttoned his jacket and placed his hand on the highly polished brass handle, and entered the inner sanctum of the leader of the British government.

The Prime Minister sat in one of the four wing-backed chairs that stood in a circle at the centre of the room, a pile of documents on the small coffee table in front of her.

Bookcases lined the shelves, while lamps cast a yellowish hue upon the shuttered windows and illuminated the patterned carpet under Knox's feet as he approached.

'Good afternoon, Prime Minister.'

He hovered next to the chair opposite hers and kept his hands clasped behind his back.

The PM flung the report she'd been reading onto the coffee table and glared at him over the top of her glasses. 'Well, Knox – I have to say today's events are an unmitigated disaster.'

'Yes, Prime Minister.'

'We'll be a laughing stock in Europe. Not what we need at the moment. Weakens our position, you see?'

'Understood, Prime Minister.'

She sighed and waved a hand at him. 'Sit down, then. Let's hear your version of events.'

He chose the seat opposite hers, rather than sitting right next to her and having to twist around, then cleared his throat and proceeded to give her a precis of the incident at the park.

'Were you aware your man was attempting to meet with Delacourt?'

Knox glanced down at his hands. 'I've had him under surveillance for a few weeks now. It would appear that he thought *I* was the leak in the Section, and instead approached Philip Petersen for guidance.'

The PM emitted a sharp intake of breath, and Knox raised his gaze.

'Does your man know he made a mistake in trusting Petersen?'

'I strongly suspect he does now, yes.'

'Do we know who placed the Code One on Eva Delacourt?'

'I have evidence to suggest that was also Philip Petersen's work.'

The PM cursed. 'I thought he was under surveillance and medicated?'

'It would appear he's been fooling us all.'

Her eyes narrowed. 'Not all of us, Knox.'

'Prime Minister.'

She sighed. 'I presume you've got a plan to sort this mess out?'

'Yes. Probably best I don't share the details with you, with all due respect. Deniability, and all that.'

'Understood.'

'What about the threat from Maxim Kowalski? I'd be happier if we could give our colleagues in the Czech Republic some sort of warning.'

'Let the Czechs deal with it themselves. Put a dossier together and have your office deliver it to mine before close of business tomorrow. I'll ensure it's sent to them straight away.'

'Prime Minister, with all due respect, we don't have time to bring them up to speed on the events of the past month. Moreover, there are certain operational protocols we'd have to divulge into order to do so. May I suggest an alternative?'

'What?'

'I have a man on the inside. With Eva Delacourt.'

The PM's eyebrows shot up. 'You're in contact with them?'

Knox shifted in his seat, and avoided her eyes. 'Yes.'

She drummed her fingers on the chair armrest, the movement causing the light to reflect off the rings on her fingers.

'All right,' she said eventually. 'Maintain that contact. Stop Maxim. Without embarrassing the British government. And get that damn Code One retracted. Immediately.'

'Yes, Prime Minister.'

'Issue an all ports alert for them, just as a formality, mind. Might as well keep an eye on them.' She dismissed him with a wave of her hand, and he nodded, before rising from his seat and hurrying to the door.

'And, Knox?'

'Prime Minister?'

'Deal with Petersen. Properly this time.'

'Yes, Prime Minister.'

# THIRTEEN

Eva hugged her coat across her chest, then reached up and adjusted the backpack on her shoulder.

Her breath fogged in the crisp air and she resisted the urge to yawn.

Late the previous night, they'd eventually agreed that Miles would return to the Section to report to Knox after cleaning the flat to ensure no trace of their existence remained, and then meet them in Prague.

She'd been incredulous at first when Decker had suggested they bring the current Section chief up to date with their plans.

He'd reached into the canvas bag he'd brought with him, and extracted a mobile phone before handing it to Miles. 'I think you'd better phone Knox and bring him up to speed.'

'Are you kidding me?' Eva had launched herself from the

chair and snatched the phone from his hand. 'We can't trust the Section. Any of them.'

'We *have* to,' said Decker. 'We can't do this on our own, and Knox needs to know about Petersen. If Miles is right, and Petersen is communicating with Maxim, he needs to be stopped before he compromises our mission. Now. Permanently.'

She, Decker, and Nathan had been on the move since before dawn, working their way up the Essex coastline in a vehicle Decker had stolen on the outskirts of Romford.

She could only hope Miles Newcombe was as good as his word.

They had taken turns driving, keeping to the minor roads and passing through sleepy villages as a weak sunrise crested the horizon.

They had eventually dumped the car east of Ipswich, taking to footpaths and lanes to reach their destination.

At first, Eva had questioned Decker's insistence on keeping away from the Kentish coastline. It had been her intention to return to the continent via Dover once more.

He had argued the point.

'Too risky. We got away with it once. I doubt very much we'll get away with it again.'

Instead, they had headed for Felixstowe with the intention of catching a ferry to Rotterdam.

Now, the three of them huddled in the shadows, away from passing traffic and faced the large freight terminal that dominated the horizon.

Despite it being a little after two o'clock in the morning, the area was a hive of activity, the roar of truck engines and hydraulic braking systems carrying over the concrete apron towards their position behind a temporary construction office.

'Remind me again why we dumped the vehicle? Don't we need it to board the ferry?' said Nathan, his eyes scanning the scene before them.

Decker shook his head. 'It's too risky to try and cross the North Sea on our fake passports. It might have worked crossing the Channel two days ago, but after what happened in Hyde Park, they'll be looking for us. It's better this way.'

'And which way is that?'

Decker pointed at the parked trucks that were waiting to enter the ferry terminal.

'We catch a lift in one of those.'

'What, just walk up to one of the drivers and ask if we can grab a ride?'

'Not exactly. You'll see.'

Nathan coughed out a laugh. 'You have heard of border security, haven't you? The truck will be searched.'

'It's risky, that's true,' said Eva. 'But, they've usually got their hands full with trucks arriving in the UK, not leaving it. I think Decker is right. This is the best chance we've got to get out of the country undetected.'

She heard Crowe exhale, and buried her chin into her scarf so he wouldn't see her smile.

She was quickly learning that the IT expert would

question her or Decker in any situation that was unfamiliar to him, but that it wasn't because he was scared – it was simply the way his analytical mind worked.

It was similar to how she once worked. She would assess the location for a hit from every angle, often spending days observing the buildings around her chosen pinch point while keeping an eye on people around her. It enabled her to mitigate the risks – both for egress, and for her target's security team that might be conducting the same assessment.

Except Nathan had never worked in the field.

She could sense Decker's impatience with the questions being bombarded at him, and took pity as Nathan huffed and shoved his hands in his pockets before staring out at the articulated vehicles parked side by side.

She tapped him on the arm to get his attention once more.

'It'll be okay. Just do what we do.'

He nodded in reply, and looked away.

Eva held her wrist closer to her face and angled it so she could read her watch from the dull glow of a gantry light several metres away.

'It's nearly half past. What time's the next ferry due to leave?'

'Six o'clock. They'll be boarding soon.'

'Then we need to get a move on.'

Decker didn't respond, but moved away from the fence and began to follow its path around the perimeter of the ferry terminal, Eva and Nathan at his heels.

Every few steps, Eva checked over her shoulder to make sure that they hadn't been followed, but it seemed Decker's hunch was correct – the majority of the security patrols were over by the arrivals terminus, away from the freight carriers that were due to leave the UK.

Once they reached the large roundabout that intersected the main road in and out of the port, they kept to the shadows once more and away from the pyramids of light caused by the streetlights above.

The illuminated logo of a fast food restaurant loomed ahead, and Decker slowed his pace before turning to Nathan.

'This is where we leave you. Stay here, stay out of sight, until we come and get you.'

Nathan's brow creased. 'Hang on – where are you two going?'

Decker grinned. 'Don't worry, I'll bring you back a cheeseburger.'

Eva ignored the sigh that the IT expert emitted and hurried after Decker.

'What's the plan?'

'We need to find a driver who's going to be travelling with a trailer to Rotterdam. We're not going to be able to hitch a ride in a trailer – we won't be able to get away with it because of the security seals on the doors, and we have no idea when those trailers might be leaving the dock at the other end. We'll grab a coffee, so keep your ears open for anyone who's leaving here from the roll-on roll-off terminal.' He jabbed his thumb over his shoulder. 'All the trucks are parked back there, so it makes sense the drivers are here having a break before they get on the ferry.'

'Okay.'

Eva had no idea that Decker could drive a truck, but it didn't surprise her. He was the sort of person that liked learning, and when they had last worked together he had told her that it wasn't just firearms skills he learned in between jobs.

It seemed his diligence and attention to detail would give them the best chance of escape.

There were only a handful of cars in the restaurant car park, and Eva suspected most of those belonged to the staff working in the twenty-four-hour fast food outlet.

Decker held the front door open for her, and as she made her way to the counter at the far end she cast her eyes over the half dozen men sitting at tables scattered through the room.

A sleepy-looking teenager stood next to the till, and forced a smile as Eva approached.

'Can I take your order?'

Eva asked for two coffees and a couple of burgers, then joined Decker at a table towards the back of the room while she waited for their food to be prepared.

From their position, they could hear the conversations around them, but also keep a lookout for anyone else entering the restaurant.

'What am I listening out for?' she murmured.

'We need something that isn't dangerous goods. Something that won't be checked too closely. A regular driver, someone who has a swipe card to get through the auto gate system. All we have to worry about then is getting his ID, the keys and the swipe card. After we get through the auto gate, we still have to get through the police gate but that's usually just a check against the vehicle's registration number with the police Automatic Number Plate Recognition system. That's why we couldn't bring our own vehicle. We need a truck that's already got a booking on that ferry.'

Eva glanced up as her order number was called, collected their coffee and food and returned to the table, where they ate in silence.

Around her, the conversations ebbed and flowed as the drivers chatted amongst themselves, laughing and joking as they readied themselves for the early morning ferry crossing, or recovered from a recent arrival before heading out across the UK's network of motorways.

She could hear different accents – German, Polish, and English, but it was evident that there was a camaraderie amongst them, even if they hadn't met before.

It was these three drivers she honed in on, and noticing Decker shifting in his seat, she knew he'd picked up on the same people.

She sipped at her coffee slowly, knowing it could be a long wait to find the right driver.

After half an hour or so, one of the drivers near the front of the restaurant rose from his seat, picked up his mobile phone, and made his way through the restaurant towards Eva.

She held her breath as he passed, wondering if she had been caught staring, but he pushed through the doors to the toilets without looking at her, and she breathed a sigh of relief as the door swung shut behind him.

'Back in a minute,' said Decker. 'I need to take a piss.'

Eva took another sip of her coffee to disguise her smile.

The truck driver reappeared first, made his way to the counter, and ordered coffee to go.

Decker appeared moments later.

'We're going. Now.'

Eva wiped her lips with a napkin, screwed it up and dropped it to the table before following him out the door.

They edged around the side of the building before altering their course, making their way back out to the road.

'What happened?' said Eva.

'He's the one. He's got the truck we need. I got chatting with him, said we were waiting for a passenger ferry in the morning but that we'd arrived too early. I asked him where he's heading, and he's taking a load of bed mattresses to Germany. It's our best bet for getting on that ferry without being stopped.'

'So, we ambush him before he gets to his truck?'

'Exactly.'

He reached the point where they had left Nathan, and emitted a low whistle.

The IT expert emerged from the undergrowth, brushing off his jeans, his eyes hopeful in the gloom.

'Shit,' said Decker.

Nathan's face fell. 'You forgot my burger, didn't you?'

## FOURTEEN

A loud belch signalled the imminent arrival of the truck driver from the direction of the fast food restaurant, and Decker waved his hand behind his back.

Eva and Nathan dropped into a crouch, ready to spring when Decker gave the command.

They had positioned themselves at the entrance to the truck park. It resembled a large lay-by rather than a formal parking area, which suited them just fine. It was unguarded; the trucks were in darkness, and most had curtains pulled around the windscreens and windows as the occupants slept off the effects of driving through the night.

The man's footsteps were unhurried, and from where Eva crouched she could hear him talking on his phone.

Decker moved further into the shadows, unwilling to startle the man while he was speaking to someone else.

There was no sense in alerting others to their plans, not until they were far away.

As the man drew closer, he finished his phone call muttering under his breath. He picked up his pace as he passed them, seemingly eager to get back to his truck cab now that he had a full belly. He slurped from a take-out coffee cup.

Nathan emerged from the shadows in front of the man, causing the truck driver to rear back in fright.

'What do you want?'

'Your truck,' said Decker, closing the distance between him and the driver, and wrapping his arm around the man's neck in a chokehold.

Eva ran up to them and helped Nathan manhandle the driver into the undergrowth, his struggles becoming weaker as his oxygen supply was cut off.

Eventually, he slumped against Decker, who let him tumble to the ground before rolling him over and checking for a heartbeat.

'Did you kill him?' said Nathan, his eyes wide.

'No. He's just out cold. Quick, we need to move.'

Eva and Decker moved efficiently, the older assassin patting down the man's clothes until he found keys, identity papers, and the all-important card that would operate the auto gate system to let them into the ferry terminal.

He took the man's mobile phone and wallet, and then stood while Eva tied a makeshift gag around the man's mouth and ensured he could still breathe through his nose.

Nathan reached into the backpack he carried, and handed Eva the loops of rope she'd stuffed into the bottom of it before leaving Prague.

'Do you always pack your bags like this when you go away?'

'Admit it. You're impressed.'

'Let's go.'

Decker led them to where the trucks were parked, leading them to a green coloured cab and silver trailer parked at the end of the line.

Eva ran her eyes over the livery emblazoned along the side of the trailer.

She didn't need to ask if they had the right one – the logo of a well-known bedding store took up most of the trailer's side panel, accompanied by a cartoon-like drawing of a pile of mattresses.

'Shame we can't sleep on those on the way over,' said Nathan.

Decker chuckled. 'Nice thought, but we can't risk breaking the seal on the trailer. It will be the only thing that gives us away.'

He inserted the key into the lock, opened the door, and stepped back.

Eva held her breath, but no alarm sounded.

'All right,' said Decker. 'That's the easy part done.'

He climbed up into the cab, and Eva watched as he began to run his hands over the sleeping compartment at the back of it. He lifted cushions away, and then turned back to her.

'You're both going to have to squash into here. I can let you out once we're on the ferry, but you're going to have to stay hidden while I get through security. There's enough room if we strip out everything he's got stored here and dump it.'

Eva nodded. 'Okay, pass everything down. We'll hide it in the bushes over there. Quick – before anyone sees us.'

When they were done, Decker held out his hand and helped Eva into the cab, shuffling over to one side while she balanced between the seats and lowered herself into the compartment.

Decker wasn't kidding – the space was cramped, and by the time Nathan had climbed in next to her and Decker had placed the cushions back on top, sealing them into their temporary hiding space, sweat was already beginning to itch at her scalp.

'No talking now.' Decker's voice sounded muffled through the upholstery. 'I'll tell you when it's safe.'

Eva heard him turn in his seat, and then the engine rumbled to life.

Moments later, Decker eased the truck from its parking bay and she reached out and placed a hand either side of the box-like structure to steady herself.

She heard Nathan swear under his breath.

'Shh. You can moan about it afterwards.'

The rumble of the engine vibrated through the walls of the cab, and Eva ignored the cramping sensation in her calves.

No doubt by the time they got on the ferry, she'd be in agony, but they had to get there first. The automated gate system at the ferry terminal wasn't a problem, but once the truck was parked and waiting to be loaded onto the ship, they could do nothing to raise the suspicion of the border security patrols.

The hydraulic brakes groaned, and the vehicle eased to a standstill, the engine still running.

She realised Decker had reached the barrier, and heard a faint beep as the swipe card they'd stolen from the driver was accepted by the computer at the gate.

The truck began to move forward once more, and she breathed a sigh of relief.

'We're through the first gate,' said Decker. 'No noise now. This is where it gets risky.'

The truck braked to a halt after what seemed only a few seconds, and Eva heard the electronic whirr of his window being lowered.

'Morning,' he said.

Eva strained her ears, but couldn't hear the other person's voice. She held her breath.

'That's great,' said Decker. 'Many thanks.'

The window raised, and she heard him murmur under his breath.

'That was the police gate. They haven't found the driver yet – we just passed the ANPR cameras. Now we have to get on the ferry.'

Eva could feel the twists and turns of the truck as Decker

followed the signs through the terminal apron and into the correct parking bay for the roll-on roll-off ferry.

She twisted her wrist in the darkness – the glow from her watch showing they had half an hour to spare before the ferry would start to be loaded.

By the time Decker started the engine once again, the temperature inside the hidden compartment was several degrees hotter, and Eva could hear Nathan's heavy breathing as they both gasped for air.

Thankfully, the people running the ferry service were fast and efficient in loading the trucks, and from the way Decker changed down a gear moments before she sensed an incline, Eva realised they were entering the ferry's loading dock.

The sound of engines and machinery around them slowly dissipated as the ferry was made ready for departure. From the research that they had done the night before, she knew that most of the freight would be taken to Rotterdam without drivers. The ferry company used small tractors to pull the trailers onto the ferry and load them in position so that the weight was evenly distributed around the ship. Trucks with drivers such as theirs were then loaded on the upper deck, the advantage being theirs would be the first off the ferry at the other end.

When they had been debating their means of escape the night before, Nathan questioned why they simply couldn't hide in a trailer, and it was Decker who pointed out that they might end up in a trailer that was left at the ferry terminal in

Rotterdam for several days before being collected. They wouldn't be able to escape.

Eventually, Decker switched off the engine, and Eva heard him shift in his seat before movement above her head reached her ears.

The cushions were removed from the upper framework of the cot, and she and Nathan gasped at the fresh air that swept over them.

Decker helped them to their feet, although they could only crouch in the cramped space of the cab.

'Keep your voices down,' he said. 'I've got the curtains pulled across the windscreen and side windows, so no-one will see you, but we're packed in like sardines.'

Eva nodded, and concentrated on working the kinks from her legs. She turned to Nathan.

'Okay?'

He nodded, and wiped his sleeve over his brow. 'Thank God that's over.'

'All right, well I didn't get questioned on my way here, and there are only three other drivers on board,' said Decker. 'None of them were at the fast food restaurant, so I'm going to get the lie of the land.'

'What about CCTV?' said Eva.

Decker shook his head. 'Haven't seen any cameras, but I'll keep a look out. The cameras are usually on the outside of the ship, to assist with docking and the like. I'll see you in a bit.'

With that, he left the cab and locked the door behind him, whistling.

'What's he looking so happy about?' said Nathan.

'He's the only one of us who's going to get a hot meal,' said Eva. 'The canteen just opened.'

Decker glanced over his shoulder and grinned at the truck as he began to ascend the steel staircase out of the hull, evidently guessing they'd be watching him through the gap in the curtains.

'Bastard,' said Nathan. 'He's done it again.'

# FIFTEEN

*Prague*

Eva inserted the key into the lock, and pushed open the back door of the bookshop, her legs weary.

After arriving in Rotterdam, she and Nathan had climbed back into the compartment behind the driver's seat of the truck as Decker drove the vehicle off the ferry and away from the terminus.

Half an hour later, she'd felt the vehicle swerve to the right before braking to a standstill, and the engine died.

Decker had parked in a secluded lay-by off the main road, hidden from passing motorists by a thin line of trees that shielded the occupants of the truck as they climbed from the cab.

The older assassin locked the doors and hid the keys under the wheel arch.

'No sense in him getting into more trouble,' he'd said.

Eva had smiled as she and Nathan had followed him through a gate into a neighbouring field and begun their hike towards a distant village.

Decker could be one of the most frightening assassins she'd ever known, but every now and again he let his guard down and became the man he must have once been.

If people didn't deserve to die, or be inconvenienced by his actions, he made sure he looked out for them.

It was what made her turn to him when she was in trouble.

They'd stolen a car on the outskirts of the village and had spent eight hours taking it in turns to drive away from The Netherlands, across a quiet unmanned border gate in the countryside and then through Germany towards the Czech border.

Switching vehicles, they'd then made their way to Prague, ditching that car three miles away from the safe house.

Now, Eva staggered up the stairs, punched in the security code, and led the way into the apartment.

'Food,' said Nathan, and began to sort through the refrigerator and cupboards.

Soon, the aroma of garlic and onions wafted through the room, and within half an hour they were sitting around the kitchen table, eating their way through a large pot full of spaghetti bolognese.

Eva eventually pushed back her plate, and reached out for her wine glass.

'That was great – I feel human again.'

'What do we do now?' said Nathan. 'Wait until we hear from Miles?'

Decker shook his head. 'We need to keep moving. All the intelligence seems to suggest that Maxim is planning an imminent attack. We need to work on the basis that we're working alone. Despite what Newcombe said.'

'I agree,' said Eva. 'We can't rely on anybody but ourselves. The sooner we can get over the border into Poland, the better. It's too risky to leave it until Maxim's men reach Prague. We have to take the fight to them.'

'But there's only three of us!'

'We can use that to our advantage,' said Decker. 'We stand less chance of being spotted by any guards that Maxim has placed around the facility.'

'Doesn't sound like much of an advantage to me.'

Eva pushed back her chair, carried the plates over to the sink, and dumped them in the soapy water before turning back to the two men.

'There is one person who might be able to help us with regard to what's going on at that facility, or at least how many men Maxim has there, given that Miles suspects him anyway.'

Nathan's brow furrowed. 'Who?'

'Scott Lancaster.'

'The guy from the gallery? The one who probably set us up, and got me shot?'

'Well, we can't get to Petersen, and someone told Maxim's hit squad that we were in town. Lancaster is an arrogant prick, but there was something else that time – it was like he knew he'd be putting our lives in danger, and he did it anyway. So, that makes me think he knows more about Maxim's operation than we thought. I think Miles is right about him.'

Decker reached for the wine bottle, and topped up their glasses. 'We'd need to recce the American Embassy first. Watch his movements, find out which cafés he frequents for lunch, that sort of thing. We don't have a lot of time.'

'So,' said Eva, 'we start tomorrow. What do you think?'

'I think it's time to have another word with Scott Lancaster,' said Decker, a gleam in his eye.

# SIXTEEN

Eva sipped an espresso, and turned the page of her book before raising her gaze to the group of three men sitting on the far side of the café.

Despite Nathan's misgivings about the lack of time they had available to them, and the fact they still needed to travel to Poland, Eva was adamant that they make sure Scott Lancaster divulged any information that they could use to their advantage before they went. If that meant waiting another twenty-four hours, she was content to do so – as it was, for a tactical operation, she couldn't help feeling that they were rushing ahead blind.

She had no doubt that Lancaster knew more about the laboratory facility, given his connections with the CIA.

And, the more she and Decker discussed tactics the previous night, a sense of justice began to prevail – she was sure Lancaster was somehow involved in the hit on Douglas three years ago, and she intended to make him pay for it.

They needed as much information as possible to finalise their plans for their assault on Maxim's base first, though.

The up-to-date satellite images provided by Knox gave a sporadic account of movement on the ground; they needed actual figures and a proper sense of the layout. The satellites could only tell them so much – no doubt Maxim had camouflaged as much of the facility as possible from prying eyes, let alone what was buried underneath ground level.

Lancaster had appeared from the embassy building an hour before. He wasn't senior enough to warrant a security detail, and given the way he took a convoluted route to the café, he was doing his best to implement his own counter surveillance tactics to compensate.

Eva and Decker had taken turns following the man, acting as a tag team until he finally approached the café where he now sat, greeting the two men as if they were old friends.

Decker had retreated to the opposite side of the road and taken photographs, messaging them to Nathan back at the bookstore, who had then run the images through the database.

Eva had received a text message ten minutes before, confirming the two men worked for a manufacturing firm in France who were hoping to bid for work through an American subsidiary.

She had relaxed then, satisfied that they posed no threat to her.

She turned another page in her book, and smiled at the waiter as he brought her a fresh pastry.

Lancaster's tradecraft had become sloppy over the years – she had noticed at the gallery that he had put on weight, and he had relaxed too easily upon meeting the two men at the café.

Now, despite it being another thirty minutes until the rest of the city's workers took their lunch break, the three men were indulging in a second bottle of wine.

She texted an update to Decker.

An inebriated target could either be a blessing, or a curse.

She had to rely on Decker's ability and strength once their plan had been set in motion.

She picked at the pastry, and let the rest of her coffee turn cold.

Loud laughter from Lancaster's table caught her attention.

The embassy official rose unsteadily to his feet, shook hands with the two men, and then buttoned his jacket and turned to leave the café.

Eva tucked some Koruna notes under the plate in front of her, and then sauntered towards the door, letting it swing shut in front of her before she followed.

She couldn't afford to let Lancaster know she was there – not yet.

She pulled her phone from her pocket as she stepped onto the pavement and dialled Decker's number.

'He's on his way. He's taking the shorter route back, but he'll still be at the pinch point within two minutes.'

She didn't wait for an answer, and ended the call before tucking the phone back into her pocket and concentrating on the man several paces in front of her.

She planned to weave in and out of the crowd without being noticed by Lancaster should he glance over his shoulder. In case he turned around, she had tied her hair back and pulled a woollen beanie onto her head. She looked nothing like the person Lancaster had met at the art gallery a few weeks ago.

As predicted, he turned left into a cobbled street that was quieter than the main thoroughfare.

Eva let him gain some distance – she had no intention of letting him hear her footsteps, or sensing that someone was following him. She was more exposed here, and took a moment to crouch next to a rack of bicycles to tie an imaginary shoelace, even though she kept an eye on his progress.

He wavered a little; obviously the effects of the wine were beginning to take hold.

She wondered how effective his work would have been in the afternoon – not that he was going to see his office again.

A white panel van turned into the street at the far end, the rumble of its engine echoing off the sides of the buildings.

She glanced up, but it seemed that it was all residential housing along the street, with no shopfronts or brass plaques signifying offices tucked away.

Bright coloured laundry hung from several of the ornate balconies, and somewhere she could hear an exotic songbird tweeting from one of the apartments.

She rose to her feet and picked up her pace as the van drew closer.

Now, she could make out Nathan behind the wheel, a baseball cap pulled down low over his eyes.

She had worried at first about bringing him out into the field like this, but there was no other way – all three of them had to be a part of this to make it work.

Ahead, Lancaster's gait began to slow as the incline of the street took its toll on the poor physical condition of his body.

As Eva drew closer, she could hear his laboured breathing.

A moment later, he was level with the van, and all hell broke loose.

Nathan swerved the vehicle over to the pavement and braked, a moment before the side door was wrenched open and Decker emerged.

Eva ran – it was imperative they bundled Lancaster into the van before anyone saw what was going on and raised the alarm.

At the sound of her running feet, Lancaster spun around,

his eyes wide, as if he was only then realising what was happening.

He opened his mouth to cry out, but Decker was onto him too fast, slapping his hand over the man's mouth as he began to drag him backwards towards the vehicle.

Lancaster fought back, twisting and grasping at Decker's arms as he was hauled closer to the van.

Eva used the forward motion she had gained from running towards the two men to punch Lancaster in the stomach.

He dropped instantly, the air escaping his lungs in a loud gasp before he fell to his knees.

'Help me,' said Decker.

They manhandled Lancaster into the back of the van, and Decker slammed the door shut.

Eva braced herself against the opposite side of the vehicle, and then called out to Nathan.

'Go, go!'

## SEVENTEEN

Eva paced the floor as Decker adjusted the bindings that held Lancaster to the wooden chair placed on top of a sheet of clear plastic, and then turned to Nathan.

'I saw an old office back along the corridor there. Why don't you go and wait for us inside?'

His face paled, and his expression became troubled. 'Why?'

'I think you can guess why. You might not want to see this.'

She didn't admit it to him, but she also didn't want him to see *her* like this.

Especially when she knew someone she had trusted had endangered her life – and that of someone she cared about.

Nathan's eyes travelled over the unconscious man, and then back to Eva.

'What's going to happen to him?'

'That depends on what he tells us. And whether we think he's lying. We need answers, Nathan – and we're running out of time.'

'This isn't right. We can't do this.'

'We don't have a choice. Like I said, it's best if you leave us alone for a while. We'll find you when we're finished.'

The sound of a slap reached her ears, and Nathan winced as a groan emanated from Lancaster as he recoiled from Decker's strike to his cheek.

'I think you're probably right,' said Nathan, and began to walk away. After a few paces, he stopped and turned back to her. 'I keep forgetting this is your job.'

Eva folded her arms across her chest, and ignored the expression on his face. He looked as terrified as Lancaster.

'This is who I am.'

She waited until the door closed after him, then stepped over to where Decker stood over Lancaster, the double agent's eyes glazing over briefly before he shook his head and glared up at them both.

'You can't do this.'

'Want to bet?'

Decker moved over to the corner of the room, returning with a coil of hosepipe and a thin towel which he tossed to Eva.

Lancaster's eyes darted between them, his breathing ragged.

'What do you want?'

'What's your involvement with Maxim Kowalski?' said Eva.

'You've got to be kidding me.'

He hawked a gob of spit at her, and she stepped back, her footsteps crackling on the clear plastic.

Decker closed the distance between him and Lancaster in an instant, swiping his hand across the man's face.

Eva heard the crack moments before Lancaster spat out part of a tooth.

'That's no way to talk to a lady,' said Decker. 'So, mind your manners.'

Eva wrapped the ends of the towel around her hands and moved until she was standing behind Lancaster.

His shoulders heaved with the effort of his breathing, and she reckoned he was sobering up fast after his early lunchtime drinking session.

She raised her gaze to Decker, who nodded once, and then she swept her hands up and over Lancaster's head and pulled the towel flat across his face, forcing his head backwards.

Decker didn't hang around – he turned the hosepipe on and held it so the water flowed over Lancaster's covered face.

The man began to struggle against his bindings, and Eva had to use all her weight to stop him from moving his head from side to side to try to escape the water that cascaded over him.

After twenty seconds, Decker turned off the water and

jerked his chin at her.

'Let's see if he's a bit more talkative now.'

Eva swept the towel away, wringing it out to lose the moisture.

Lancaster's head fell forward, a coughing fit sending spasms through his body before he spat out the water from his mouth.

Decker sneered at him. 'Right, let's have some answers. What's your involvement with Maxim Kowalski?'

Lancaster snuffled, his eyes red. 'I can't tell you. He'll kill me.'

'Who's your contact in the Section? Who's feeding you information to pass on to Kowalski?'

Lancaster swore, and dropped his head to his chest.

Eva held her breath and waited.

Then Decker signalled, and she grabbed Lancaster's hair.

Jerking him backwards, she slipped the towel over his head again as Decker advanced with the hosepipe.

A muffled cry escaped the thick cotton material before the man began to struggle once more.

She lifted her eyes to Decker, noticing the grim expression on his face.

His jaw clenched, and then he stepped away and held the hose to one side, water splashing onto the concrete floor and plastic sheeting.

She loosened the towel and pushed Lancaster's head upright.

He leaned forward and vomited between his legs, his

breathing ragged.

'We've got all day,' said Decker. 'How long do you think you can keep this up?'

Lancaster's eyes shot to the water spouting from the hose as sweat poured down his face.

Decker leaned closer. 'It's a bit different when you're on the receiving end, isn't it, Scott? Did you ever think about what it was like when you tortured those innocent souls in the Middle East?'

'I wasn't in the Middle East.'

"Course not.' Decker waved his hand. 'You had illegal sites for this sort of thing, didn't you?'

Lancaster bit back a sob.

Eva moved until she was within the man's line of sight, and began to wrap the towel around her hands.

His eyes opened wide, and then a sigh escaped his lips.

'All right. Stop. I'll talk.'

'What sort of weaponry does Maxim have?' she said.

Lancaster swallowed. 'Nothing too heavy. Handguns, semiautomatics. They're stashed away from site, underground. He's too paranoid about an uprising, so no-one that has access to the lower levels of the bunker is armed. Only Maxim, and about ten guards have weapons at any one time.'

Decker picked up the hosepipe and circled the chair so he was standing behind Lancaster, and then bent down to his ear.

'I don't believe you. Maxim would never leave the facility

so lightly guarded. He's got too much invested in this.'

Lancaster tried to twist around in his seat, but his bindings held him tight.

'It's true! It's because the forest around the facility is full of traps. Tripwires, landmines – that sort of thing. It means he doesn't need a lot of guards around him. You've got to remember, he's paranoid.'

'What about the leak in the Section?'

He snorted. 'I've got no idea what you're talking about. Mind you, it wouldn't surprise me – someone put that Code One on both of you. Makes me think someone wants to keep you quiet.'

Decker dropped the hose to the floor and signalled to Eva, before walking towards the door, turning off the water faucet on his way past.

Eva tossed the sodden towel into Lancaster's lap and hurried over to join him.

He lowered his voice as she approached.

'I don't think we're going to get anything more out of him. He's obviously been dealing directly with Maxim but I think he's telling the truth about not knowing who the leak is in the Section.'

'I think you're right. We're done here.'

Decker opened the door for her, and they made their way along the corridor until they reached the office.

Nathan spun round in the chair he had found, his face ashen.

'Is it over? Did he tell you anything?'

Eva hovered at the threshold. 'Yes, we've got some useful information about Maxim's base, especially the sort of weaponry and guards that he has. Better than going in blind.'

'We need to get a move on,' said Decker. 'We should get back to the apartment and start to make plans to go to Poland.'

Nathan rose from his chair and brushed down his jeans. 'All right, let's go.'

He swept past Eva without meeting her gaze, and began to walk along the corridor towards the exit.

Eva glanced down as Decker's hand wrapped around her arm.

He pulled her to a stop, and let Nathan walk on ahead of them.

'Petersen can't be allowed to warn Maxim. We need to get a message to Knox.'

'Agreed.' She glanced over her shoulder at the sound of sobbing from the other room. 'What do we do about Lancaster?'

'He's too much of a risk. You and I both know the moment he gets out of here, he'll either try to contact Petersen – or worse, Kowalski.'

'Do want me to do it?'

He shook his head. 'I know you want justice for Douglas, but so do I.' He jerked his chin towards Nathan, who was waiting by the double doors, his eyebrow raised. 'Take him. I'll see you back at the bookstore in half an hour once I've had a chance to dump the body.'

# EIGHTEEN

Two hours later, the three of them were sitting in the apartment above the bookshop, poring over all the information that they had gleaned to date.

Nathan had his laptop open, and Eva glanced up as he emitted a surprised grunt.

'What is it?'

'A message from Miles. He says he's just landed here.'

'Give him the address for the bakery at the end of the road,' said Decker. 'Tell him to get a taxi. I'll wait out of sight for him to make sure he hasn't got a tail before bringing him back here.'

He grabbed his jacket while Nathan's fingers flew over the keyboard.

'Are you absolutely sure we can trust him?'

'I don't think there are any absolutes in this whole

situation,' said Eva, 'but as I said before, we can't do this on our own.'

Decker disappeared out the door, his footsteps echoing down the stairs before she heard the outer door slam shut.

She wandered over to the window and peered through the net curtains, watching as he shoved his hands in his pockets and disappeared from view.

'You never did tell me how you found out about the threat on my and Alex's life in Cyprus,' she said.

She heard Nathan's typing stop, and turned to face him.

He stared at her defiantly.

'What? You think I'm the traitor in the Section? Are you going to start torturing me now?'

She crossed her arms over her chest.

He sighed. 'Look, I'm not a mole. The week before the attack, I was reviewing a whole heap of communiqués that had been collated by other analysts – people like me. I guess I saw something I wasn't meant to, because when I tried to find it again it had gone missing. It was just a two-line message that had been sent to Petersen. I was surprised, because given his ill-health I didn't think he was still being sent weekly updates. I couldn't prove anything – the report I then sent to Knox was simply a precis of what I'd seen, but without the proof I guess it wasn't taken seriously.'

Eva dropped her hand to her sides and wandered over to where he sat, sinking onto the cushions as he shuffled over to make room for her.

She leaned forward, placed her elbows on her knees and ran a hand through her hair.

'I'm sorry. I've been doing this for so long, I don't know *how* to trust anyone – let alone who to trust.'

He reached out and wrapped his fingers around hers, and waited until her eyes met his.

'You can trust me. I would never do anything to harm you, or Alex and Grace. When this is all over, you and I need to have a long talk.'

She nodded, and bit her lip.

He smiled, squeezed her fingers, and then let go and pointed at the screen.

'In the meantime, I'm going to see if I can find some more up-to-date information about the terrain around the laboratory to help us.'

Thirty minutes later, Eva heard footsteps coming up the stairs, and then the tell-tale *beep* of the security mechanism.

Decker appeared, Miles at his heels.

He held a canvas holdall in one hand, and a laptop bag was slung over his opposite shoulder. He dropped both onto the coffee table and removed his coat before throwing it over the back of a chair.

'All right. Knox is on board and expecting our call. Secure line through to his private number as soon as you can, Nathan.'

'Before we do that, are we sure we want to get someone like him involved?' said Nathan. 'The three of you all have field experience – Decker here is, frankly, terrifying. Surely it would be better if we just do this ourselves?'

'I'm an assassin. I've never been part of an assault team. I'm used to working alone, working out how best to kill someone without being caught, and not drawing attention to myself.' Eva waved her hand at the maps and satellite photographs strewn across the table. 'By comparison, this is suicide.'

'However much it pains me to admit it, she's right,' said Decker. 'I haven't got a problem attacking the place, but I want to go in fully equipped. We don't have the time or the money to put together the sort of assault that's needed to finish off Maxim once and for all.'

Miles pointed at Nathan's laptop. 'Get Knox on a secure video call. I've got some ideas about how we do this that I want to discuss with him while all of you are in earshot.'

Moments later, Knox's face appeared on the screen.

Compared to when Eva had last seen him, his appearance was haggard, and he made them wait while he ensured the door to his office was locked and the blinds pulled down across the window behind his desk.

'The biggest problem we've got is lack of weapons,' said Eva, once they'd updated him. 'And, given that I'm sure Lancaster has been reported as missing by now, any attempt by us to approach contacts that you might have here is going to raise a bloody big flag.'

Knox pinched the bridge of his nose, then aimed his glare at Decker.

'You couldn't have just roughed him up a bit?'

'He was a traitor.'

'Yes, but the Americans are meant to be our allies. It does make things a little... awkward, doesn't it?'

Decker sighed, and ran a hand over his cropped hair. 'I had a feeling you'd say that. You'd better let them know they can find him in a dumpster in an alleyway behind the US Embassy.'

Eva frowned, then turned to him. 'You mean – you didn't kill him?'

Decker shrugged. 'I figured it might cause more problems than he's worth.'

Knox exhaled. 'I'll make some discreet calls once we're done here. We'll have to deal with the fallout later, but in the meantime, I'll let Lancaster's countrymen know about his treachery and ensure they hold him at a secure facility until our business with Maxim is taken care of.'

'We still need weapons,' said Eva, 'and neither Decker nor me have anyone we can speak to here, or over the border in Poland. So, what are we going to do?'

'I can get us assault rifles, handguns, grenades – pretty much anything you need,' said Miles.

'And how, exactly, do we get that sort of equipment?' said Decker.

'Alan Greene, currently with Interpol.'

Eva raised an eyebrow. 'Since when do Interpol have that sort of remit?'

'They don't,' said Miles. 'Greene is NSA and has been

after Maxim for years. If we tell him we know where to find him and what he's capable of, it'll be like dangling the biggest carrot in front of Greene that he's ever seen. He won't be able to resist helping us. Not with what's at stake.'

'I thought we didn't want to involve any other parties?' said Nathan. 'Won't Greene try to keep the smallpox for the American government?'

Miles shook his head. 'Greene doesn't work like that. Trust me. I'll vouch for him. We worked together—'

'In South America. Right.' Eva held up her hands. 'I swear blind, Newcombe – once this is all over, you *are* going to tell me what you got up to down there.'

She was rewarded with a sly smile.

'All right. What about Petersen?' said Eva. 'Any ideas, Knox?'

A mirthless chuckle reached her ears.

'Leave him to me.'

# NINETEEN

*London*

Knox left his car parked several streets from his ultimate destination and began the laborious walk up the steep uneven pavement towards the park at the top of the road.

A light drizzle peppered the evening air, and he relaxed a little. The inclement weather would keep people indoors, where they would remain warm and dry after their late afternoon commute, blissfully unaware of the spy that passed by their homes.

A chilly breeze flapped the ends of his overcoat, and he shoved his hands in his pockets as he hunkered down and considered his options once more.

There weren't many.

A heavy weight rested over his heart, and he shifted uncomfortably as he reached the crest of the hill.

He turned and surveyed the blinking lights of the business end of the city laid out below. The borough sprawled out each side of the road he'd followed, trees on either side rocking gently as the wind increased and whipped branches and leaves.

Knox exhaled, and cut through an alleyway that passed between two large houses before depositing him in a neighbouring street.

Privet hedgerows lined the cul-de-sac, enabling its residents to protect their privacy at all times.

Knox had maintained a watching brief on the house that backed onto the far end of the dead end street for a long time now; off the books, and entrusted to no-one.

There were some jobs better done alone.

He checked over his shoulder, but no-one followed; no-one hesitated in the shadows. The cars parked alongside the pavement were as familiar to him as their owners.

Nothing was out of place.

Everything was as it should be.

He placed a gloved hand on the low wooden gate, and pushed.

It swung open easily, on recently oiled hinges, a legacy of Knox's last fleeting night-time reconnaissance.

He prided himself on his foresight. It was something he'd honed over the years out in the field, and something that he'd successfully applied to his meteoric rise to Section chief.

Though prepared, he was disappointed it had come to this.

He stepped through the gate, ensuring his shoes fell on the soft grass verge of the footpath, not the mud, and closed the gate behind him.

Despite the guest the home concealed, there were no security patrols on the grounds. A CCTV network of cameras surrounded the facility, but Knox knew none of those faced the copse of trees. He'd been the one to arrange the system's upgrade, after all.

A shuffling sound to his right caught his attention, and he froze, stock-still, until a young fox cub bounded across the path, a small rodent between its teeth.

Knox followed its progress with his eyes, briefly reminded of his childhood in the Berkshire countryside, and silently marvelled at the animal's presence in the urban sprawl.

He inhaled the aroma of pine needles and damp leaves underfoot, and then began to move once more.

As the trees gave way to the lush grass of the retirement home's manicured lawns, Knox slowed his pace and began a reconnaissance of the grounds.

He took his time; there was no need to rush. Dawn was still hours away, and he was willing to wait if he had to.

He'd spent the afternoon reading the files on Petersen's guards.

The old man had picked them himself; a last act of defiance before Knox claimed his job from him.

He used a copy of the building's keys to enter through the kitchen door, then made his way through the reception area and crept up the stairs, his senses alert for any movement above.

The house was silent, its residents asleep and oblivious to the assassin that crept past their rooms.

He reached the door to Petersen's room, and held his breath.

Closing his eyes, he recalled the layout of the room, putting himself in Petersen's place and tried to anticipate whether the old man would be fast asleep or expecting a visitor.

He opened his eyes. Petersen wasn't a fool, despite the impression he gave to the other residents and to those who had taken his career away from him.

The knowledge made Knox's job easier to bear.

Petersen had to die.

There was no other way.

He pushed against the door, and in a split second the shock of it giving way on his touch hit him, and he realised he'd been fooled.

The old spymaster was ready for him.

He'd waited, biding his time for the past three years in order to exact his revenge.

As the door swung open, Knox dropped to the floor, but too late.

Fire ripped through his shoulder a moment before the muted cough of suppressed gunshot reached his ears.

A muffled curse came from the window, and he swung his own weapon up, firing twice.

A cry, a stumble, and a body crashed to the floor before him.

Knox staggered over the threshold, weapon raised.

Petersen had fallen against the side of a plush armchair next to a floor-to-ceiling window, clutching his stomach.

As Knox advanced, the man spat blood onto the ornate carpet and glared at him.

'You should've stayed out of this, Gerald.'

'Why? Why betray your country?'

Knox kicked at the man's leg, satisfied when it caused a judder through Petersen's body and made him howl in pain.

'What was it? Money?'

Petersen smiled through the pain. 'You'd never understand, Gerald. That's why you were never allowed to become involved. There's a power shift happening in Europe, and I was going to lead the British side.'

Knox blinked. Black specks formed at the corner of his vision as the sound of sirens in the distance filtered through the window.

His orders had been received from the upper echelons of the Section – execute Petersen, rather than have the agency and any dignitaries remotely connected to it publicly embarrassed by a criminal prosecution.

He couldn't afford to be found here, not like this.

The Section worked out of sight, and there had already been too much activity surrounding the secret agency of late.

He raised the weapon until he had Petersen's forehead in his sights, and then took the final, lethal shot.

Knox turned and staggered towards the hallway, clutching his shoulder and all too aware that the blood seeping between his fingers would lead the police straight to him.

He had to act fast, but in his weakened state, he knew that if he failed to get away only one option remained.

He tested the weight of the weapon in his other hand, and wondered if he'd be able to pull the trigger on himself.

Movement at the end of the passageway caught his eye, and his hand jerked up, sighting the barrel on the figure at the top of the stairs.

One of Petersen's bodyguards stood facing him, his own weapon raised.

# TWENTY

Eva wrapped her fingers around the strap fixed above the passenger window of the old four-wheel drive and braced her feet against the floor as Decker drove the vehicle through another shallow river bed.

A muffled curse from the back seat reached her ears, and she checked the wing mirror to her right to make sure no important parts were now hanging off the vehicle.

Such as the exhaust pipe.

Twilight hugged the trees on each side of the narrow track, and her gaze fell to the map she held in her other hand.

The village was another mile away, and they would have to stop soon, or risk the noise from the engine creating unwanted attention.

Eva ran through the plan once more in her mind, making sure she hadn't overlooked anything.

It was risky, and she wouldn't get a second chance, but they couldn't work out another way to get close to the testing laboratory.

Decker swung the car over to the right and as the vehicle bounced between gnarled tree trunks and brambles, Eva began to concentrate on her breathing, keeping her heart rate low.

Once she left the relative safety of the vehicle, she would be on her own.

Decker killed the engine and rested his hands on the wheel.

'Are you sure you want to do it this way?'

'Yes. It's the best chance we've got. We can't turn back now.'

He nodded before she opened her door and lowered herself to the ground.

Nathan emerged from the back seat and held out one of the handguns that Alan Greene had sourced for them earlier that morning.

She shook her head. 'If I walk in there armed to the teeth and I get stopped, no-one is going to believe my story. We have to assume that I'll be searched.'

He replaced the gun in the bag with the others, but didn't look happy.

'No weapon, no comms, no phone – we have no way of keeping in touch with you once you leave here. What if it goes wrong?'

Eva jerked her thumb over her shoulder at Miles, who

had climbed out of the vehicle and was leaning against the back of it, listening to their conversation.

'Then he and Decker make a decision whether to proceed with the rest of the plan or not. We've already agreed all this. Give me two hours, and if you don't hear from me, assume it's all gone pear-shaped. Don't hang around. We have to stop Maxim.'

With that, she pulled on the old coat Decker handed to her and shouldered the backpack she had brought with her.

'I'll see you in a couple of hours.'

She paced back through the undergrowth towards the rough track, and then turned right and began to pick up her pace to close the distance between her and the village before night fell.

After the noise of the city, the forest held a deathly silence, and whereas in Cyprus – or England – she would expect to hear birdsong at this time of late afternoon, there was nothing.

It was as if even the wildlife had abandoned the area.

She wondered how the villagers managed to eke out a living, and then realised they were probably responsible for providing Maxim and his men with food supplies, and that the community probably lived in fear of retribution if they didn't comply.

As she walked, an idea began to form – an improvement upon the plan she and the rest had made the previous day with Knox.

It would be risky, but she reckoned she stood a better chance than trying to steal a vehicle without being seen.

She checked her watch, and realised half an hour had already passed. She would reach the village soon.

A renewed awareness of her surroundings swept over her. The location of the testing facility was still some miles away, but if she was Maxim, she would have guards posted around the village to keep an eye on things.

She slowed her pace and altered her stance from that of a confident and deadly assassin to one of a downtrodden woman, on her last legs.

With no electricity in such a remote and forgotten area of the country, it was some time before Eva noticed the first lights from the tiny community.

An enterprising person had lit oil lamps at the end of the track where the first houses hugged the roadside.

Eva slipped into the shadows, keeping her back to a dilapidated stone wall that bordered the first of the properties.

Through the shutter-less window, she could see a family sitting down to an early evening meal, light from candles in the centre of the table reflecting on their faces.

She drew a little closer, safe in the knowledge that they wouldn't be able to see her through the glass.

A family of three sat around the table – an older couple, and a boy of about thirteen. All three bore the signs of malnutrition, their cheekbones hollow and their eyes sunken. Despite this, they took their time eating and Eva realised they were doing so to savour every mouthful.

She moved away, and edged down the side of the track to the next property. Again, no-one seemed to worry about privacy – it was evident that once the sun began to sink below the horizon, people returned to their homes and didn't venture outside in the freezing weather unless they had to.

The thought caused her to check over her shoulder once more, to make sure that she hadn't been followed.

The road behind her was silent and empty, and she turned back to the sight before her.

She frowned. Once again, a family sat around a table to their evening meal, this time with two boys – one about the same age as the kid in the first house, and the other a few years younger.

She hurried to the next house, a thought occurring to her.

As she peered through the window, her concerns crystallised.

There didn't appear to be any teenage girls or young women in the village.

Eva realised that her best bet to find out what was going on was to speak to one of the older women.

She edged her way around the back of the house, to find that the building and the neighbouring properties all backed onto the forest. There were no gardens.

Outside the back of the buildings, smaller shed-like

structures had been built, and as she approached one of them, the stench assaulted her.

Realising that the houses shared communal toilets, she hunkered down in the undergrowth close by to wait.

Cramp was beginning to seep into her muscles when the back door to one of the houses opened, and a woman hurried towards the shed nearest to Eva, hugging a shawl around her shoulders against the cold.

Eva stayed in the shadows while the woman occupied the shed.

She had hung a lantern outside the door, and Eva realised this was because it was unsafe to have a naked flame anywhere near the open cesspit.

She fought down the urge to move away, to put a safe distance between her and the natural explosives, and concentrated instead on the noises she could hear.

When it seemed that the woman was ready to vacate the shed, Eva move closer.

The door opened and the woman emerged, but before she could reach up to and hitch the lantern, Eva's hand snaked around her mouth and pulled her towards the undergrowth.

The woman's muffled cries subsided, and her body grew limp in Eva's arms as if she'd lost all hope.

Eva lowered her mouth to the woman's ear, and spoke in Russian, hoping the old woman would understand, given her age and the fact the language had been spoken by Communist occupiers until only a couple of decades before.

'I'm not going to hurt you. I'm here to help. I'm going to take my hand away from your mouth. Don't scream. Okay?'

The woman nodded, and Eva released her, ready to strike if the woman changed her mind.

'Who are you?'

'A friend.'

'You're not from around here, are you?'

'Is my Russian that bad?'

A bitter snort reached Eva's ears before the woman spoke again.

'If you were from one of the bigger towns near here, you'd run away and not come back.'

'I haven't got much time. Will you help me?'

'Why should I?'

'Where are all the young women? I haven't seen any. There are loads of boys, but no girls – none that are older than teenagers, anyway. What's going on?'

The woman wiped at her eyes and pulled her shawl tighter around her shoulders with shaking hands.

'The guards take them.'

'From the testing facility?'

The woman nodded, her bottom lip trembling. 'When they are fourteen, the men take them. There's nothing we can do. If we try, they shoot the boys.'

Eva clenched her fist, and took a step back. 'I'm presuming they're taking all your food as well.'

'Yes. We are allowed to keep a quota, but it's not enough. We are starving.'

Eva reached out and placed her hands on the woman's shoulders. 'I can get the girls back. I can stop the guards. But I'm going to need your help, and you can't tell anyone that you've seen me.'

The woman held her gaze for a moment, and then spoke.

'What do you need me to do?'

## TWENTY-ONE

Eva held the binoculars to her face and hunkered lower in the long grass.

A slight breeze ruffled the leaves of a dandelion plant next to her, the sweet scent of dead and rotting leaves that carried on the wind evoking a brief memory of a childhood in the countryside before it was gone, the wind direction changing once more.

Beside her Decker remained still, his face passive behind the scope of the rifle, the sleeves of his jacket rolled up to his elbows despite the early morning chill.

They'd arrived in darkness, walking the distance between the van where Nathan kept watch on their progress via satellite and their current location. Neither had spoken during the transit, both too busy concentrating on avoiding the tripwires that criss-crossed the forest floor.

And the fact Decker was still angry with Eva.

The old woman from the village had slipped back into her house the previous night, returning half an hour later with a set of keys.

'My husband is passed out, drunk. He has a van, it's old, but you'll be able to get close to the facility because it's the one we use to transport fresh vegetables there every week.'

Decker's temper when she'd returned driving the old panel van and announced she intended to rescue the girls before the facility was razed to the ground could have been best described as ballistic.

Eventually she'd calmed him down enough to tell him and the others about the rest of the conversation she'd had with the old woman, and passed him the map she had drawn for her – a rough sketch of the area, complete with as much information as possible about the traps that had been set around the perimeter to ward off potential attacks.

Then he'd fallen silent for a while, his jaw clenched, before a fresh torrent of abuse filled the air – this time aimed at Maxim and his guards.

'How does she know all of this?' said Nathan, the doubt in his voice echoed in his eyes as he snatched the map from Decker.

'Apparently, the men from the village poach rabbits and small deer from the forest around the facility,' said Eva. 'They have to – they're starving. So, they've worked out where the tripwires and other traps are.'

Miles had risen from his position crouched next to the back wheel of their four-wheel drive, and slapped Decker on the shoulder.

'All right. We all feel the same way about the situation, but now we need to enhance the plan Eva has, to make sure Maxim's bioweapon is stopped, and that the only people who leave this place alive are those girls.'

But, in the middle of the night while Eva took the opportunity to get some sleep for a while, he had disappeared.

'Says he's got another trick up his sleeve, and that he'll see us later,' Nathan had explained when she'd asked.

Paranoia threatened once more, and Eva wondered if the man had simply decided that it was too risky to be with them and had turned tail and fled – taking the four-wheel drive vehicle with him.

She'd woken as Nathan had started the van's engine and pulled away from their hiding place, Decker's eyes glinting in the low light cast by the dashboard dials. She doubted he'd slept at all, but she knew better than to ask.

Now, and despite a fitful sleep in the back of the van, Eva's senses were alert.

Although the old Cold War bunker appeared abandoned to outsiders, they'd agreed that Maxim would have guards on patrol in the surrounding woodland, and they would take no chances.

There was too much to lose.

As they'd climbed the tree-lined embankment from the road, the soft purr of the van's engine receded into the distance as Nathan took up his position, blocking the guards' vehicles in their parking spaces under a canopy of trees that had been invisible to the satellite imagery. Thanks to the old woman, all the vehicles had been accounted for.

At least, that's what Eva hoped.

In case anyone asked, Nathan's instructions were to puncture one of the back tyres of the van to disable it. To work around his lack of Russian, he'd simply pretend to be deaf.

'Stop worrying. He'll be fine.'

Decker's voice cut into her thoughts, low and barely above a whisper.

She frowned and swept the binoculars to her right, over a disused shed with a dilapidated lean-to hanging off its side, until she could see the beat-up farmhouse that huddled against the west side of the clearing.

'Yeah,' she managed.

She exhaled, trying to let some of the tension out of her system before lowering the binoculars and twisting her neck from side to side.

The sweet scent of pine needles and leaf rot tickled her nostrils.

A faint mist lifted beyond their position, a curling strip of grey-white that flattened along the length of a stream that separated them from Maxim's boundary and imminent danger.

A young girl had appeared at first light, a blanket around her otherwise naked figure, and had made her way over to a small box-like structure off to the left.

She'd returned to the farmhouse after five minutes, knocked on the door, and disappeared back inside.

Miles had groaned when she'd told them about her plan to rescue the kidnapped women from the camp, but had acquiesced. None of them wanted to leave them behind, not after what Maxim and his men had done to them, but it added risk to an already fraught operation.

Eva and Decker had agreed that Maxim was likely in the farmhouse, but until they confirmed it, they were working on assumptions.

So they sat and waited, and counted off the guards they saw moving around the forest camp.

'Here we go.'

She raised the binoculars once more. Sure enough, an armed man had appeared against the opposite tree line, his rifle slung over his shoulder and a cigarette between his lips as he rested his hands on his waist and stretched.

Eva checked over her shoulder.

A large tree provided a shelter behind them, obliterating any chance someone would have of sneaking up on them, but they couldn't afford to make a mistake.

Not now.

She twisted back round until she was facing the clearing.

Decker hadn't moved.

His forefinger graced the trigger, ready to fire if he needed to.

'I still hate this plan,' he muttered.

'We're not leaving the girls behind to die.'

'You could die trying to free them.'

She sighed. 'Decker, I've spent most of my life killing people. It'd be nice for once to do something good, don't you think?'

They fell silent as the guard meandered back towards a low-slung building that had been placed between the main farmhouse and a smaller hut.

They had only counted a dozen guards in total, and Eva realised that Maxim deliberately kept the numbers small to avoid knowledge of his secret facility becoming known. Any more than twelve guards, and he would likely have incurred the risk of dissidents and a power struggle.

The guard placed his hand on the door latch, and Eva heard Decker exhale.

'Get ready to run.'

She raised herself to her feet, keeping low so as not to alert the guard to their position, and held her breath.

A red spurt of blood exploded from the guard's head a moment before the suppressed cough from Decker's rifle reached her ears, and then she was running, heading for the hut and the imprisoned girls.

Guards poured from the accommodation block, weapons raised as they tried to flush out the man who had killed their colleague.

Panicked commands were issued as they began to run away from Decker's line of fire, and Eva took advantage of the confusion.

She took a deep breath and launched herself towards the smaller hut.

# TWENTY-TWO

Eva ducked behind the woodpile as gunfire chattered from the guard's accommodation block, quickly followed by a volley from Decker's position.

She crawled to the far end, took a deep breath, then edged around the corner, weapon steady.

A girl of about seventeen crouched beside the back door, a younger version of herself hunkered close by, eyes wide.

They turned at Eva's low whistle and she put a finger to her lips, then scuttled closer to them, keeping her back to the wooden slats of the building.

'How many of you?' she whispered in Russian.

'Only six now,' came the reply. The older girl wiped at tear-streaked eyes. 'Anya died two weeks ago. He made us bury her in the forest.'

A sense of dread swept over Eva as she wondered if Maxim had already released the weaponised smallpox.

'Was she sick?'

The girl bit back fresh sobs, then shook her head. 'Maxim and his men raped her.'

Eva reached out and squeezed the girl's shoulder before eyeing her younger sister.

'I'm here with friends. Three men. We're going to end this once and for all, but you need to be brave, and you need to do as I say, okay?'

Both girls nodded, and Eva relayed the plan.

The girl's hand shook as she took the rough map the old woman had drawn.

'This is my grandmother's handwriting.'

'It's because of her bravery that we're here,' said Eva. 'She wanted to help us free you.'

The girl sniffed. 'He told us all they were dead, so we wouldn't try to escape to get back to the village.'

Eva pulled the girl into a fierce hug, and then pushed her away, her grip tight on the girl's wrist.

'I *will* kill him for everything he's done to you. Now, go and round up the others, and be ready for the signal.'

The older girl moved towards the door. The younger of the two followed her sister, then hesitated and glanced over her shoulder.

'Will we hear your signal?'

Eva smiled. 'Oh, yes – I guarantee it.'

She waited until they'd disappeared back into the building, their muffled voices soon lost amongst the gunfire that streaked across the clearing.

Eva ran to the end of the building, circling back towards her original position, and wondered where the hell Newcombe was.

Despite the weaponry provided by his NSA contact, and the fact Maxim's guards had evidently never seen active service, the adrenalin coursing through her veins was beginning to wane, and she fought down an urge to panic that was both alien and frightening.

She had to get the girls to safety.

She needed the distraction Newcombe had promised, and they needed it—

Eva was knocked off her feet by the force of the blast that tore through the farmhouse and sent a hot, fierce fireball several metres up into the air.

She rolled, covering her head with her arms as she sought cover from the projectiles that peppered the clearing, hot shrapnel that smoked and burned as it descended.

Movement out the corner of her eye roused her dulled senses, and she saw the two teenage girls emerge from their hut, stunned expressions on their faces.

She signalled to them to get moving, to use the guards' temporary confusion to their advantage in order to get to safety, and then turned her attention to providing covering fire.

It was evident from the way the guards scattered that without Samuel Parkes to issue orders to them, they were either too high on drugs or too stupid to provide much of a response to the attack.

To her relief, Nathan emerged from the undergrowth and signalled to the girls to run to him. She watched as he spoke to the older of the two girls Eva had assigned as a team leader and gave her directions back to the van while avoiding the tripwires.

Eva turned her attention to the flames licking the sky from what had once been Maxim's farmhouse.

She wondered where Miles was, and whether he had escaped the blast. Evidently, the farmhouse used propane gas for heating – or at least, cooking – and he had used these to his advantage. The stench of scorched flesh reached her nostrils, and she wondered how many guards had been taken out by the explosion.

Decker's covering fire had withered out, and at a low whistle from him, Eva glanced up to see him running along the outer edge of the clearing. He signalled to her to make her way to the bunker entrance, and she nodded in understanding.

They had to somehow destroy the facility before the sound of gunfire reached any other guards patrolling the vicinity – and before anyone from the bunker tried to escape.

She, Decker, and Miles had agreed that no-one would be allowed to live. They simply couldn't risk the knowledge from Maxim's bio engineering project being ransomed to the highest bidder.

It had to end here.

She sensed movement behind her a split second too late.

A hand snaked around her head and clamped over her mouth, and she felt a pinprick at her neck.

'You bitch.'

Eva cursed under her breath. She had been so intent on getting the girls to safety, and making sure that Decker wasn't overpowered, that she had let her guard down.

Rasping breath reached her ears, as she recalled that Maxim Kowalski was not a well man. Crazy, yes. But not as strong as her.

She slumped against him, her whole body screaming defeat.

He chuckled. 'So, this is the woman who managed to escape my team in Cyprus, and outsmart Parkes. I guess your luck has run out.'

Eva ran through her options in her mind. She couldn't get Decker's attention – he was already too far away, closer to the bunker; she could hear the report of his gun as he picked off the remaining guards.

'Where are my twins?' said Maxim.

Eva frowned, and her shoulders slumped.

Maxim cackled. 'You never realised, did you? You thought they were the engineer's children.'

Realisation dawned on Eva as the man lowered his mouth to her ear.

'It wasn't just secrets that bastard stole from me. He stole my *family*.'

Eva shifted her weight, and drove her elbow backwards.

She heard the air escape the man's lungs, before his hand

fell away from her mouth. She spun around, slamming the heel of her hand into his nose.

He fell back staggering, and she saw the knife glint in his other hand.

She didn't hesitate – she threw herself to the ground, rolled, and collected her weapon from where it had fallen, swinging it upwards and firing before Maxim had recovered.

He cried out, clutching his shoulder as the knife clattered to the earth moments before his body slumped and he fell to his knees.

Her breathing hard, Eva crossed the distance between them and placed the barrel of her gun against his forehead.

His eyes found hers and in that moment, she knew she was looking at pure evil.

There was no remorse, no guilt, and no fear.

A smile began to form on his lips, and as he opened his mouth to speak, she fired.

Breathing heavily, Eva ejected the magazine from her gun, reached into her back pocket and slipped a fresh one into the weapon. Her ears rang from the combined assault of shouting and gunfire, and she spun round at a tap on her shoulder, weapon raised.

Decker held up his hand, then grabbed her shoulder as she lowered her weapon.

'Can you hear it?'

She shook her head, and tried to listen.

At first, she could only hear the crackling of flames from

the burning farmhouse and the cries of the women as Miles led them to the edge of the forest.

'Where's Nathan?' she yelled.

'Already gone,' he said. 'Come on!'

Then, as her hearing returned to normal, she heard it.

A low buzzing noise, similar to the approach of a helicopter, but higher in pitch – and getting closer.

Miles heard it then, too, a moment before he shoved the last woman onto the path and beckoned to Eva and Decker.

'What is it?' said Eva.

'Drone,' he yelled. 'They're going to hit the bunker. We need to get out of here. *Now.*'

Eva didn't need further encouragement.

She took off towards Miles, Decker at her side as the tone of the aircraft changed.

'It's on its final approach,' said Decker. 'We've got seconds.'

Eva gritted her teeth and forced another burst of energy into her legs, her lungs beginning to burn despite the adrenalin rush she'd experienced since they began the assault.

A low whine filled the air, and Eva tumbled into the undergrowth moments before the shockwave scorched overhead.

# TWENTY-THREE

Decker stood with his hands on his hips and surveyed the smoking hillside, then shook his head and turned to Miles.

'I guess you'd better thank the NSA for us. There's nothing left of the facility.'

'That wasn't the NSA. That was one of ours.'

'The Section has drones?'

'Not on paper, no.'

'We have to get out of here before the authorities arrive,' said Decker. 'I don't think they'll be too impressed that the British government blew this place up, and I don't fancy spending the next ten years answering their questions in a remote prison.'

Eva ignored the banter between him and Miles as they walked along the track, the sound of an engine reaching her ears.

She glanced over her shoulder, and breathed a sigh of relief as the van appeared, Nathan behind the wheel.

Evidently, he hadn't needed to puncture the tyres, which was just as well given the number of passengers the van now carried.

Nathan slowed as he neared them.

'Jump in,' he said. 'I'll give you a lift to the four-wheel drive.'

Eva joined Decker and Miles as they scrambled through the side door and into the back of the van, sitting on the floor amongst the rescued women.

Their eyes wide, they appeared stunned, mute, until one of them cleared her throat.

'Thank you,' she said.

Eva nodded, and closed her eyes.

She rubbed her fit hand over her arm and tried to ignore the frantic beat of her heart.

Despite the successful mission, she felt a sense of dread.

A wave of sickness engulfed her and she fought it down, placing her hands on the hard floor of the van while sweat pricked at her hairline.

Eventually, Nathan drew the vehicle to a standstill and Decker slid open the panel door.

They'd arrived at the outer fringes of the village, and as Eva blinked in the bright winter light, she spotted the old woman she'd met the night before hurrying towards her.

Eva swung her legs over the side and gulped in the fresh air.

Despite the layers of clothing she wore, she was shivering and as she staggered to her feet, her vision blurred.

'Are you okay?' said Nathan, resting his hand on her arm.

'Sure.'

She nodded and forced a smile as the woman approached.

'You found them, thank goodness.'

Eva held up her hands, warding off the hug she knew would be imminent.

'That's okay,' she replied in Russian. 'Without you, we'd have never got out of there in one piece.'

'We heard an explosion. Is it done?'

'Yes, it is done. They are all dead. You are safe now.'

The woman turned back to the small crowd and relayed the message. A moment later, a cheer erupted from the people gathered around, and Eva resisted the urge to sigh with relief.

Instead, she turned to Decker.

'We need to leave. Now.'

'You don't want to stay and celebrate with your new friend?'

'Decker – I mean it.'

He frowned at the tone of her voice. 'Everything okay?'

'Get me out of here now, and I'll explain once we're on the road.'

She staggered back to their vehicle and clambered into the passenger seat as Decker rounded up Nathan and Miles, their excited voices carrying over her in a wave as they said their farewells to the villagers.

Eventually, Miles got behind the wheel of the four-wheel drive, and once Decker and Nathan had climbed into the back seats, he started the engine and steered the vehicle back along the track.

Eva estimated they'd reach the Polish-Czech border in a few hours.

She bit her lip.

She wasn't sure she'd make it.

A fresh wave of sickness struck her, and she reached out for the door handle.

'Stop. I need to get out.'

Miles slammed on the brakes and the vehicle skidded on the wet muddy surface.

Eva didn't hang around – she slipped off her seatbelt and launched herself out of the four-wheel drive and stood on the verge, her hands on her knees.

She felt movement behind her, and Nathan approached, a bottle of water in his hand.

'All right, what's going on?'

She blinked, and reached out for the water before taking a long drink.

She kept hold of the bottle, the sides of her vision blurring as she took in the concerned faces of Decker and Miles from the car windows.

'When Maxim cornered me, I thought I'd felt him put a

knife against my neck before I disarmed him because he was holding one when I shot him, but I'm wrong. He must have stabbed me with a syringe,' she said, her throat constricting. 'I think I'm infected with the weaponised smallpox.'

## TWENTY-FOUR

'Eva. Eva?'

'She can't hear you.'

'Yes, she can. Her eyelids moved.'

Eva blinked, and then raised her hand to shield her eyes from the bright light streaming through the room.

As her vision adjusted, she licked her lips, her throat parched.

She was lying down, and as she focused on her surroundings, two figures appeared next to her.

'Told you she was waking up.'

Miles stood at the foot of the bed, his hands in his pockets and the skin at the corners of his eyes crinkling.

'How are you feeling?'

'Where am I?'

'London.'

She turned to find Gerald Knox standing beside her.

'What are you doing here?'

'It seemed appropriate, given that one of my best operators has been in a coma for the past two weeks. You're lucky. We found an antidote in time.'

'The twins?'

'Safe. And, thanks to them, you're alive. The medical team here managed to extrapolate a sample of their blood and infuse you with it to fight off the infection.'

'Where are the twins?'

'Staying with me and my wife,' said Miles. 'We're working with the authorities to see if we can adopt them. Give them the childhood they deserve.'

Eva frowned, and pointed at the sling Knox wore.

'What happened to you?'

'Petersen fought back.'

'He's…?'

'Dead, yes. Although Petersen was allowed to choose the men who guarded him, they still reported to me. More importantly, Douglas can be exonerated from any wrongdoing,' he said. 'We've been spending some time going through the events of three years ago, and together with what you've uncovered, we've concluded Petersen was the one who first made contact with the engineer, some two weeks before the conference took place in Prague. He persuaded him to keep quiet about their meeting – laid it on thick about not wanting to alert the Russians – and instead, suggested to the engineer that he approach Douglas instead.'

'Why? Surely if Petersen believed the engineer had vital

information about a biological weapon, he'd have wanted full control of the operation to help him defect?'

A sad smile crossed Knox's face. 'Eva, Petersen had no interest in helping the engineer defect. He realised he could make a fortune selling the knowledge on the black market. His days were numbered in the Section, and he wasn't going to agree to retirement without a fight. Cost-cutting, downsizing – call it what you want, but Petersen was on his way out the door, and he didn't like it. As soon as he heard what was on offer, he decided to start a bidding war for that information.'

'I don't understand.'

'Petersen *used* Douglas. He needed to be able to keep an eye on the engineer, but at arm's length. He couldn't be seen to be closely involved, otherwise the minute the deal went sour, he'd be a dead man. In the meantime, Maxim wanted his children back. We can only assume the engineer and his wife decided to rescue them from a horrific fate at the hands of their father.'

A chill crossed Eva's spine, and she held up a hand.

'Hang on a minute. What deal?'

'Petersen made a deal with Scott Lancaster at the US Embassy that the engineer – and his secrets – would be handed over to the Americans. For a large sum of money.'

'What went wrong?'

'The engineer decided to evade his security detail, and got himself shot.' Knox turned his gaze to the pale blue sky beyond the window, and Eva noticed how exhausted he appeared.

'What happened?' she whispered. 'Did the Americans kill Douglas?'

He shook his head. 'No – although they probably wanted to, given what Petersen did next.'

'What?'

'He knew he had to cover his tracks, so he made some phone calls, explained to the Russians what had happened, and assured them the engineer told us nothing. It wasn't good enough for them. They wanted retribution. An eye for an eye.'

Eva sat back in her seat, her mouth open.

'I'm sorry, Eva,' said Knox. 'I've been trying to expose him for the last three years for what he did.'

'He sacrificed Douglas to the Russians?'

'They'll deny it, of course. Douglas was innocent, Eva. He wasn't the traitor. Petersen was.'

Eva exhaled, her thoughts churning. Her mentor, the man who had trained her, had betrayed her and killed her lover.

Knox's tone softened. 'You'll tell Decker?'

'Of course.'

'We could use him back here, you know.'

She glanced at Miles, but he shook his head.

Evidently Decker had disappeared again.

'That's a conversation you can have with him. When you find him.'

Knox cleared his throat, and lowered himself into the chair next to the bed.

'Eva, the Section was created to deal with situations that, for whatever reason, can't be dealt with by MI5 or MI6. We're the ones who go after the people who fall between the cracks. The sort of people that can't be negotiated with.'

'You mean the sort that would cause embarrassment for the politicians.' Eva held up a hand to stop him interrupting. 'I know, Knox. You forget I was part of the glorified clean-up squad for a long time.'

'And a very valued part,' said Knox. He shifted on the chair, tried to get comfortable, then gave up and removed the sling and let his arm rest in his lap. 'Have you thought about what you're going to do when you get out of here?'

She shook her head. 'Not really.'

'There are always going to be people who are a threat to us, Eva. People like Maxim Kowalski, and with you in hiding for three years, we've had to continue our work without one of our best operators.'

He rose from his seat and crunched up the sling in his hand. 'All I'm saying is, don't make a hasty decision.'

Eva didn't respond, and instead watched him leave the room, waiting until he pulled the door shut and she could hear his footsteps receding along the corridor away from her.

Knox might have pretended to be on her side, but she understood full well the threat behind his words.

The Section didn't offer a retirement plan – it was why

Decker had taken so much care to establish a remote bolt hole so that until recent events, even she didn't know its location. As it was, he would move again in case the information was gleaned from her or Nathan.

She sighed, closed her eyes, and rested her head against the pillow.

Until she could work out her own escape plan, it seemed she'd remain employed by the Section.

———

Eva was discharged from the hospital two days later, the medical staff content that she was no longer infectious and wouldn't present a threat to the public.

As the lift doors opened and she stepped into the lobby in the late afternoon, a familiar figure strode across the space towards her and enveloped her in his arms.

'I thought I'd lost you,' said Nathan.

Eva relaxed into his embrace. 'You have to try harder than that, nerd.'

'Come on. The Section have arranged a hotel room for you until we can sort out somewhere for you to live.'

She slipped her hand into his and followed him out through the double doors.

'Fancy a walk?'

'Yes – I need some fresh air after being cooped up for so long. What have you been up to?'

She let his voice drift over her as they made their way

along a narrow street that wound between the hospital grounds before opening out next to the Thames River.

Nathan led her along the Embankment until they reached Hungerford Bridge, and then stopped her and reached into his jacket pocket and held out his hand.

Four broken squares glinted in the light.

Eva frowned. 'What are those?'

'The memory chips from the computers at Maxim's headquarters. They contain all the information to replicate and distribute the smallpox,' replied Nathan, his breath fogging in the night air. 'Once we got you on a repatriation flight to the UK for treatment, Decker went back to what was left of the bunker and managed to retrieve them for me.'

'What are you going to do with them?'

'This.' He held his arm out, then turned his palm and let the pieces of metal fall into the raging Thames River below.

Eva watched the last remnants disappear under the water's surface, then turned to Nathan.

'They've taken samples from my blood and the twins' antibodies, haven't they?'

'They had to, Eva. Don't worry – they're secure, at Porton Down. We're the good guys. You have to believe that.'

'What about you? What are you going to do now?'

He smiled, and then reached out and cupped her chin in his hand, before kissing her.

She pulled away, and then laughed.

'You didn't answer the question.'

His mouth twitched. 'I heard there was a bookshop for sale in Prague.'

Eva crossed her arms and raised an eyebrow. 'Did you, now?'

'Well, someone has to look after the place. I heard the current owner once threatened to burn it down.'

She laughed again.

'It's yours,' she said, then looped her arm through his and led him away from the bridge. 'But first, you can buy me dinner.'

## THE END

# FROM THE AUTHOR

I hope you've enjoyed the stories and the concept of this **English Spy Mysteries series**.

If you have, I'd be delighted if you would consider leaving a short review for each of the episodes in this paperback omnibus on Amazon or Goodreads – it all helps to spread the word and help readers discover my stories.

If you'd like to stay up to date with my new releases and writing projects, please join my Spy Novels reader group: http://smarturl.it/SpyBooks. I will never share your email address, and you can unsubscribe at any time. You can also find out more about me at www.rachelamphlett.com.

Thanks again for your support.

Best wishes,
Rachel Amphlett

Lightning Source UK Ltd.
Milton Keynes UK
UKHW01f1154020518
321990UK00001B/405/P